M000202396

DARK WINGS RISING

To Leah Nelson,
Wishing you joy & peace in
life's journey!
Dwain Cassady
1/6/21

Dwain Cassady

ACKNOWLEDGMENTS

I am grateful to all of you who encouraged me along the journey of writing this novel. I am especially grateful to Marilyn Chambers for serving as my editor in chief and so graciously giving her time to apply her knowledge and skill to ridding the manuscript of its grammatical and stylistic errors. I appreciate Cindy Chaffin, B. J. Myers-Bradley, and Yvette Summerour for taking the time to work through the manuscript and share your insights. Each of you helped to make this a better novel! I also want to thank Kristen Hornung, a fellow writer, for taking the time to offer her advice and wisdom. I am thankful to Brandi Doane McAnn for her creativity and patience in designing the cover. Finally, thank you to each reader who has picked up this novel and allowed me to share this story with you.

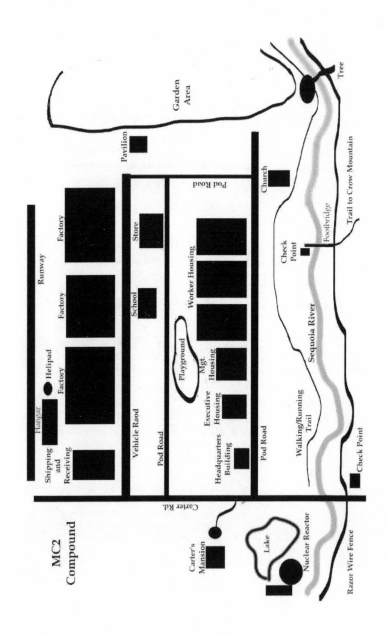

MC2 Compound

Garden Area

Pavilion

Runway

Hangar

Shipping and Receiving

Factory

Helipad

Factory

Factory

Vehicle Raod

Pod Road

School

Store

Pod Road

Playground

Worker Housing

Church

Check Point

Footbridge

Trail to Crow Mountain

Tree

Executive Housing

Mgt. Housing

Headquarters Building

Pod Road

Walking/Running Trail

Sequoia River

Check Point

Carter's Mansion

Carter Rd.

Lake

Nuclear Reactor

Razor Wire Fence

DARK WINGS RISING

Chapter 1

THE NEAR FUTURE...

Sam chuckled to himself, "Half-breed! Well, look at me now!" Stretching back in his new office chair, hands behind his head, Sam thought, "I have proved them wrong!" He was remembering his high school days when the school bullies taunted him, saying he would never amount to anything because he was a "half-breed." As of today, Sam had achieved more than anyone else in his class. He surveyed his corner office and grinned, almost wanting to giggle like a kid. At thirty-two years of age, he had just been promoted to Chief IT Officer for MC2, the energy conglomerate for the whole United States. He relished the moment as he settled in for his first day.

Sam looked around with pride at his new surroundings. He had windows overlooking the Sequoyah River and Crow Mountain in one direction and the factory section of the compound around the corner. "If I turn my desk just right, I can look out at the mountain," he thought. Sam slid the desk so that it was facing the east window rather than the door and sat down. "I like it!" It was a fine office, large enough to say he had made it but functional, too. With excitement, he began to arrange his personal items in the desk.

"I told Evie this would be a good move for us," Sam thought, "And I was right!" Being the IT chief of a big company was one of his life goals, and he had a hunch that MC2 was a place where he could accomplish that when he and his wife, Evie, moved to the compound two years ago. So, as he placed his set of colored pens in the drawer, he wondered why he was still nagged by what she had said when they drove through the check point that first day? "This is a dark place," Evie had said. She had said it as a matter of fact, as though it should be obvious to anyone.

Sam had often thought that if they lived in Ireland, Evie would have been considered fey. She seemed to be able to see and know things that other people missed. Sam shook his head, "I'm not going to let that bother me today!" He went on about the fun business of setting up his office. Yet, the thought still hovered in his mind, probably because he knew Evie was almost always right.

The phone interrupted Sam's preparations. "Mr. Carter would like to see you now." Sam noticed the emphasis on "now" and felt his guts tighten. He hadn't expected to meet Mitch Carter today! Mitch, short for Mitchell, was the owner of MC2, and one of thirty ultra-rich businesspeople in America who controlled just about all commerce. "What? Why? What should I say?" Senseless phrases raced through Sam's mind as his hands started to shake. "Wait, I have to calm down. Why wouldn't the owner want to meet his new IT chief?" Taking three slow, deep breaths, Sam regained control and walked up the two flights of stairs to Mitch Carter's office.

As Sam walked into the outer office, the woman behind the desk stood. "I'm Mary Stein, Mr. Carter's secretary. It's nice to meet you," she said and offered her hand. Sam reached across the desk and shook hands with Mary, an efficient looking woman in her fifties with sensible brown hair, stylish glasses, and a smart business suit that complimented her colors. "If you will have a seat, Mr. Carter will be with you in a moment. An unexpected call just came," Mary explained.

Not surprised at having to wait, Sam took a seat in one of the luxuriously upholstered chairs and willed himself to wait calmly. He began to rehearse what he would say and how he would greet Mr. Carter. "I am so grateful for the chance to serve MC2 as your IT chief." That sounded good. Not cocky, but not too obsequious, either. So, when Mary ushered him in, that's exactly what he said.

Mitch Carter smiled a pleasant smile and said, "I like to hear the word serve! People who strive to serve an organization are valuable." Sam felt welcomed and began to relax in Carter's presence. Carter had a heavy brow, thick brown eyebrows, and a fleshy face with slight wrinkles that turned down from his eyes. Gray mingled with his brown hair, overtaking the part at his temples. Carter was about six feet tall and pudgy, giving him an intimidating and unpleasant appearance.

Sam looked around and noticed the emptiness of the huge room. There was an exquisite chess set on a table with two chairs by one of the ceiling to floor windows, a couple of bookcases, Carter's large carved mahogany desk, and a few chairs. The floor was dark slate with lighter gray granite on the walls. Sam realized Carter was talking to him.

"If you will keep that attitude, you will go far. Wait, you have already gone far, haven't you?" Carter laughed. "Now, a few expectations: I expect my IT chief to stay on top of things, anticipate problems and start solving them before they happen. I need you to keep this operation running smoothly. You have a lot of resources at your disposal. Don't be afraid to use them. Your performance so far says you are up to the task. I don't expect to be disappointed."

"Thank you, Sir. I will give it all I have," Sam replied.

Carter asked if Sam had any questions at this point. Wanting to make a little small talk, Sam asked, "Where did Johnson go so suddenly?" referring to his predecessor in the IT Chief role.

"Let's just say he decided his loyalties lay elsewhere," Carter said. As Sam watched, the smile and congeniality washed away from Carter's face, being replaced with stone. "You had better get busy, now." Carter sat down without another word. Sam understood that the interview was over and left quietly, feeling a little unnerved by the change in Carter's demeanor. Back in his office, Sam took two more deep breaths and then smiled. "I can't believe this is really happening!"

Sam had two desks and a small, six-person conference table in his office. One of the desks was executive style; the one Sam had positioned to be able to look out at the mountain. The other was a workstation with a mountain of monitors on the wall in front of it. Sam had a hunch he would be spending more time at the workstation than looking out at the mountain and river. As he continued to place his personal items, he came to the ceramic totem Evie had made for him on their first anniversary. This was his most treasured possession.

The totem was a replica of his clan's totem. At three feet tall and about a foot in diameter, the totem was an impressive piece of art. Sam thought it was museum worthy, but Evie had said that he was just biased. The totem generated conflicting feelings in Sam, but he realized that these conflicts were the essence of his life and being.

Sam should have been born of the Raven moiety of the Tlingit people near Sitka, Alaska. His father should be following his grandfather as chief, making Sam next in line. But Sandra, a beautiful, courageous photographer and journalist from Chicago had stepped off a boat one day to do a story on Tlingit people. Against the wishes of Sam's grandfather and grandmother and against the norms of his people, Sam's father broke tradition and married Sandra, throwing away his, and Sam's, chance to be chief.

Sam had lived with that regret and the fallout from his dad's decision. He grew up with loving parents, but the other children derided and teased him, calling him half-breed and saying he was polluted. Sam was proud of his Tlingit heritage. Its respect for women was something he cherished and had lavished on Evie. His grandfather had won peace with the clan so that his father and mother had been accepted as part of the community. But that didn't stop the teasing and bullying.

Sam ran his fingers through his thick black hair as these memories flashed through his mind. He looked Tlingit, except for his piercing blue eyes. The eyes had done nothing but stoke the bullying in his youth. It wasn't that Sam was a runt. His five-foot ten-inch frame was stocky and muscular. But as a teenager he had not yet been able to incorporate being different, being a biracial child, into his identity. The least taunt inflamed his anger, and the other kids fed off his reactions. From his teenage years, Sam's first goal in life was to get out and away.

The totem somehow held all of those experiences and memories for Sam, shaping them into a whole for his life. With a flood of emotion, Sam tried to decide where to put the totem. He started to place it on the executive desk, but his back would be to it from the workstation. He felt that he needed to be able to see the totem. It anchored him. He decided to put it on a small chest to the right of the workstation. He could see it from both desks, and it would be one of the first things people saw as they entered his office. Satisfied, he placed the totem on the chest and paused. He was now ready to start his day.

* * *

Evie was supposed to be packing, but she found herself sitting and staring into space. It was a fine summer day. She had seen Sam off for his first day as IT chief and gone for a three-mile run. After showering, Evie put her thick, curly auburn hair into a ponytail and surveyed her summer freckles, her emerald green eyes examining critically. She had taped the bottoms of five boxes, and now here she sat. Because of Sam's promotion, they were being moved to the executive housing complex, but Evie's heart resisted. It would be a nicer apartment with more room, but she had a few friends in this building. That wasn't really it, though. She realized that moving to the executive complex felt like moving closer to the darkness she sensed in the compound.

Evie shook her head, hoping to ignite some action synapses in her brain. "What to pack first?" Evie took a box and walked to the bookshelf. A few minutes later, she realized that she had sat down and was staring into space again. The box was only half full.

Evie had been remembering moving as a child. It happened frequently and usually at night. Her mother would say, "We have to stay one step ahead, Evie," as if that explained the moves. As she grew, Evie came to realize that her mother was carefully timing the moves to stay ahead of an eviction while getting as far behind on the rent as she dared.

Looking at the half full box, Evie said to herself, "You have to stay one step ahead, girl. You have to get busy." Evie was an artist, and it was hard for her to do anything if her heart wasn't in it. She had taken the position as art teacher for the compound school when she and Sam came. School was currently on a brief summer break. The break should make moving easier since she had time to pack, but her heart just wasn't in it. That seemed to be a theme for these last two years. Evie had struggled ever since they moved into the compound.

The MC2 headquarters was pitched as one of the finest places in America to live. Sitting in a gorgeous river valley in the Blue Ridge Mountains of Virginia, it was idyllic. The river cut in close to Crow Mountain on the east, and the valley opened with gentle rolling hills to the west. The mountain wore a soft green shroud over its hard, granite core. The compound boasted recreational facilities of all types. One could hop a jet ski on the lake used for cooling the nuclear fuel in the reactor, kayak the river, or get a pass to leave the compound grounds to hike the adjacent mountains. Evie realized that this should have been a place that fueled her creative energies. "Why is it sapping me instead?" she wondered.

Evie found herself rubbing her upper arm, a habit she had developed ever since the ID chip had been inserted. "Most people would be excited to be here," Evie thought, "Why do I always feel so down?" What she felt like doing was ripping the chip out of her arm. She willed herself to stop rubbing it, realizing that the thing in her arm was part of the problem. While it had its conveniences, like checking out at the stores by just scanning the chip or using it as ID to get through check points, the mandatory chip felt onerous. Evie felt owned rather than free, and the chip that signaled her every move to the compound security force was a symbol of what troubled her spirit. The idea that someone sitting in a surveillance room could locate her on the compound at any moment frazzled her nerves.

Evie decided to take a break from packing, at least from attempting to pack. Maybe she would call Sam and see how his day was going. She pulled out her phone and hesitated. "I should call Sam. At least, I should want to call Sam." She mustered her resolve and dialed Sam's cell phone. When he answered, she summoned more energy to her voice than she felt. "Hey, Sam! How is it going so far?"

Sam told her about his visit with Mitch Carter, where he put the totem, and how he was now going through the different software systems in use. "I haven't found any notes from Johnson, though, about things that need attention," Sam said.

"Well, congratulations again! I'll see you when you get home," Evie said feeling awkward at having to force herself to sound upbeat.

Evie thought she felt the tension in their relationship more than Sam. She also thought it was her fault since she was the one feeling down. "Sam is doing great things at this company and has been promoted to the highest position he could hope to achieve. I need to get more excited about that. I have to quit this pity party and get on board." Evie summoned her resolve and tore into packing, stuffing books into boxes with an angry energy.

With books packed, Evie moved on to knickknacks. When Evie was in this kind of mood, she could get things done in a hurry. Pictures were next. She went to remove one by the living area window and noticed a bluebird perched on the ledge, its bright blue back and russet sides gleaming in the sun. The bird appeared to be studying her. She walked slowly to the window, trying not to frighten it. She bent down and looked into its eyes.

Evie felt a connection with the bird, as though it sensed her angst, and then it flew away. "What a pretty bird!" she thought. "I think it likes me!" Her heart felt lighter after her encounter with the bluebird, and Evie resumed her packing with less fury.

Chapter 2

After hanging up from talking to Evie, Sam felt happy. She had called him! He knew their relationship was struggling since they had come to MC2, but he hoped that it was improving. He had made a list of things that he thought needed to be addressed for work, the most pressing being the program from NOAA to analyze weather patterns and predict long term climate conditions. He did not see any documentation that it had ever been vetted as free of malware. Sam remembered the day the NOAA computer folks had come to install the program. It was the day before Johnson disappeared. Everything else seemed to be running fine, so Sam decided he would examine the code for the NOAA program.

Sam began scanning the code, looking for anything suspicious. After about 10 minutes, his computer suddenly went blank, and the phone rang. "Mr. Carter needs you in his office, NOW!" Mary ordered. Sam feared that all of the computers had shut down like his, but he didn't have time to explore. "If Carter would just leave me alone, I could find out what happened."

As Mary opened the door for Sam to enter Carter's office, Sam saw Carter hurl a tennis ball at his office window. It struck right at the spot where a blue jay sat. It screeched a grating squawk and flew off. "That bird is driving me nuts!" Carter said. "It always seems to show up when bad things are happening." Sam noticed an open drawer with several tennis balls and surmised this must be a regular occurrence.

Carter leveled his eyes at Sam and seemed to be composing himself. "Sit down," he finally said, and Sam obeyed. After a moment Carter said, "You probably noticed that your computer shut down. That was me. I have an indicator that lets me know if someone is messing with programs that they shouldn't be. I have agreed to host the NOAA program on our computers to give them increased computing power. What do you think it would look like if word got out that we had tampered with their program? I want you to consider that program off limits."

Sam could feel his heart speeding up and began to sweat. He said, "I noticed that there is no documentation that the program has been vetted as malware free. Even though NOAA seems a trustworthy organization, I think we need to examine the program to make sure there is nothing that will interfere with MC2's operation or compromise our processes or intellectual property." Sam realized he had spoken with more force than he meant, and he sweated a little more.

Sam saw a slow smile grow on Carter's face. "That's laudable of you, Hanson. But I can personally assure you that there is no malware in the program. Do you need me to sign something to assuage you?" The smile disappeared, and Carter said, "Leave that program alone."

Sam's spine stiffened. He managed a "Yes, sir," as he rose to leave the office. Walking back to the elevator to go down to his office level, Sam noticed the stairs. His adrenaline was racing, so he decided to walk down the two flights. On his way down he found himself muttering, "How would he know if there is any malware in the program? He probably has never seen computer code! Unbelievable!"

By the time Sam reached his office, he felt calmer. His computer was back up and running. "This is ridiculous!" he thought. "Am I just a puppet?" Sam plopped down in his chair in front of the computer. There was a message scrolling across the screen. "Just let the NOAA program run. It will automatically send reports to their offices." "It looks like Big Brother is on the job!" Sam thought with exasperation. Sam sensed that something was amiss, but what could he do about it? "OK, let's see what's next," he thought resolving to put the incident behind him.

* * *

Sam finished his first day and walked out of the building. He pulled out his phone and summoned a pod to take him the half mile home. A dome-shaped transportation vehicle with a door on each side, two seats in the front and two in the back facing each other, and windows all around pulled up to the curb. Except for the color, which was MC2's signature bonfire red, Sam thought the pods looked like half a baseball on wheels. Sam hopped in, and a computerized woman's voice said, "Hi, Sam! Where do you want to go?" Sam replied, "Home," and the battery-powered device pulled out and whisked him there.

Sam opened the door to the apartment to find a jungle of boxes. "Wow! You've been busy!" It was Monday, and the move wasn't scheduled till Friday. It looked like Evie had already packed everything.

Evie hopped over a box as she came into the room, her green eyes sparkling with more life than Sam had seen in a while, "Guess what happened today!"

"You packed everything?" Sam responded.

"No, I had a close encounter with a bluebird! It was sitting on the ledge of that window watching me. It let me walk all the way up to the window and look into its eyes before it flew away."

Sam felt Evie's energy and was pleased to see her excited. So often when he came home he found her seeming sad and tired. Maybe she had come to peace with the move. Without realizing it, Sam's analytical mind kicked in, and before he could stop himself, he said, "I wonder if it was just seeing its reflection in the window."

Sam realized his mistake when he saw the change in Evie's eyes. Transforming from bright and alive to the old, familiar dullness, Sam heard Evie say, "Why do you always have to put down the things I tell you?"

"I'm sorry, Evie. It's just my nature to try to figure things out."

"Well, I know that it was looking at me because it turned its head and followed me as I crossed the room. So there!" Evie said.

Sam, hoping he could rekindle the energy and excitement that he had dampened, said, "I guess it was looking at you then! What do you think it wanted?"

Evie said, "I think it was trying to connect."

Sam felt like laughing but knew better than to let out a chuckle. Seeing Evie's eyes narrow, he realized that she had read what he was thinking. She turned and stomped out of the room. Sam felt frustrated. "How am I supposed to deal with her when she can read my every thought? Should I follow her or let her cool down a bit?" While Sam was trying to figure out his next move, he heard a knock at the door. Torn between answering the door and feeling that he needed to follow Evie, Sam found his feet stuck to the floor. At the second knock, Sam uprooted his feet and answered the knock.

Opening the door, Sam saw the smiling face of Pastor David. David McCutcheon had been assigned to the compound church two months ago, fresh out of seminary. At thirty-five, he had felt the call to be a pastor after a stint in the army, a stint that involved losing three of his friends on the battlefield. Tall, wiry, and pale from too much indoor work, he gave the appearance of a lanky gazelle. His unruly brown hair over soft brown eyes added to the gazelle theme. "Hey, Sam!" David said. "I just wanted to come by and congratulate you on your new position."

Torn again, Sam hesitated. Embarrassed by the disarray of his apartment, he started not to ask David in. But that felt rude, so Sam opened the door a little wider and said, "Thanks,

David. Come on in. Just watch the boxes! They may attack." David chuckled and walked into the apartment, slightly tripping on the first box he met. "Evie, David is here!" Sam called toward the back of the apartment. Evie popped through the door with a smile on her face, her green eyes beaming. Sam breathed again, seeing that Evie had put away the anger. He didn't want David to know they were in the midst of a row.

"Hey, David," Evie said, "Thanks for stopping by."

Sam was surprised at how chipper Evie sounded. "Was this an act, or had she gotten over her feelings from a moment ago?" he wondered. He found that Evie had a way of keeping him off balance.

"I see you are busy packing. It hadn't dawned on me that you would be moving. I will miss you here," David said. David lived in the same building as Sam and Evie, the building that housed professionals and lower-level management. There were seven buildings in a row down the street. For the first three, each building got larger and taller, and the apartments got smaller as one went from executive housing to professional/management to worker buildings. The last five were all worker buildings and were the same size.

"I wish we didn't have to move," Evie said. "I think Sam should ask if we can just stay here."

"We've been over this, Evie. We have to move," Sam said. "It's expected."

"Well, it couldn't hurt to ask."

"I'm sorry, David. Evie and I have a disagreement over this move thing."

"Change can be a difficult thing," David said. "But I'm sure you two will figure it out. I should go and let you get back to packing."

Evie said, "I'm absolutely sick of packing! Won't you stay for supper? It will just be burgers, but I can easily add a third one."

Sam had noticed that David had a way of showing up at people's houses near supper time. He supposed that David's being single had something to do with that. "That's a good idea! It will be nice to have some company," Sam said. Sam also hoped that David's presence might help him get back into Evie's good graces.

"Why don't you two stack some of those boxes so we can walk without killing ourselves, and I'll get supper started," Evie said.

"We're on it!" David said. He and Sam began to organize the boxes, stacking them in a corner out of the way.

Seated at the table with burgers, broccoli, and blueberries, David asked how Sam's first day went.

Sam told him about getting settled in and where he had put his totem. "And I got called in to Mr. Carter's office for a pep talk!"

"Wow! You met the big man!" David quipped.

Sam felt a sense of pride and was glad that David was impressed. He said, "Then..." and stopped. He found himself uncertain as to whether or not he should say anything about the NOAA program.

Evie sensed his dilemma, "What is it Sam? Go ahead and tell us."

Sam was caught, so he began, "There is a program that was installed on our computers for NOAA the day before Arnie Johnson left. It is a weather and climate change prediction program that we are hosting so that NOAA can use our super computers for additional processing power." It felt good saying "our!" "I noticed that it had not been vetted as free of malware, so I started looking over the code. The next thing you know, my computer shut off, and I got a call to come back to Carter's office. He told me to leave the program alone."

"That sounds suspicious," Evie said. "Why wouldn't he want you to check it out?"

"He assured me that it was free of malware and offered to sign something saying so. But I doubt he would have any idea whether or not there was a problem with the code."

"This sounds like a genuine spy novel!" David pitched in and rhyming the last syllable of genuine with spine.

"I don't know about that, David, but it is odd that he doesn't want me to examine the code. I wouldn't change anything."

"They have probably fixed it so that no matter what conditions are put in, it will spit out a rosy picture of the climate forecast," Evie stated in her matter of fact way.

Sam felt a chill run up his spine. It was one of those fey things that Evie had a habit of saying that usually turned out to be accurate.

"Oooh! Juicy!" David said. "Is there any way you can tell if that is the case?"

A wave of embarrassment washed over Sam. He would have to admit that he was under Carter's control if he told the truth. Nevertheless, he said, "Carter has a program that alerts him when anyone is looking that the NOAA program. He warned me that he would be watching."

"I wonder if Johnson's leaving is tied in with this program. Do you know where he went?" David asked. "Maybe we could call him."

Sam thought, "This guy seems to be all about intrigue!" and said, "Carter was tight lipped about that, too."

"I could ask around to see if anyone knows where he went," David offered.

Evie spoke up, "I told you this was a dark place, Sam. I think Carter and his cronies are bad players. You need to be careful with them."

"OK, folks! I think we are getting carried away here by a series of circumstances. Let's relax and talk about something else."

"Still," David said, "I think I'll ask around and see if anyone knows where Arnie went. It will seem natural since he used to come to church. It will be like I just missed him this past Sunday."

Desperate to change the subject, Sam said, "Evie, why don't you tell David about your bird?"

Chapter 3

It was ten o'clock on Wednesday morning. David was working in his office in the church, which was located near the north end of the compound, just before the garden areas where workers grew vegetables and next to the river. David had thought it fitting that the church was located at the place that joined sustenance and work. He had allowed himself two hours to work on Sunday's sermon and two hours for tonight's Bible study, strict schedules being a product of his military training.

Having finished the two hours on his sermon, David stood up and stretched. He went for a second cup of coffee. Looking out the window at the river and mountain, David felt drawn to the scenery. It dawned on David that he had not been out of the compound even once since he arrived two months ago. On the spur of the moment, he ditched the coffee idea and decided to go for a hike. "Maybe the mountain will give me inspiration!" he thought.

David had always loved the outdoors. His father was a ranger for the National Park Service and had been stationed at what was Rocky Mountain National Park until Max Gunther, the owner of Ameridirect, America's shipping industry conglomerate, had managed to purchase the park from the government. Gunther renamed the park Ameridirect Majestic Destination Area and continued to run it as a vacation and wildlife area. Gunther had retained the services of the people in the National Park Service, so David and his family had been able to continue living in the midst of the mountains he loved. While

Crow Mountain was small in comparison to the Rocky Mountains in whose shadows he had grown up, it still beckoned to him.

David stuffed his Bible, note pad, and commentary on the Gospel of Luke into the backpack he carried between his apartment and office and headed out the door. He realized he might get hungry before he was ready to come back, so he stopped into the compound store for a drink and energy bar. He waved his left arm at the scanner to make the purchase and started to leave. Seeing the store manager, who was a church attendee, David walked over and asked, "How are you doing, Sylvia?"

"Just fine," she said.

"I didn't see Arnie on Sunday, and now Sam has moved into his position. Do you know what happened to him?"

"The word I heard was that Arnie up and quit to go to another company."

"Did you get to talk to him before he left?"

"No," said Sylvia, "and I don't know anyone who did. It was like he just disappeared. It must have been a sudden change. Of course, the boss doesn't like it if anyone wants to leave, so I bet he hurried Arnie out the door."

"Thanks," David said. "I was just wondering where he might have gone." A new cover sprang to David's mind. "I'd like to send him a card and wish him well, so if you hear anything, please let me know." David took his leave and headed out the door.

There was a check point to get to the mountain trails about a quarter mile south of the store. David walked briskly, excited to get out of the compound and onto a mountain. The check point was located just before a foot bridge that crossed the river. David recognized the guard, another church attendee. "Hey, Bobby! How are you today?" David said as he approached.

"Just fine, Pastor David. How about you?"

"I'm excited! I decided it is time to go for a hike. I've been cooped up in the office long enough."

"Great! That should be fun," and Bobby began typing in his computer. Bobby, with jet black skin was thick and muscular, making it a marvel that his fingers could move so smoothly over the keyboard. "I don't see a leave approval. Did you submit a request to leave the grounds for your hike?"

"A request?" David went blank. Then his eyes lit up. "Oh no, I forgot all about that. Now I remember I'm supposed to get that approved first. Is there a way to submit the request now?"

"It usually takes a couple of hours for approval to be granted," Bobby responded.

David felt disappointed, and it apparently showed. "Man! I had gotten excited about this hike. I guess I'll have to try another day."

"Do you have your phone?" Bobby asked.

"Sure."

"Go ahead and submit a request. I'll call security and see if they will process it right now."

David whipped out his phone, asked Bobby to show him how to find the request form, and filled it out. When he submitted it, Bobby called security and made his plea. "The pastor is standing here at the check point and wants to go for a hike. Can you make that happen, like right now?" Hanging up, he told David, "They're getting on it."

"Thanks!" David said with a big smile. While waiting for the approval, David asked Bobby if he knew where Arnie Johnson had gone. David saw a shadow come over Bobby's face, but he composed himself quickly.

"I have no idea. He just left." Bobby looked back at his computer screen, and David sensed a little nervousness. "Ah, you're approved. Just wave your chip over the scanner, and you're free to go."

Moving his left arm toward the scanner, David said, "Thanks, Bobby! If you do hear where Arnie went, please let me know. I would love to send him a card to wish him well." David walked through the check point and across the foot bridge over the river. When he got to the other side, he heard an electronic click as Bobby buzzed him through the gate in the fence that ran all the way around the compound. David followed the trail that began to skirt up and to the right along a shoulder leading to Crow Mountain. It felt good to be outside, and David relished the moment.

David turned to look back over the compound before making a turn in the trail. The sun was hot on his back, but a gentle breeze blew. He surveyed the ten-foot fence, complete with razor wire at the top, running along the river. He could see the neatly planted garden area beyond his church to the north, the factory section rising above the housing complexes to the south, and the exhaust stack for the nuclear plant beyond that. David had a strange sensation as he looked at the fence, thinking, "From this angle the compound looks like a prison."

As if cued into his thoughts, David heard the roar of MC2's three Apache helicopters as they zoomed past on a surveillance mission. At least that is what Bobby had told him they were doing when he asked the first week after moving in. Bobby had said that the militia captain, Zeke Starke, liked to keep a check on the area to make sure no other militias were building up forces nearby. "He says he wants to make sure no one tries to sabotage the nuclear plant. Personally, I think it is just a good excuse to keep the helicopters up and running," Bobby had added. David smiled as he watched the helicopters fly into the distance. He had always liked helicopters and fondly remembered when his buddy had coached him through flying one back in his army days.

The trail led David southeast, gradually climbing the face of Crow Mountain till it turned slowly east around the mountain's shoulder. He walked through a thick stand of mountain laurel and marveled at the beauty of dead moss-covered logs lying down the mountain in a frenzy of ferns. David continued walking, mesmerized by the beauty around him. It was a warm summer morning, but in the shade, it felt good. After walking over, around, and under large granite outcroppings, he finally thought to look at his watch. He had been walking for an hour. Making another turn in the trail, David came across a noisy stream in a thicket of rhododendrons. The water leapt from rock to rock on its way down the mountain. He spied a perfect sitting rock just off the trail and said, "This is it!"

David sat down on the rock, pulled out his notepad, and found himself just gazing at the stream and the rhododendrons with their gnarled trunks and thick green leaves. He felt like he was in an ancient place that was full of deep life. "Lord, thanks for showing me this place!" After a few minutes, David realized that, while this was nice, it wouldn't get him ready for tonight. Pulling out his Bible and commentary, he read through the chapter for the study, Luke 10, and opened the commentary. While he was reading intently, he heard a rustle in the leaves and looked up to see a crow sitting on a rhododendron branch a few feet away. David noticed that the bird was eyeing him with one ebony eye then went back to his studies.

A couple of minutes later, David heard another rustle in the leaves. He looked up and saw two ebony eyes. The eyes were seated in a woman's face with brown skin and wild raven hair. Surprised, David stood-- he had been trained to stand when you meet someone-- and tried to find words. Finally, he blurted out, "Hi. I'm David." His eyes locked on the woman's. David was startled as the crow flew right at him. Black feathers and claws filled his vision. He stepped back to get away and plopped down on the rock on which he had been sitting. Shaking his head, he looked back to where the woman had been standing. Nothing. She was gone.

David puzzled for a minute, and then stood back up. He listened for footsteps but heard nothing. "I should try to find her. She might need help," he thought. Then he noticed the crow sitting on a low branch of an oak tree. It had been joined by a second crow. They eyed him a moment, cawed to each other, and flew away. David began scanning the area but saw no movement. He walked up the trail a bit then realized he had seen her coming out of the rhododendrons. He went back to the spot where he had seen her and pushed through the branches and leaves. On the other side there seemed to be a bit of a trail, but it disappeared about a hundred feet back, ending in nothing but forest. David walked to the end of it and looked for tracks.

"Nothing," he muttered to himself. "Where could she have gone? What if she is lost?" David realized that last thought was a bit chauvinistic. "She obviously knows her way around well enough to get away from me," he thought.

David sat back down on his rock and picked up the commentary. "Now where was I?" He was looking at words but seeing ebony eyes. He read a couple of more sentences and found himself trying to decide what she was wearing. "What did she have on? It seemed like an animal hide." After about five minutes of trying to wrestle his mind back onto the track of preparing for tonight, David gave up. "Could I have imagined the woman? I guess I'll just have to wing it tonight. With the parable of the Good Samaritan, that shouldn't be too hard."

David pulled out his drink and energy bar and thought as he began to munch. "How can I leave this woman out here by herself and go back and talk about the Good Samaritan?" He got up and decided most likely she went back in the direction she had come. He followed the short trail and kept going around the mountain, keeping at the same altitude level so as to not lose his way back. He walked for five minutes but saw nothing. "Lord, I hope I wasn't hallucinating!" Giving up, he went back, finished his snack, and walked back to the compound.

David got back to his office about 1:30. Thanks to the energy bar, he wasn't hungry. Guilt spurred him to empty his backpack and try to study again, but all he could think about was the woman on the mountain. David resolved to go back and spend more time looking for her. Maybe he would ask for volunteers to help tonight at Bible study.

That evening David stumbled through teaching as best he could. He meant to ask if people wanted to help him look for the lost woman but found that he had managed to forget. Evie was the last person to leave. "Evie, before you go," he called out. He started to tell her about his encounter, but he just couldn't. He covered by saying, "Tell Sam we missed him tonight. Oh, and I asked a couple of people about Arnie, but neither knew anything. Have a good night."

Chapter 4

Sam had skipped the Bible study to work on a project. Ever since Carter had told him to leave the NOAA program alone, he had been trying to think of a way to examine it without Carter's knowing. He had decided to try creating a cloaking program that would let him access the system without being detected. The week Sam and Evie moved into the compound, Sam, in a bit of rebellion, had modified one of his personal computers by removing the MC2 tracking device. He partitioned part of his older computer's hard drive, copied the hard drive and operating system from his newer computer onto it, and then switched the tracking device so that it was connected to that part of the old computer. To MC2, it looked as if both computers were still accounted for.

Sam opened the computer and began typing code that would make the computer invisible to the system. After about twenty minutes, Sam stopped and scratched his head. "How will I know if this is going to work without risking getting caught?" he thought. Sam was a gifted computer scientist and confidence had never been a problem for him. He had graduated third in his class at MIT, not because he was trying for the position, but just because he was that good. He had hacked into many a system in his day, but the consequences of being caught had never been so dangerous.

Sam leaned back in his chair, feeling tense. He was beginning to realize that the stakes were high if he got caught. "Maybe I should just leave this alone and do my job." Sam realized that he was pacing frantically. "OK, I guess that's my answer. I'll just leave it. Well, it won't hurt to finish writing the program." Feeling calmer, Sam sat back down at his computer and continued working. Writing programs was fun for him.

Oblivious to everything but his thoughts and computer screen, Sam nearly jumped out of his chair when Evie said, "Hey Sam! I'm back... What in the world? Did I scare you?" Evie said.

"I was so zoned in on this program that I didn't hear you come in." Sam got up and stretched. He wanted to give Evie a hug but found himself holding back. She was already walking toward the bedroom, anyway. Sam sat down and resumed writing his code. Evie was used to Sam working at home, a lot, and he knew that she would just assume he was finishing something from work. He wanted to tell her he was trying to find a way to investigate the NOAA program. "She would be happy to know that," he thought. But, since he had decided it wasn't worth risking his job over, he felt that telling her now would just be a disappointment. He felt his own disappointment as he settled into finishing the code.

* * *

The phone rang as soon as Sam walked into his office Thursday morning. It was Sheila, one of his three IT sector heads. "The payroll program has gone haywire again. This time it's at the Oregon plant," she said. "They need to be able to process it by tomorrow."

Sam had been in Sheila's position before his promotion. He had wrestled with that program the entire time he had been at MC2. "Great!" he said facetiously, "I assume you have called Solumatics to get them on it."

"I have. They promised to make it their top priority but couldn't tell me when they would have the problem resolved."

"Thanks, Sheila. Keep me posted." Sam hung up the phone and thought, "I don't think I'll wait on Solumatics to get their act together. I'm going to have a look at that program myself." Sam opened his computer and started to access the code for the payroll program when it dawned on him that someone would be watching. Sam now knew that some poor militia guard was assigned the duty of monitoring when and who was accessing the computer systems at MC2. He couldn't imagine a duller job.

Sam called up the IT surveillance room. "Surveillance. Jonathan here. How may I help you?"

"Hi, Jonathan, this is Sam Hanson, Chief of IT operations."

"Good morning CHIT, how are you?"

"Chit?" Sam responded feeling puzzled.

"Oh yeah, you're new. We have always called the Chief of IT CHIT for short."

"Well, CHIT it is then. We are having problems with the payroll program again. I wanted to let you know that I am going to look into the program and see if I can figure out what's wrong." As Sam was saying this, a thought popped into his mind. "Oh, and I am going to compare someone's file from the Oregon plant with someone who no longer works here to see if I can see any differences."

"Thanks for letting me know so I wouldn't think you were up to something suspicious," Jonathan chuckled.

Sam hung up and wondered if he could get away with it. "It sounds sensible to me," he thought. The idea that had popped into his mind was to look up Arnie Johnson's payroll file and see if it had any forwarding information. Sam began to examine the program. He could see so many patches that had been applied to correct problems that it was almost impossible to sort out what was operational and what had been discarded. He pulled up a worker from the Oregon plant and then pulled up Arnie Johnson's file. The Oregon worker was listed as active and enabled. Johnson's file simply ended as "Terminated." "That sounds ominous," Sam thought. But he also realized that might just be the way the program identified someone who was no longer on the payroll.

Not wanting to spend too much time looking at Arnie's file, Sam glanced over it one more time. He noticed that Arnie's last paycheck had not been distributed. Sam felt a flash of anger. "Good grief! Why didn't they pay him?" he thought. He looked for a notation that the mistake had been corrected but found none. "I'll have to point this out to the payroll department," he thought making a mental note.

Looking over the code, Sam became more and more frustrated. "This is ridiculous!" he thought. "A middle school kid could write a better program." Sam made a decision. "It is time we write our own payroll program." Feeling invigorated with the idea of improving his company, Sam sent off an email to his three sector heads calling a meeting at 1pm today in his office. He also called Jonathan back to let him know that he was out of the program.

Sam spent the rest of the morning preparing a proposal for writing the payroll program. He listed everything that the program would need to address. He could feel himself getting excited. This was the kind of thing for which he had trained! Sam called the head of human resources and told her what he was thinking.

"Thank God!" Audrey Jackson exclaimed. "Solumatics has been nothing but a nightmare for us."

"Will you help me pitch the idea to Carlisle?" Sam asked, referring to the Vice President of Operations.

"I will be happy to. He can be a challenge."

"My sector heads are meeting at 1pm today to discuss the idea. Could you come over and give us your thoughts?"

"I'll be there with bells on!"

At one o'clock, Sam and the three sector heads were gathered around the small conference table in his office when Audrey walked in sporting a smart, black business suit. A tall, slim fifty-something, she greeted everyone with energy, and tossed her black hair over her shoulder. Sam pitched his idea for writing their own payroll program and discussed the possibilities for the structure of the program. Audrey was able to fill in a lot of details that the program would need to be able to do. Sam ended the meeting with, "I'm off tomorrow for the move. Please be brainstorming this program, and we'll get back together Monday at 1pm to see where we are."

As the meeting broke up another idea popped into Sam's head. As the sector heads were walking out the door, Sam piped up, "Audrey, I have one more question for you." When they were alone he said, "I have been trying to find out where Arnie Johnson went. People at the church are asking, but no one seems to know where he is now."

"I'm afraid I can't help you, either. It is like he just walked out the door and never came back! As far as I know, no one knew he was leaving. He just disappeared."

"Are you aware that his last paycheck was not distributed?"

"Are you kidding? I will have to correct that," Audrey said, her face tensing.

* * *

Sam arrived home to a sea of boxes and a tired-looking Evie. "Hey! How's it going?" he asked. The look Evie gave him chilled his soul.

"I'm sick of packing! How did we end up with so much stuff? I'll never get this done by tomorrow," she said with exasperation.

"I'm off tomorrow, so I can help," Sam reminded her. "You look like you need a break. Why don't you do something relaxing while I fix supper?"

"Thanks, Sam, but I need to get out of this place. Let's go out."

Sam didn't really want to go out, but he could see that staying in was not an option. The compound had several restaurants. There was one in each of the housing complex buildings, a nice seafood restaurant by the river, and a cafeteria up near the gardening area. "OK, but you have to pick where we go," Sam said. Sam suspected Evie had already decided where she wanted to go, and he didn't want to set off fireworks by picking the wrong place when she was so tense.

"Seafood. I'm going to shower and change." Evie marched off to the bedroom.

Sam set down the brown leather bag he carried between work and home and started looking for something he could do to be helpful. There had been so much tension at home lately. Maybe when the move was behind them it would get better. Sam started picking boxes up and stacking them in organized rows, adding to what he and David had done the other night. By the time Evie was ready the living area looked less like a tornado zone. Evie surveyed the change but said nothing. "Are you ready?" she asked.

They were early enough to get a table by the windows overlooking the river. The pod ride had been quiet. Sam was searching for something to start up conversation when the waitress came with menus. "Perfect!" he said. "Let's see if we can figure out what we want." Relieved, Sam began scanning the menu. "It used to be so much fun when we went out to eat," he thought. "I don't understand what has happened." Sam realized that his eyes were looking at the menu, but his focus was on his thoughts. He pulled himself back to the restaurant and said, "What do you think you'll have?"

Evie sounded flat when she said, "I think I'll have grilled shrimp tonight." She usually went for the trout.

Sam's eyes lighted on the salmon, and it looked good. "I'll have the salmon."

The area where Sam and Evie were sitting jutted out over the river. There were small bowls of fish food and chutes about 2 inches wide that had little swinging doors in the wall. Sam watched as Evie picked up a few pieces of the fish food, pushed open the door, and let them roll out the chute. They both watched as the food hit the water. Within seconds, trout were swimming around and gobbling it up.

Sam looked around and started to say something, but the waitress came. They ordered, and when she was out of earshot, Sam said, "We had a problem with the payroll program today."

"I don't really want to hear about work woes tonight," Evie said crossly.

"I think you might want to hear about this," Sam said a little more angrily than he meant to.

"What then?"

"While I had the program pulled up, I looked up Arnie Johnson's payroll record."

"OK, I'm listening," Evie softened.

"All that the file said was that he had been terminated." Sam was delighted that he had Evie's attention. "There was no forwarding information, and his last paycheck was never distributed." Sam looked into Evie's eyes. He had always loved the little brown flecks that floated in the green sea of those windows to her soul.

Evie's eyes met Sam's, and she said, "Obviously he didn't just leave, or they would have paid him. He must have done something really wrong to get fired and not paid." A serious look came over Evie as she said, "They would have had to pay him if he were fired, though. The only reason not to pay him is if he was dead. Even then, the check should have been deposited into his account."

"If he had died, why wouldn't everyone know?" Even as he said it, Sam felt the hair on the back of his neck stand up. He looked to make sure no one could hear. "Do you suppose they killed him?"

"Unfortunately, that's the most sense you've made in a long time."

"No, that's ridiculous," Sam said. "Why would they do that? Who would do that? It's not like there are a bunch of murderers running loose in the compound. If he's dead, I'm guessing it was suicide, and anyone who knows is keeping quiet about it." Sam wished he felt as confident as he sounded.

The waitress came around the corner with their food, so Sam and Evie hushed. Sam felt anxious as he unrolled his silverware and got ready to eat. "What if I had tried that cloaking program and gotten caught?" he thought. "It might have been more than my job I was risking." Sam looked up and saw Evie looking at him. He knew she could sense his thoughts and mood. "Should I tell her?" He felt the conflict in his gut. He needed his confidant but didn't want to add to Evie's worries.

Silence settled over the supper, and they both picked at their food. Finally, Evie broke the silence. "Sam, I don't think you should do any more snooping. I have a bad feeling about this place. I wish we were moving away from here instead of next door."

Sam reacted defensively. "But I can't give up this job. It's what I have wanted all my life. Surely you wouldn't take that away from me."

"You and your precious job!" Evie glared at him and put her fork down. Sam tried to continue to eat. He could not find a response and didn't want an argument. Retreating into his thoughts Sam began to wonder, "Do I value this job over our relationship? I have put in a lot of hours since we have been here. But that's what it takes to do what I do and get where I am. Can't she understand that?" They returned to their boxed-up apartment in a chilly truce.

* * *

The next morning, they got up early, and Sam began packing what was left. "Since you're on packing detail, I'm going out for a run," Evie said. She went out the door and down to ground level. Evie liked to run along the river trail, down past the garden area and back. It was an even three miles. As she took off in the cool summer morning air, her body felt better than her spirit. She found herself wondering how much longer she could stay here. "That would mean leaving Sam, too, I guess. He'll never leave that job. I just need to get away from here! Maybe a trip would help. But school starts back the week after next."

Evie's mind was accustomed to roam while she ran, but usually it meandered over more pleasant thoughts. She began to huff and puff and realized she was running way too fast. Coming out of her depressing thoughts, she willed herself to slow down the pace. She also noticed a bluebird on the lamppost up ahead. As she approached, the bird flew to the next post. Evie found herself talking to the bird as she ran, "Hey birdie." At the next post, "Whatchya doing?" The bird stayed with Evie all the way into the garden area and then flew up to a huge oak tree that leaned over from the other side of the river.

As Evie ran under the shade of that tree, she said, "Bye," to the bird and continued her run. As she came back, the bird did the same thing for five lampposts and then flew back to the tree. Evie was puzzled but found herself feeling joy after interacting with the bird. "This is a rare feeling these days," she thought. She suspected it was the same bluebird that had landed on her window.

When Evie walked back into the apartment, she was smiling. Sam said, "You must have had a good run!"

"It was great! The bluebird I saw at the window joined me. It was precious!"

"It sounds like you have a new buddy!"

Evie related how the bluebird had flown before her from lamppost to lamppost.

"That's interesting," Sam said. "But, we only have till one o'clock to be ready to roll."

"OK, let me shower, and I'll get back to packing drudgery."

It was eight o'clock when Evie emerged from the shower. She surveyed the situation. Sam had "packed" his clothes in some boxes, emptying closets and drawers. She observed that they were more stuffed than packed and said, "I'll get my clothes. There is plenty in the kitchen that still needs to be packed. Just save out something for lunch."

As Evie began to place her clothes neatly in boxes, she realized she was humming. She always felt better after running, but she hadn't felt this good in a long time. She kept thinking about the bluebird. The little creature's antics made her feel she finally had a connection here. Her thoughts and humming were interrupted when Sam poked his head through the bedroom door smiling. Evie looked up and saw him just looking at her. "What?" she asked.

"You were humming, and I just wondered, what was so much fun?" Sam said.

Evie felt embarrassed and blushed. "Can't a girl hum while she is packing?" she asked rather defensively.

"Sure!" Sam said. "I'm glad to hear you sounding happy!"

Evie finished the bedroom packing, tackled the bathroom, and began labeling boxes according to the room in which they needed to be placed at the new apartment. She carried the floor plan from box to box. In the living area, where Sam and David had stacked boxes, she got flustered because she couldn't remember what was in each. The move began to feel overwhelming again. It was 11:30, so she called out, "Sam, let's go ahead and eat lunch." Sam agreed.

Over a quick peanut butter and jelly sandwich, Evie said, "Sam, I can't remember what is in which box in the living area. I should have labeled them when I packed them, but I didn't think to." She pulled her ponytail tighter in frustration and guilt.

"Let's just label them for the living area in the new apartment since that's where they are coming from."

Evie felt a rush of anger and knew that it showed. "Why didn't I think of that?" she asked. Sam seemed to make it so easy.

"That's why we make a good team," Sam said. "We yin and yang!"

Evie found herself smiling. "You know, you're right!" She hopped up, rounded the table, and planted a kiss on Sam's cheek.

Evie was still labeling boxes when the movers showed up at 1pm. The movers were a detail of eight men from the militia.

Evie felt a little overwhelmed as they all piled through the door. Wasting no time, John, the crew leader, said, "Where do you want us to start, Ma'am? It is usually best to load boxes first."

Evie pointed to the mountain of boxes she had been labeling, and the men began piling them on hand trucks. Evie felt a wave of anxiety, watching her belongings being whisked away in such a flurry. Everything she and Sam owned just flew out the door. Without all the trappings of life, she had only her inner self left. Somehow, that felt empowering.

The crew had the entire apartment deposited in the new space by 4:15pm. Evie and Sam did a little cleaning and then walked to their new apartment in the building next door. John handed Sam the keys as he and Evie entered. "Have a look around and see if we need to move anything."

Evie felt overwhelmed. "Look at this place!" she gasped. Their new apartment was very upscale and luxurious. Evie made an effort to keep her jaw from dropping as she moved from room to room. She directed the men to change a few pieces of furniture, but for the most part liked where they had placed it. When the crew left, Evie gave herself permission to look around and be amazed. "Wow! It looks like a palace!" Evie exclaimed.

Evie found herself flooded with memories of her childhood. She had grown up poor. Her single mom had done the best she could to provide for the two of them. Her father had left, just left, and they never saw him again. Growing up as a latchkey kid had been lonely. Evie had longed for a brother or sister to help fill the emptiness. She had learned to fill the void with her inner life. It was both a hardship and fuel for Evie's creative spirit.

Evie and her mother had struggled along. Not being a part of one of the A-30 corporations, the huge conglomerates that controlled just about all of the industry and commerce in America, her mother never really had much of a chance to get ahead. Just trying to survive had been the reality of her life. Evie's break came through her artwork. It was so good that she won a full scholarship to Savannah College of Art and Design. She had never even entertained the notion that one day she would be moving into an executive housing complex.

Neither Evie nor Sam had ever experienced the luxury that now surrounded them. Elaborate crown molding, a stone fireplace with gas logs, and high ceilings wowed Evie as she took her tour. She felt a little intimidated as she walked through the kitchen, with its island, granite countertops, and gourmet features. Even the bathrooms were amazing, like something she had seen in a fancy hotel. Evie felt guilty about her resentment toward moving now that she saw the apartment. "What do you think, Sam?" Evie asked, her eyes wide and a big smile on her face.

"This is amazing! I love it!" Sam responded. He ran over and gave Evie a big hug. "I hope you are happier than you thought you would be."

"I'm sorry I was such a grump about moving. Now that I see this apartment, I can't imagine not wanting to live here." She hugged him back.

Chapter 5

Saturday morning, David got up, had breakfast, and pulled out his computer. "I have to get something going on my sermon," he thought. He was behind after going back to the mountain Thursday and Friday to try to find the lost woman. Reading through his scripture passage, he leaned back and hoped some ideas would come to him. What did come was an image: ebony eyes that seemed burned into his memory. "What if she is hungry? She could have starved to death by now. At least she knows where water is."

He shook his head. "That is not helping at all." Trying to tighten the reins on his mind, he forced himself to think about the verse for his sermon, Luke 11:33-36, about not lighting a lamp and putting it in a cellar and the eye being the lamp of your body. "Our inner selves shine through our expressions and actions. And, what needs to be shining in our eyes is love, the love that comes from God and is empowered by God. That's a good start! Now, to build it into a sermon."

David's mind started to click as he searched for ways to illustrate the sermon. "What had I seen in the lost woman's eyes?" Searching his memory, David realized that it wasn't desperation or fear. It was more like curiosity. "Good grief! I can't stop thinking about that poor woman!" Frustrated, David convinced himself that he would be putting his sermon into action by trying one more time to find her.

David stood and walked to get his backpack. Guilt and reality crowded back in his mind. "I still have to preach tomorrow. I know! Maybe it is time to pull out the sermon I wrote in seminary on the Good Samaritan. Since we just studied that, it will be a natural!" Realizing that he was actually talking to himself, David veered to his file cabinet and located that sermon. "I can try this one on hiding the light for next week."

David stuffed a lunch, some drinks, and a notepad into his backpack. He looked out the window and saw fat clouds draping the mountain, their gray ghostly fingers drifting down toward the valley. "I'd better take a poncho," David thought, and stuffed one in the backpack. He punched in a request to exit the compound for his hike and then dressed for the occasion, complete with hiking boots. David started to summon a pod to ride to the exit checkpoint but decided he should walk to give his request more time to be processed. Bobby was on duty at the checkpoint and told him that he was likely to get wet today. David agreed and headed on his way.

Walking up into the cloud felt surreal. Things seemed extra quiet. Mist moved between David and the trees in an eerie way. He scanned the mountain up and down as he walked, but it was hard to see far. While hiking, little ideas popped into his head. "I could talk about how we read faces to tell how someone is feeling. If someone reads our face, what do they see? Maybe this is what I needed to get this sermon going!" David kept walking and thinking.

He was pulled out of his thoughts by a bird singing a beautiful song. Locating the sound, he saw a tiny brown bird sitting on a limb and singing for all it was worth. David continued his climb up the mountain trail and noticed the same song coming from up ahead. It looked like the same bird, but he supposed there could be two birds singing to each other. This was turning out to be a great hike, even if he didn't find the lost woman.

David reached the stream where he had first seen the woman and sat on the same rock. It was a little on the damp side, but he didn't notice. He pulled out his notepad to jot down the thoughts that had come to him while walking and a drop of rain splatted on the page. David heard the downpour coming and rushed to put on his poncho. He stuffed the notepad under the poncho just in time for the deluge. Hunkered down under his poncho, David began to pray. Not really directing thoughts to God, just sitting there and being. It was a way of praying that David enjoyed.

David was startled out of his prayer by the words, "What are you doing!" He jerked his face up and saw the lost woman standing there. David was so surprised that his mouth opened, but nothing came out.

"Why do you keep coming here?" the woman demanded.

"I have been looking for you... to see if I could help you."

The woman looked David up and down and chuckled, "You don't look like much help! Why do you keep bringing books and paper to a stream?"

"I work on..." David felt puzzled and stopped. "Wait, have you seen me more than once?"

"I come for water. You are here."

"Why haven't I seen you then?"

The woman smiled and said, "You don't know how to see."

David felt perturbed and felt his eyes scrunching. He regained his composure and started to speak as the rain stopped suddenly. The little brown bird tuned up again.

"Your bird tricked me," the woman said.

"What do you mean tricked you?" David responded. "And what do you mean, my bird? I guess it has been flying with me today."

"It kept singing, making me think no one was here. It tricked me on purpose."

"OK," David thought, "This person is a little odd."

"The crow tricked me last time you saw me. It obviously wanted me to see you."

David vividly remembered the crow that flew at him, knocking him back down. Then David realized he was staring. He watched as the woman lowered a covering from her head that looked like an animal skin. There was something fluttering in his gut and his heart was beating wildly.

"What you do with paper and books at a stream? You never answered."

Her light Spanish accent was pleasing to David's ear. "I work on Bible studies and sermons."

"You write words here so you can talk them at church? I think I call you Word Man."

David laughed and asked, "What is your name?"

She hesitated and looked down. Then locking her eyes on David, she said, "Viviana."

David thought he saw a blush, as though sharing her name was something very personal. "Viviana," David repeated. As he said it, the name sank into his soul, as though there was a spot that had needed that particular name to fill. Feeling totally overwhelmed, David struggled for a response. He felt himself blushing and looked away to hide the feeling. After the awkward silence, he said, "That's a beautiful name. Why did you not run away this time?"

"I need water. Besides, the birds insist that I meet you."

"You need water?" The realization slowly sank in. "Oh, this is where you get water," David said dumbly. "Wait, does that mean you live out here? What do you mean the birds insist that you meet me?"

"Silly Word Man. You do not understand the birds." Viviana pulled out some kind of pouch and bent down to the stream and filled it.

The little brown bird began to sing again. David looked up and said, "So little bird, were you actually leading me here?" trying to show he was getting the idea that the birds were playing a role in this meeting. When he looked down, Viviana was gone! He had heard no sound. Looking desperately in every direction, he searched. No sign of movement. He finally called out, "Viviana!" No response. David tried to sit down, but too much adrenaline was coursing through his veins. He needed to find her. He wanted to find her. He paced. He walked one way a bit and then the other, all the time knowing he would not see her. He began to wonder if he had imagined it all but knew better than that. When he noticed two crows sitting above his head, he wondered again about his sanity.

Finally, David gave up and started the walk back to the compound. Feelings rushed through his body. One second he felt angry that she disappeared. The next he felt worried for her safety. Then he felt sad that she was gone. By the time he got back to his apartment, he was exhausted, not physically, but emotionally.

David managed to put down a few more thoughts on the sermon that would wait for next week and then embarked on his next mission. He had decided to take a meal over to Sam and Evie's since they had just moved. He put potatoes on to bake, pan seared some chicken strips, and put together a quick salad. With the potatoes wrapped in dish towels, the chicken in an insulated container, and the salad in a plastic bowl, David headed to celebrate Sam and Evie's move.

* * *

Sam and Evie were unpacking boxes in the living area when they heard a knock on the door. Simultaneously, they looked at their watches, discovered it was 6:25pm, and said, "David!" Evie put down the picture she had in her hands, ran fingers through her hair, and headed for the door. She found David standing there with a basket.

"I brought supper," he said with a big smile on his face. "I hope you are hungry!"

Evie said, "How thoughtful of you! Come on in."

As David walked in, Sam stood up from digging in a box by the fireplace. He smiled and said, "Hello David! Welcome to our palace!" as he dramatically spread his arms wide open and spun around. He whacked the back of his hand on the corner of the mantel. The molding on the short side of the mantel flew off and blood began to run down Sam's hand. "Yow! Oh! Ouch!" Sam began to dance. He grabbed his hand and realized it was bleeding.

"Grab a paper towel so you don't drip blood on the carpet," Evie commanded.

Groaning with pain from the smack, Sam obeyed, heading for the kitchen, "I'm dying, and you're concerned about the carpet!"

"First things first!" Evie said.

Sam knew she was joking as he tried to corral the blood in his hand while going for a paper towel. He also knew that he should wash the cut, so he stuck his hand under the water. It smarted seriously. Sam quickly pulled it out and patted it dry.

David set his basket down on the only bare space on the counter and said, "That looks like it will need a bandage. Can I find one?"

"I'm sure they are in one of the boxes in the bathroom, but I don't think they are unpacked yet. Evie will have to hunt it down." Sam started to call for Evie when he noticed her standing in the doorway. He looked up to see his wife standing there ashen faced and holding a rolled-up piece of paper in her hand. "What's wrong? You look like you've seen a ghost!"

"Is this the apartment where Arnie Johnson lived?" Evie asked, her voice barely audible.

"I haven't thought of that, but I suppose it could be," Sam replied.

"I found this paper rolled up and stuck in the mantel where you knocked the molding off." Instead of handing over the paper, Evie just stood there, and her arms dropped to her side.

Sam felt a sense of dread and knew Evie had found something awful. He had trouble getting his words out this time but finally managed, "What is on the paper? Are you going to share it?" David looked on in silence.

Evie started to hand the paper to Sam, but he held up his hands with the left one pressing the paper towel onto the back of his right one and shrugged his shoulders. Evie said, "OK, I'll read it to you. 'Aug. 14: Tomorrow promises to be a hard day. NOAA is coming to install their weather and climate modeling program on our computers. Carter informed me that he wants me in his office as soon as the NOAA people are gone. I don't know why, but I have a bad feeling about this. Lord, help me to sleep tonight so I can face the challenges tomorrow brings.' Then, at the bottom in shaky, scrawled letters it says, 'The worst has happened! I have to le'"

Sam and David stared at Evie for a moment, and she stared back. David broke the silence, "Could I see the paper?" He read it, flipped it back and forth, and said, "This looks like it could have been ripped from a diary."

Sam's guts tightened and he forced himself to breathe. He felt the room shrinking and compressing him. While the kitchen was amply large enough for the three people, Sam said, "I need some space," and walked back to the living area. He sat down on the couch, feeling shaken. "I wonder what happened," he said, so softly Evie and David barely heard.

Possibilities started flying around the room and bouncing off the walls. Evie, "Maybe they wanted him to do something bad, and he had to leave in a hurry to get away."

David, "Maybe he did what they wanted, and they then ushered him out to make sure no one found out."

Evie, "Maybe they were coming to kill him, and he knew it!"

David, "Why would he hide a note in the mantel? Maybe it was a suicide note."

"Why would you hide a suicide note?" Evie asked.

"Or maybe he did something to sabotage the program, and they arrested him," David went on.

Sam found he was massaging both sides of his head, running his fingers through his thick black hair and rubbing his scalp hard. The blood had stopped oozing on the back of his hand. He remembered what Evie said when they first arrived. "Evie, you may have been right. This may be a dark place," Sam said feeling shaken. The note seemed to have whisked away any legitimacy to the idea that Evie and David had been overreacting to the events. It dawned on Sam that he was at the epicenter of whatever had happened. "Could my life be at risk, too?" he wondered. He dared not speak those thoughts because they would terrify Evie. They were terrifying him! What Sam did say was, "What are we going to do?"

Silence and tense faces filled the room. Finally, David said, "I know! Let's eat! I brought some marvelous chicken, baked potatoes, and salad. It won't stay warm forever. Well, everything but the salad. The salad is not warm, at least I hope!"

Sam seized the opportunity for a diversion. "You're right, David. Let's eat! I hope we can find dishes!"

"Sam, how can you think of eating at a time like this?" Evie scolded.

"Well, we have to eat sometime, don't we? And David went to all this trouble, so we shouldn't let it spoil. Besides, we can ponder this thing while we're eating just as well as while we are standing here." Sam led the way to the kitchen. Evie took over, directing whom to take what to the table and pointing to its location.

David said a blessing over the meal, "Thank you dear Lord for this food, these friends, and your love. Please guide us through this mess we have found. Amen." They passed the food around. Silence had fallen, except for silverware clicking on plates. Sam noticed how stressed Evie looked. Next he noticed the slightest smile sitting on David's face. He thought, "David must really like this kind of thing." After a few more bites, Sam noticed the smile was a hint larger. "David, you look almost happy," Sam said feeling puzzled.

David's eyes widened as though he had been caught. "Well, I do have some news. More intrigue, I'm afraid."

Evie had been staring at her plate, but looked up, now. "Well, go on," she said, sounding almost irritated.

David related the story of how he had seen the woman at the mountain stream on Wednesday, gone back looking

Thursday and Friday, and then had seen her again this morning. "She was getting water today, so apparently that is the place she goes for water. I'm afraid she needs help, but she keeps disappearing. I don't know what to do. Do you think we could get volunteers from the church to search and see if we can do anything for her?"

Sam saw the smile slowly spread across Evie's face. She said, "I think our pastor is smitten!"

"What? Why do you say that?" David asked, as a flash of red touched his cheeks.

"Your eyes say things your mouth doesn't," Evie said.

"Does this mystery woman have a name?" Sam asked.

"Viviana," David said.

"What does she look like?" Sam asked.

"She has dark eyes. She is Hispanic with long black hair. Probably about our age. I think she was wearing some kind of animal skin. It was raining today, and she carried another skin as kind of an umbrella. But don't you think we should look for her and see if we can help? Where could she be living? What does she eat? What about when it gets cold this winter?"

Sam and Evie both chuckled, looked at each other, and said, "Smitten," at the same time.

"I am not smitten!" David proclaimed. "There is someone lost out on the mountain, and I think the church has a responsibility to help. I think I have a responsibility to help."

"Speaking of responsibility, what are we going to do about this note?" Evie asked.

Heaviness sank back into Sam's soul as Evie jerked them back to their recent discovery. Thoughts were racing through his mind. He half listened as David was rattling on about how he didn't think they should turn the note over to the militia security team because they may have had a hand in killing Arnie. All the while Sam felt his muscles getting more and more tense. He feared they were holding dynamite and might be placing themselves in danger if they pursued this. Sam was drawn back out of his thoughts when he heard Evie mention the FBI.

"We could turn this over to the FBI," Evie said. "But, you know they would never prosecute someone like Mitch Carter. He probably has the director on his 'payroll,'" Evie said, making air quotes.

Sam started, "I think the best thing we can do is forget about the note and…" All three jumped at a loud knock on the door. Wide eyed, Sam looked at Evie and David then went to the door. John, the head of the move detail, strolled in.

"Just checking to make sure everything is OK," John said. He scanned the room and noticed the damage to the mantel. "What happened here?"

"Sam got carried away and banged his hand on the mantel," Evie said, sliding the note down under the table.

Sam held up his hand sporting its bandage, "I'll get some nails and put it back."

"Nonsense!" John said. "I'll have maintenance come by and tend to it. It may take a few days, though. You haven't found any other… problems?"

Sam noticed the slight pause before John said "problems," as if he were searching for the right word. "No. This place is marvelous!" Sam responded.

"I'm glad you like it. I won't bother you anymore. Just call if you need anything." With a nod of his head, John left. Evie took a deep breath and exhaled slowly. Sam and David looked at each other with somber faces.

"Do you think that was a coincidence?" Evie said. Then she whispered, "You don't think they have this place bugged, do you?"

"Like I was saying, the best thing for us to do is hide the note and forget about it. This can only bring trouble, and if we find that Arnie was murdered, what can we do about it?" Sam whispered.

"We can get out of here!" Evie said.

Chapter 6

Zeke Starke arrived at his office as usual at 6:30am. He didn't mind long days because the pay was good, and he liked his job. He lived for his job. Zeke had retired from the army at the rank of lieutenant colonel. A former Army Ranger, he had continued to be disciplined with regard to his body and maintained his fitness with a home gym and cardio workouts. Tall and very muscular, Zeke presented a formidable appearance. In his mid-forties, Zeke was right handsome with a weathered face, close cropped black hair, and steady blue eyes.

Zeke Starke was captain of the militia for MC2. He tended to all the details of security, maintaining order in the compound, and keeping the militia ready for any eventuality. Starke was Mitch Carter's right hand man and confidant. He almost always dressed in the MC2 militia uniform of black nylon cargo pants and bonfire red polo shirt with the MC2 insignia.

Zeke's first mission every morning was to check in at the surveillance room. Walking down the hall, he heard laughter. It sounded like all three guys were falling out of their chairs. "Someone must have told a good one," Zeke thought and smiled.

He opened the door, and the laughter stopped. All three men snapped to attention. "At ease, men." Zeke ordered. "Are you going to share what was so funny?"

"You have to see this, sir," said Trevor and pointed to the monitor overlooking the garden area. "A bird landed on the camera and keeps looking at us!"

Zeke could see black movement on the screen, then, suddenly, a bird's eye. The three men laughed again, and Zeke found himself laughing, too. The bird pivoted so that they were looking at its back end. "Don't you dare poop on that camera!" Kyle said through his laughter. The bird did poop, but nothing got on the lens.

"Whew! That was close!" Joe, the third man in the room, belly laughed.

Zeke recovered from laughing and asked if they could get the bird off the camera.

"I could try moving it," Trevor said. He punched some buttons and used a joystick to move the camera back and forth a few times. The bird pivoted again and looked into the lens but didn't fly off. Trevor punched a couple more buttons to return the camera to its original position. "I think it likes the ride!" Trevor commented, and the laughter commenced again.

"I trust this was the only incident for the night," Zeke said.

"That's correct, sir," Kyle responded. "It was a quiet night."

"Don't forget to check the other cameras, even with your bird show," Zeke commanded as he strode out of the room.

All three men responded with, "Yes, sir" to his back as he closed the door.

Zeke went back to his office to tend to a few things before his weekly Monday morning meeting with Carter. Every Monday, Wednesday, and Friday, when he was in the compound, Carter wanted to meet with Zeke for an update on security and any other issues with the militia. He seemed particularly proud of his militia. Zeke guessed it was a power thing for Carter. Having risen to the rank of lieutenant colonel in his army days, Zeke had gotten used to powerful men. But it was different with Carter. He seemed obsessed with his power and ability to control things.

At ten minutes till eight, Zeke grabbed a notepad and headed to Carter's office so he would be there five minutes early.

Mary, punctual as usual, arrived just after Zeke had positioned himself to wait by the door and ushered him in. Zeke stood while Mary buzzed back to let Carter know he was here. "He'll see you now," Mary waved him back.

Zeke walked into Carter's cavernous gray office and almost stepped on a tennis ball. He noticed several scattered around the floor. "I see the bird has been back," Zeke commented.

"The thing started squawking just before the sun came up! Come in and sit down, Zeke, and tell me what's going on."

"Apparently a bird has taken a liking to one of our cameras. It had the surveillance crew laughing their heads off this morning with its antics. A few folks have been asking about Arnie Johnson, but that's understandable. Other than that, everything is running perfectly."

"I think it's best that we just let people come to their own conclusions about Johnson, rather than releasing a statement."

"Agreed," Zeke stated.

"You know I'm leaving this morning for the A-30 gathering in Chicago. We have a presidential election to sort out. I don't know if we will continue with a Republican or let a Democrat have a turn this time. I assume the jet will be ready," Carter prompted.

"It's already fueled and on standby for you," Zeke responded.

"Thanks, Zeke. I like the way you keep things going smoothly around here. This is capitalism at its finest. You know, this is the way things are supposed to work. Most people don't have the intellectual or financial resources to take care of themselves."

"Oh no," Zeke thought, "He's waxing philosophical this morning. I'm going to be here a while."

"It makes sense that those with the ability and resources, like the thirty of us who will be gathering for this meeting, should set things up so that people can live and have the resources they need to survive. Look at what we have done here, Zeke. The workers have everything they need to live on and nothing to worry about but doing their jobs. They are happy, aren't they?"

Zeke knew better than to disagree. He also knew it was pointless to try to change the subject. So, he said, "Yes, sir."

"That's good to hear. I use my intellect and resources to take care of all of these workers. In return, they provide me with what I need to continue doing that. It's a beautiful system. What do we have, like ten thousand people in this compound alone? And they are all doing OK."

Zeke knew the real figure was a little over eight thousand, but he let the exaggeration slide.

"Just look at the poor souls outside the compounds. They are hungry and struggling. I'm telling you, Zeke, this is a beautiful thing."

"Yes, sir," Zeke responded.

"I'm telling you, Zeke, it will only take us three days in Chicago to decide who should be the next president and plan the next four years for this country. Three days! Can you imagine what would happen if we really left it up to the people?"

Zeke had somewhat tuned out and thought that the question was rhetorical. He noticed Carter looking at him as though awaiting a reply. "No, I can't, sir."

"Just look back twenty or thirty years ago, and you will see, Zeke. There was nothing but fighting between the two parties. There was no governing going on, just bickering and posturing. The A-30 came in and took the helm, and now everything is as smooth as glass."

Zeke felt the irritation rising but kept his face placid. Sometimes he really didn't like his boss. He was so arrogant! But, whether he liked him or not, Zeke would be loyal.

"Zeke, my friend, I will be back Wednesday afternoon. Of course, you are in charge of security and personnel issues. But, let the VPs run the business side of things," Carter chuckled. "I couldn't run this place without you, Zeke. Thanks for all you do."

"You're welcome, sir." Zeke stood, hoping to seize the opportunity to leave. Carter didn't start up again, so he headed out the door. Zeke was relieved that the lecture was over but found himself wondering about some of the things Carter had said as he walked back to his office. He agreed with the statement that people were better off in the compound, knowing that people who were not employed by one of the A-30 corporations were struggling to survive. Being fired from a compound job was essentially a sentence to a slow death.

"But are they happy?" Zeke thought. "I don't think so. People do what they have to do to survive and tolerate what they have to tolerate." Back in his office, Zeke called to make sure the Boeing Max 9, Carter's personal jet, was in fact ready. He knew he would never hear the end of it if Carter were late to the A-30 meeting, short for American 30. This group of thirty ultra-rich men and women who owned the businesses providing services and products for the country did not do tardy. Receiving assurances that the jet was ready and waiting on Carter to arrive, Zeke hung up.

"But are they happy?" the question ping ponged around Zeke's mind again and again.

Chapter 7

Sam heard the engines roar and twisted in his seat to see the jet lift off and rise into the air. "I guess Carter is on his way to Chicago," Sam thought. He watched till the jet was out of sight, then spun back to his desk. An idea popped into Sam's head. Feeling bold with the boss gone, Sam decided to pull up the NOAA web site and look at the reports being generated by MC2's computers. "He couldn't object to my looking at their web site," Sam thought.

The first screen that popped up was a global view of earth's surface temperatures. It was an interactive screen on which he could spin the globe, click on a spot, and zoom in showing ground level temperatures. Sam clicked over the United States, and the screen zoomed to the lower forty-eight states, showing a topographical map of temperature variances over the land, lakes, and oceans. Sam noticed a distortion in West Virginia. The image had a black spot. Sam clicked on it, and the screen zoomed to the state outline of West Virginia. The spot was still there.

Sam realized this meant there was no data for that hole. "That's odd," he thought. "Why would there be one spot that is not displaying data?" Sam clicked through a couple more screens and came to one that compared today's temperatures to those from one hundred years ago. Since the temperatures were reported in Celsius, they didn't seem that big of a rise. But Sam knew that introducing that much energy into a system the size of the planet was huge. He clicked out of the web site and went back to preparing for the one o'clock meeting with his sector heads.

Sam scooted back to the apartment for lunch and found Evie collapsing boxes. She had finished the unpacking. "Sam, I hid the note from Arnie in your 'Lord of the Rings' book. It's on page 417."

Sam smiled, knowing the page number was the date of their anniversary. "Good thinking, Evie! It wouldn't do for someone to find that."

"Sam, what are we going to do?"

Sam looked up and saw tears rolling from Evie's eyes. "What's wrong?"

"This stress is killing me! I'm worried about you. I'm worried about the note. I'm worried about us." Evie put her face in her hands and headed to the bathroom for a tissue.

Sam followed. "What do you mean that you're worried about us?"

Evie grabbed him in a bear hug and said, "I don't know how much more of this place I can take, and I know you won't leave your job to come with me if I have to go."

Sam hugged Evie back but felt the shock deep in his soul. He knew she had not been happy but had not realized it was this bad. He was torn, knowing that she might be right. How could he leave his dream job? He thought things had gotten better with the move, but today the dam broke. "We'll get through this, Evie," Sam assured. "We will stay together no matter what. I promise. We are not involved in whatever happened to Johnson, so I don't think we have anything to worry about. Maybe school starting back next week will help."

Evie's sobs eased. She took Sam's cheeks in her hands, looked deep into his eyes and said, "Don't you dare do any snooping on the company computers. Promise me that!"

Sam said, "I promise, at least not without your permission."

Evie smiled and hugged him again.

Sam had a quick sandwich and headed back to the office, arriving at 12:50. His team arrived promptly at 1:00pm. Seated around the conference table, each person opened a laptop to the task sharing program. Sheila took the lead, explaining what they had come up with so far. Sam had been distracted by his encounter with Evie when the meeting started, but he found that getting absorbed in the program they were creating took over and pushed his distress aside.

After an hour of hashing out potential pitfalls and bugs in the program, Sam felt pleased with their results. He assigned Sheila the task of finalizing the program and assisting him with presenting it to the VP of Operations. Sam called the office to request a meeting.

"William Carlisle the Third's office, this is Janice speaking. How may I help you?" the secretary answered very formally. Sam explained the purpose of his call and requested a meeting. Janice responded, "Let me check his calendar. He has an opening a week from Thursday at 9:00am. Will that work?"

Sam felt irritated at the delay but pushed it back and responded, "That will be great, thank you." He sent off an email to Sheila with the date and time of the meeting. He started to send one to Audrey but decided to call her. The secretary patched him through.

"Hey, Audrey, this is Sam Hanson."

"Hey, Sam, what's up?" Audrey replied.

"We have a meeting date to pitch the new payroll program to Carlisle. It's a week from Thursday at 9:00am. Will that work for you?" Sam asked.

"Wow! That was quick! Let me see..." Sam assumed she was pulling up her calendar. "It looks like I am free, so I'll be glad to join you. We will need compelling reasons to convince Carlisle to make a change. I'm going to make a list of all the problems we've encountered in the last two years. What do you have?"

Sam replied, "Can I tell him that a middle school kid could have written a better program than the one we have now?"

Audrey laughed, "It depends on how attached he is to this program. I think I would stick with explaining some of the technical problems, but not too technically, if you know what I mean."

Sam responded, "Got it." He started to ask if she had heard anything else about Arnie Johnson's last paycheck but remembered his promise to Evie. "I'll see you a week from Thursday then."

Sam hung up, and things were starting to feel more normal. His schedule was building out with meetings. Projects were getting underway. "Maybe I can get beyond all the problems of the last week," Sam thought.

Chapter 8

As the jet circled around to line up with the runway, Mitch Carter took in the view of Lake Michigan with a smile, the water stretching as far as the eye could see. Coming down toward the runway, a castle came into view, and Carter almost laughed with delight. "He really did it!" Carter thought to himself. The plane landed, and Carter got off and walked to the waiting limousine that whisked him on his way.

Carter's destination was the very castle at which he had gawked while landing. Steve Sterling, the head of ConneX, the communications conglomerate for the USA that owned all phone, internet, and entertainment options, had built a castle modeled after the Hohenzollern Castle near Stuttgart, Germany. Sterling had added a moat to his design. It was an impressive site, though a bit odd on the Chicago lakeside. The road leading to the castle even had an operational drawbridge.

Carter watched the bridge lower as they approached and enjoyed the show. The limousine rolled smoothly up to the front door of the castle, where staff were waiting to usher Carter in and manage the luggage. Carter settled into his room and took a moment to appreciate the castle-like accoutrements, including a full set of armor. Fitting for a castle, there was a male staff member there to serve as a valet and unpack Carter's suitcase, hang his clothes, and get whatever he might need.

The valet ushered Carter down to the meeting room. Carter walked in and let his eyes take in the luxurious setting with huge paintings and wall tapestries. Statues were strategically placed around the room. But the pièce de résistance was a huge, marble round table in the center of the room, fitted with thirty chairs.

About a dozen of the A-30 members were already gathered. Carter walked up to Steve Sterling, a tall, thin, sixtyish African American with intense eyes, and greeted him with a warm smile. "I see we are the knights of the round table today," Carter said. "That is perfectly apropos!"

"Welcome to Sterling Castle, Mitch. I trust you had a good flight and got settled in well," Steve responded.

"I did, thank you. This is a marvelous place, Steve! I love it and look forward to my stay here," Carter said.

"Thank you, Mitch. And I look forward to being at MC2 next year for our meeting."

"I'm afraid that I don't possess your creativity, Steve. My set up is much more... plain."

"Make yourself at home. I see others are arriving, and I must greet them," Steve said taking his leave.

Carter looked around the room and took in the other members of the A-30. He realized that he had his secrets, secrets that no one here would ever know. But he didn't feel guilty. He assumed that each person in the room had secrets of their own. "After all, that is how big business is built," he thought with a smile.

Carter greeted four or five of the other guests before Steve positioned himself by the entry way and spoke, "As you can see, there are no name tags or reserved places. This is a round table, where everyone is equal. Please take the seat of your choice, and we will begin."

Carter literally beamed as he took a seat at the table. Steve's introduction suited Carter's philosophy very much. He liked to think of himself as being in the room with equal titans who were committed to steering the country in the best direction. Carter went to the chair in front of him and sat down between Xavier Harrison, the owner of Bodies-N-Motion, the transportation industry, and Max Gunther, the head of Ameridirect.

Steve Sterling stood and opened the meeting with, "Ladies and gentlemen, thank you so much for making the trip to Chicago for this important gathering. I welcome you to my home and assure you that if there is anything you need, my staff will take care of it. Just let them know.

"Now the election is fast approaching, and we need to decide which candidates we want to advance and list the priorities that we need them to address. I assume that we will start with the office of President, so I yield the floor to discussion."

Ying Chen, a five-foot four-inch whirlwind of energy who was known for her ruthless tactics in taking over the fashion and clothing industry, stood and said, "I think we have things very well on track for all our businesses. Everyone in our employ seems to be faring well. I am concerned about all the people outside our realm of privilege. I think it is time we look at enacting some programs to improve their lot. So many people are hungry, starving even. We need to bring them into the fold."

Xavier Harrison slid his overweight frame out of his chair and stood. "Ying, you are always concerned for these people. America is the land of opportunity, as we all know very well. They just need to take advantage of the opportunity and do something with their lives." Three fourths of the room clapped while he sat down.

Ying jumped back to her feet, and Steve stood at the same time, holding up a hand. Steve spoke first, "People, this is a round table. I remind you that in the A-30, our policy is to be open to all ideas. Please refrain from openly taking sides." He gestured toward Ying as he sat down.

"Thank you, Steve. I would just point out that the way we currently have things structured so that one has to work for an A-30 company to be successful, means that there is no opportunity for those who are not part of our businesses. I do not think we are doing the best we can," Ying responded coolly and sat down.

Mitch Carter stood up next. "I think it is time to advance the Democratic candidate. There has been a Republican in office for twelve years now. We need to present an illusion of fairness to the people. Maybe we could incorporate a little of what Ying brought up into the next four years while still advancing the cause of capitalism. The polls seem to indicate that people are in a mood for change, and I think this will let them feel that they have some control."

Max Gunther stood and said, "I am in agreement with Mitch. I think we need to present the possibility of change in order to keep people's hopes up. I agree that they will feel more empowered, too."

Side conversations broke out around the table and went on for a couple of minutes. Steve Sterling stood again and said, "It sounds like I am mostly hearing agreement around the table. Is anyone opposed to Mitch's suggestion?"

No one spoke up, so Steve said, "That was a quick consensus! We will put our political team to work on a strategy to advance the Democratic candidate, then, to assure that he wins. Now comes the fun part. We need to put together a list of priorities that we want the new president and congress to address over the next four years. As you can see, I have set up six tables along the periphery of the room, each with a sign indicating the policy that needs planning. These were, of course, pulled from the suggestions that you sent in last month. Please locate the policy that most piques your interest and begin discussing it. As always, you are welcome to move from table to table. Let's take an hour for this and then break for lunch. Remember to be as specific as possible. Our lawmakers do better when they know exactly what to do."

Mitch stood and stretched. Looking around the room, he located the table labeled "Climate Change and Natural Resources." "That's for me he thought," feeling satisfied that the gathering had liked his suggestion. He took a seat and prepared himself to do battle with the huge issues facing his business and the world.

* * *

Sam continued to check the NOAA web site over the next two days. The blank spot continued to be there. On Thursday, Sam decided he needed at least to alert NOAA to the problem, though he was sure they were aware. He found the contact information for the person in charge of the project, Dr. Nashima Jarrard. He paused before dialing the phone, "I'm not messing with the program, Carter. Just being a good host," he said to himself as he dialed the phone.

"Welcome to NOAA, Dr. Jarrard speaking."

"Hi, Dr. Jarrard, this is Dr. Hanson, the Chief of IT from MC2," Sam responded, matching the formality of his contact. "Please call me Sam, though."

"Hi, Sam. This is Nashima. How may I help you?"

"I'm just trying to be a good neighbor and call about something of which I'm sure you're already aware. I've been pulling up your web site and looking at the maps that are being generated from the program we are hosting for you. I keep seeing a hole in the data over West Virginia."

"You are right, and we are aware. I have personally been over the program several times and can't figure out what is going on. It's really a small glitch, though. We have bigger fish to fry right now, so we're not planning to spend any more time with it."

Sam responded, "I suspected you knew, but just wanted to make sure."

"Thanks for your concern and tell Arnie Johnson thanks again for his help in getting the program loaded onto your computers. That thing is monstrously large."

Sam hesitated, not sure what to say. "I'll be glad to," he lied, thinking it the safest thing to say. They hung up, and Sam felt a little unsettled after the call. He dug into his work, and soon the feeling passed.

Chapter 9

Except for Sunday, David had continued his daily treks to the mountain looking for Viviana. Today was Wednesday. It promised to be a busy day for David since he had Bible study that evening. He had not seen Viviana since last Saturday and was getting concerned. "What if something has happened? If I can find her, I have to convince her to come to the compound where she can get food and shelter."

David had decided that perhaps the most likely time for Viviana to get water would be early morning. At the crack of dawn, he had his pack ready and was walking toward the trail check point. Bobby was on duty this morning, and David greeted him as he approached, "Hey Bobby! How are you and your family doing?"

"I'm fine. The kids are about to drive us nuts. Thankfully, school starts back next week. How are you?"

"Feeling chipper!" David said with a smile.

"You are making hiking a regular habit," Bobby remarked.

David almost told Bobby about his mission but caught himself. "The mountain is inspiring!" he said, instead. "I have found a rock by a stream that is under a rhododendron thicket. I love it there!"

"I think I know just where you are talking about!" Bobby said. "I remember sitting there on one of my hikes a few years ago. Not much time for doing that anymore."

David wanted so badly to ask if Bobby had ever seen a strange woman there but resisted. "It's a beautiful and tranquil place," he said.

David scanned himself out, passed through the gate, and walked with purpose along the trail. He tried to think about his sermon as he walked, but his thoughts kept coming back to Viviana. A familiar sound drew him out of his thoughts, and he realized it was the little brown bird that Viviana had called "his." It sang and flew along just ahead, as though it were leading him. "Silly bird," David thought. "I know where I'm going."

David continued his hike, still awed by the beauty along the way, till he got to his mountain stream. The bird lighted on a branch, sang a little song, and then flew off. David pulled out his notepad and thought he would at least try to jot down something for his sermon while he waited. As he thought, he became mesmerized by the stream dancing over the rocks. He felt a connection to the water, like the blood flowing in his veins had come from that very stream.

David's reverie was shattered by a prehistoric call. He looked up to see a crow landing on an oak branch high in the tree. Thirty seconds later, Viviana stepped through the rhododendron. "Hola, Word Man. I see you are at it again," she said.

David looked at his tablet and smiled. "That I am," he said. "How are you? I haven't seen you since Saturday. Is everything OK?"

"Everything is fine. Rey told me you were coming today," and she pointed toward the crow. The crow squawked as if to confirm her statement.

"Look," David said, becoming serious. "I think... wait," he paused. "Why did you disappear last time? I wanted to talk with you."

"I no trust you," Viviana said. "You try to follow me."

"What's wrong with that?"

"I don't want to be followed."

"I just want to help," David pleaded.

"You no look like much help. You are too pale and soft."

"What?" David looked at his forearms and realized he had lost all his tan from the last seven years of book work. He had been well tanned and much more muscular during his army days. "I mean, I want to help you with food and shelter and stuff."

Viviana pointed to the crow. "The birds help me. That is all I need."

"What do you mean, the birds help you?" David ran his fingers through his hair, feeling puzzled and frustrated. He was supposed to be the one with the answers.

"The birds, especially the cuervos, help me. They bring food. They lead me places. They bring me to you. Why? I don't know. But I trust them."

"How do you get the birds to do all of this?" David asked with incredulity.

"Silly Word Man! I don't get them to do anything. They just help. They are kind and caring. Good creatures. Humans could learn a lot from them." Viviana took out the pouch David had seen her use for water and stepped toward the stream.

"Wait! Don't!" David said.

"What you mean, 'Wait. Don't?'" I need water for today."

"You disappear after you get water," David said, pleadingly.

"What you want me to do?"

"Well," David struggled. "Stay and talk."

Viviana laughed a loud belly laugh. She bent down and filled her pouch. "OK, we talk." She sat down on the rock where David had been sitting and tied a piece of thin leather around the top of the pouch.

"What is that?" David said, pointing to the pouch.

"A deer bladder."

"It holds water?" David asked.

"That is what bladders do, Word Man. What do you want to talk about?"

"Uh..... you," David said. "Do you live out here?" David felt his mind spinning, and his heart seemed large and constrained at the same time.

"That is a silly question, Word Man. Why are you out here?"

"I'm looking for you." David responded.

"Why you want to find me?"

"Look, I think you need help. You should come back to the compound with me, and we will find you a place to live."

Viviana cut him off, "Don't be ridiculous! I am happy here. Why don't you leave the compound and come live on the mountain?"

"I couldn't. How would I eat? How would I survive?"

"You are right, Word Man. You should stay in the compound." Viviana got up as if she were going to leave.

"Wait," David said. "Don't leave.... Please."

"Now what?

"Where do you live?" David was searching for anything to keep her from disappearing.

"See? I told you I cannot trust you." She crossed her arms and glared at David.

"You can trust me," David explained.

"OK. If I can trust you, then you leave, and I won't have to disappear."

David sensed that Viviana was serious. Miffed, he reached for his backpack and said, "OK. I will go so you don't have to worry. Can I meet you here again?"

Viviana laughed, and David was confused. "Are you asking me for a date?"

"No. NO! I just... Well I would like to see you again... to make sure you're OK."

Viviana laughed, "The birds tell me when you come. I will see you, again."

David stood from the log and brushed off his backside. He was surprised by an urge to reach out and touch Viviana but managed to control himself. He did find that he was reluctant to leave. Finally, he managed a "Goodbye for now," and started his trek back to the compound.

* * *

David said the closing prayer for the Wednesday evening Bible study, and the small group dispersed. Sam and Evie lingered behind, talking with David. The door to the room where they met flew open and a woman entered wailing. She cried and staggered, pushing a stroller toward David. "They are going to take my baby! They are going to take my baby!" she sobbed.

David said rather calmly for the situation, "Sam and Evie, have you met Christie Templeton? Christie, this is Sam and Evie."

Christie seemed not to have registered that anyone other than David was in the room. She staggered back a little and looked at them with bloodshot blue eyes. Her curly blond hair was swirled and partly covered her face. In her early thirties, Christie would have been quite pretty had she not been so disheveled. Her tall thin frame swayed with uncertainty as she battled to stay upright.

David went on, "Christie, I do believe you have been drinking again. Please sit down and tell me, what is the matter?"

Sam and Evie looked on in silence as David pulled out a chair, and Christie sat down.

"That social work woman said if I don't start doing my job better I will either have to resign or send Brittany to an orphanage," Christie spoke between sniffles. Then the sobbing resumed. "They can't take my baby away, can they? I can't afford to resign, either!"

"Actually," David said with a somber face, "I think something like that was in the contract we all signed when coming to work here. We'll have to read it over to be sure, though. Christie, we have talked about this. You said you had stopped drinking a few weeks ago. You know that is the real problem," David explained patiently.

"I had stopped drinking till about two weeks ago. I couldn't help myself. I HAD to start back." Christie was beginning to regain composure.

"Why did you HAVE to start back?" David asked with an edge of frustration in his voice.

"Brittany's dad disappeared, and now I am all alone. I thought we were going to get married, but he's gone. I don't even know where he went!"

"If you tell me who the father is, maybe I can help you find him," David coaxed.

"It's Arnie," Christie said, and resumed her tears.

David felt a shock run through and looked up to see Sam and Evie wide eyed with surprise. After a pause David said, "Do you have any idea where he went or what happened?"

"No. He just disappeared. He wasn't keen on our affair since he was such a bigwig. He kept saying we shouldn't be seeing each other. But he also kept saying that he loved me and couldn't help himself. He proposed the week before he disappeared." She flashed an engagement ring to prove her statement.

David responded, "Now, Christie, if I promise to help you hunt for Arnie will you promise to stop drinking and go back to work?"

"I don't know if I can," Christie sobbed.

"You will lose Brittany, too, if you can't stop," David warned, pulling no punches. "Now go home and pour out all of the alcohol. All of it! I mean it. We will start the search first thing in the morning."

"I'll try," Christie whimpered.

"No trying! Just do it!" David almost shouted.

Christie pulled herself out of the chair and walked out. David looked at Evie and Sam but didn't know what to say. He opened his mouth, but nothing came out. David saw anger flash in Evie's eyes.

She flailed her arms and said loudly, "Good grief! They don't care whom they hurt, do they?" She started pacing, stomping really, around the room. "Threatening to take a baby away from a mother! I can't believe my ears! It's like the company considers us slaves rather than workers! You know what this is like? It's like the Dark Ages, the feudal system! Mitch Carter is the king of the castle, and we are all his vassals. He can treat us however he wants and get away with it!"

"Calm down, Evie!" Sam warned. "Someone might hear."

"Someone might hear!" Evie mocked. "Someone needs to hear! Someone has to put a stop to this outrage!"

David found himself smiling. He had never seen such passion fly from Evie. "OK," he said, "You are right. Someone has to do something, and that someone is us. We have to find out what happened to Arnie, keep Christie from losing her baby, and not lose our own jobs." As he said the words, it dawned on David that he might be suggesting the impossible.

Chapter 10

The next day, as Sam walked into his office the phone rang. "Mr. Carter would like to see you in his office, now," Mary spoke what was becoming a familiar song.

Sam tensed and felt a sense of dread. "Now what?" he wondered. He put down his things and headed to Carter's office.

As Sam entered the outer room, Mary's office, she motioned him over and whispered, "He seems to be in a foul mood today." That didn't help Sam's nerves at all, and he steeled himself as he opened the door to Carter's office. Sam saw what Mary meant in the set of Carter's face.

"Sit down Hanson," Carter barked. He leaned back and seemed to be composing himself before he spoke. "A little bird told me that you made a call to NOAA while I was away."

"I did, sir. But it was yesterday afternoon. You were actually back." Carter looked as if he was going to explode but managed to maintain control.

"Do you recall my telling you to leave that program alone?"

"Yes, sir," Sam responded. "I looked at NOAA's website and noticed there was a hole in some of their data. I thought it would be good of us as hosts to let them know about it. Of course, they were already aware," Sam said defensively. "Why am I sweating?" he thought. "I have done nothing wrong."

Carter leaned back in his chair and seemed to relax. "Maybe the explanation satisfied him," Sam thought.

Then Carter leaned forward, propped his elbows on his desk and looked Sam in the eyes. "Sam do you realize what the consequences of getting fired from here would be?" He didn't pause for Sam to respond. "With one email, I could blacklist you from all opportunities with any of the A-30 companies. Just like that!" and Carter snapped his fingers.

"And," Carter went on, standing and starting to pace, "since energy production has played a role in the climate change problems we are facing, do you realize what a public relations nightmare it would be if someone were to accuse MC2 of tampering with NOAA's program? It would be a disaster!" Carter barked the last sentence with vehemence.

Sam stayed silent, sweat running down between his shoulder blades. Carter took a deep breath, paced toward the window, and seemed to compose himself. "Your actions so far with regard to the NOAA program seem only naïve. I am not under the impression that you have meant anything malicious, and maybe I did not make myself sufficiently clear last time."

Sam started to speak to defend himself, but Carter held up his index finger, "Not yet! I'm not through talking!" he spat. "I expect you to have no contact whatsoever with anyone from NOAA or to open or access the program in any way. Don't even look at the website! I want no one to be able to point a finger at MC2 to say that we are somehow trying to control the results generated by this program." Carter rubbed his temples and shook his head. "I'm starting to wish I had not agreed to host the blasted program," he said. Carter looked at Sam and, after a pause, raised his eyebrows.

Sam realized Carter was waiting for him to speak. "I'm sorry, sir. What you said is true. I have not meant anything malicious and will forget that program even exists from now on unless you directly tell me otherwise, of course."

Sam thought he saw relief in Carter's face. "That will be all, Hanson... Just don't forget!"

Sam walked out the door feeling shaken. Mary gave him a supportive smile as he left. He got back to his office and picked up his totem, looking it over carefully. He looked into the eyes of the bear, raven, and sea serpent. He could feel the fear and disquietude from the encounter with Carter letting go. The feelings were replaced with something. Was it anger? Sam felt a tear well up in his eyes. He continued to hold the totem, and the transformation continued. It was anger he was feeling. They were tears of rage.

"What is the big deal with this program? How dare Carter treat me that way! I'm not the fool he thinks I am!" Sam wasn't sure what was happening to him, but he liked it. He felt more emotional power than he had ever felt in his life. "I am going to find out what you are up to Mitch Carter," Sam said aloud, startling himself. "You are just one more bully, and I can beat you at this game!" He looked up and saw a tufted titmouse sitting on his window ledge flicking its feathers and chirruping over and over. Sam realized the bird was looking at him. "It looks like you agree with me," Sam said to the bird.

When Sam set his totem back on the cabinet, he realized something had changed deep in his soul. He wasn't sure what had happened, but he knew two things very clearly. He could not bear to lose Evie, no matter what. And he knew something very dark was going on at MC2.

Chapter 11

Sam finished his Thursday half working and half plotting. He brainstormed some ideas for how to approach discovering the truth about MC2, jotting his thoughts down on a notepad. Some ideas seemed plausible. None seemed safe. Then the thought struck Sam, "What can I do about it if I find out? Carter is so wealthy and is totally insulated." Finally, it was 4:00pm. Sam realized he was just spinning his wheels, so he decided to go home for the day.

Sam walked into the apartment and was surprised to find David and Evie sitting on the couch. David looked flustered and tense. "Hey, David! How are you?"

David looked at Evie, and she nodded. Then, hesitantly, David began to explain to Sam, "I came over to consult Evie for ideas. I talked to the social worker this morning, and she assures me that Christie has not been pulling her weight on the job. She says her supervisor is fed up with her and has given her one more chance. I went by Christie's, and she was drinking and crying. I don't think there is much hope of saving her job or her baby."

"Sam, they haven't used orphanages for a long time. I've been searching online to see if I could find one nearby. There is no such thing," Evie said.

Sam felt the rage from that morning returning. He shared his morning's encounter with Carter.

"Lovely!" David exclaimed. "This place just gets better by the minute!"

"Carter made it crystal clear what would happen if I were to be fired, and I guess that's true for any of us. We would be blacklisted from working in any of the A-30 companies. We would be ruined," Sam said, feeling a heaviness settle in his heart. "That being said, I intend to do everything I can to expose what Carter is doing here."

Sam expected Evie to be shocked and angry. He saw a tear roll down her cheek. She said, "Sam, I have never been so proud of you. But what can we do? Anyone who knows anything is part of the corruption. It's not like they are going to just tell us what is going on."

"I didn't tell you this," Sam started, "but do you remember the computer I modified when we first moved in? After Carter told me I couldn't look at the NOAA program, I came home and wrote a program that should, I hope, let me access MC2's files without the computers even knowing they have been accessed. When I hack into a system, the program will tell the computer that the user is already logged in. I think I can snoop around and see if I can find any answers."

"I will help in any way I can," David volunteered.

"I think your mission is to try to get Christie sobered up and back to work. Beyond that, I don't want to involve you because this could be dangerous."

"As a pastor, do you think I can sit by and let people be treated this way? Not on my watch!" David protested. "I'm in all the way."

"OK," Sam said and fished in his pocket, pulling out a folded paper. "Here are my ideas so far." Unfolding the paper, Sam said, "I think the best possibility is to hack into the system and look in the security files. Maybe there are some notes about what is going on."

"Sam, what if you get caught?" Evie demanded.

"That is a chance we have to take."

David interjected, "Could you try something not so sensitive first to see if they discover you?"

"Now that's an idea!" Sam lit up. "Maybe I could hack into the social worker's files and see what she has on Christie. There shouldn't be as much attention paid to that as to the security files."

"Let's do it!" David said. They gathered in the office room, and Sam booted up his contraband computer. He started typing in commands, and then hesitated.

"What is it, Sam?" Evie asked,

"If I am discovered, they will be able to tell that it came from the router covering this building. I would probably be the most likely suspect," Sam replied.

"What about at one of the picnic tables in the park?" David suggested.

"There are cameras everywhere. They would actually be able to see Sam on his computer," Evie pointed out.

Everyone pondered for a moment, then David said, "I know! Let's go visit Christie."

"What?" Sam and Evie said at the same time.

"Let's go see Christie. Evie and I can talk to her while you do your magic with the computer. At this time of day, she will probably be so out of it that she won't even realize you are there."

Sam felt hope stirring. "David, you're brilliant! That way, it would look like it was coming from Christie's building, and there are so many people in there they wouldn't know whom to suspect."

* * *

David knocked on Christie's apartment door and waited. No answer. David looked at Sam and Evie, shrugged his shoulders, and knocked again. While they were waiting, the elevator down the hall opened and two security guards stepped out. Sam's eyes popped, but he managed to squelch his panic. The two security guards were followed by two more, one supporting Christie and the other pushing her baby in a stroller.

Sam thought the baby appeared to be about a year old. Christie had obviously been crying.

Sam, Evie, and David waited dumbly as the guards approached. Finally, David said, "Hey, Christie. We were coming to see you. What's up?"

The security guard in front said, "She had requested a pass to go hiking outside the compound. When she got to the gate, she was so drunk that she could hardly walk, much less hike. We escorted her back here for her safety."

"Christie, you promised me you would pour out the alcohol," David scolded.

"It needs me," Christie slurred. She fumbled her key fob out of her purse.

David took it and touched the pad to unlock the door to speed up the process. "We will be sure she gets settled back in," David assured the guards.

"I think you would be wise to listen to this guy," one of the guards scolded. The guards handed Christie over to David and left. David held Christie by one arm and ushered her into her apartment. Evie pushed the stroller, and Sam followed, shutting the door behind him.

"Christie, you can hardly walk! How much did you have to drink?" David asked.

"I haven't been drinking," Christie barely managed to say intelligibly. "What makes you say that?"

"Well, you can hardly stand up, for one thing," David retorted.

"I think this girl needs some coffee," Evie volunteered on her way to the kitchen.

David positioned Christie in a chair at the table facing away from the couch. He looked up at Sam, and Sam understood, pulled out his computer and sat on the couch. He opened the computer and felt sweat pop out on his forehead. He had not expected to be this nervous. He took a deep breath and launched the cloaking program.

Sam hesitated, listening to David's voice in the background as he lectured Christie about the dangers of going hiking drunk. Christie kept denying that she had been drinking today. She also denied that she was going hiking.

Sam gathered his nerve and began hacking into the MC2 system. It took him only a couple of minutes to get in. He smiled and thought, "Working here makes it a lot easier, since I know the vulnerabilities." Sam did a query for "Social Worker" and got, "No results found." "That's odd," Sam thought. He tried a query for "School Calendar" to make sure he was able to use the search engine, and the calendar popped right up. "Hmmm," Sam murmured to himself. He tried "Social Services" and got "No results found."

As Sam started to speak, Evie came back with a cup of coffee. "David, she looks like she's about to pass out," Evie said.

"I agree," David responded.

"I think we had better lay her down," Evie suggested.

Sam saw David's eyes pop wide, and he looked a little panicked. Evie apparently saw the same thing and said, "Don't worry! We won't take her clothes off."

David stood up, and Sam asked, "Do you need help?"

"I think we can manage. You just carry on," David said. He and Evie nearly carried Christie to the bed. The bed was unmade, so they laid her down gently. Evie took off her shoes and covered her up.

"What was she thinking? These flats would not make good hiking shoes!" Evie said. "Wait, what about the baby?"

"There's the crib," David pointed. "I guess we put her in there?"

Evie rolled the stroller in and checked Brittany's diaper. It was soaked, so she tended to it. Brittany woke up during the diaper change but settled down and went back to sleep in the crib. Evie and David left the two sleepers in the bedroom and went back to the living area.

Sam was feeling puzzled and trying to decide what to try next when Evie and David walked in. "There appears to be no such thing as a social worker here," Sam said.

"Well, I talked to one," David countered.

"How did you find her?" Sam asked.

"Christie had a business card. Her name was Daniella Morrison."

Sam typed that name into the computer and got a hit. He pulled up Daniella Morrison's profile. "She is a member of the militia!" Sam said, feeling shocked. "In fact, she is the Commander of Security Forces, it says." Sam looked up and saw two shocked, puzzled faces looking back.

Evie's mouth dropped open. She put her hands to her face and ran back to the bedroom. Sam and David looked at each other and heard, "Christie! Wake up! Wake up, Christie!" coming forcefully from the bedroom. They ran in, and Evie ordered a wet, cold rag.

David found one in the bathroom, took it to the kitchen, and wetted it with water from the fridge dispenser. "Here you go," he said.

Christie began to move. Her eyes opened, and she slightly smiled. "Hey. You have pretty eyes," she muttered.

"Christie, this is important," Evie said. "Can you tell me what happened tonight?"

"I'm so sleepy," she said, and closed her eyes.

Evie shook her again and asked loudly, "Christie! What happened tonight?"

"I think they drugged me," she whispered before falling back to sleep.

Evie ran to the kitchen, and Sam and David followed.

"What is it, Evie?" Sam asked.

"Look at this!" Evie said, scurrying from cabinet to cabinet. She opened the trash can. "There are no signs of alcohol. She hasn't been drinking!"

A thick silence filled the kitchen, and Sam felt he had stepped onto an alien landscape. Nothing was what he had been expecting. "This is more serious than we thought!" Sam said.

"Maybe Morrison doubles as a social worker," David said not sounding very convincing.

"I think this is all tied in with Arnie Johnson somehow," Evie said.

Sam felt a bolt of panic when he realized his computer was still logged into the system. He ran to the couch and logged off as fast as his fingers could fly. Evie and David followed him into the room.

"Now what do we do?" David asked.

"I have no idea," Sam said.

"Well, I do," Evie answered. "You two go home, get some sleep so you will be ready for tomorrow. I will stay here with Christie and make sure she and Brittany are OK. Maybe we can learn something from her when she wakes up."

"You are right as always, Evie," Sam said. "We need more information before deciding on our next step."

Chapter 12

Evie was startled awake by a short scream. She popped her eyes open and sat up to see Christie standing there with her mouth covered. Evie quickly gathered her senses and said, "Good morning, Christie. You weren't doing so well last night, so I stayed to make sure you and Brittany were OK."

"What are you talking about? What are you doing in my apartment? I'm calling security!"

"Don't you remember me?" Evie asked.

Christie paused and looked at her. "You were at the church when I told Pastor David they were threatening to take Brittany."

Evie could see the panic ease. "That's right. And David, Sam, and I were here last night when you came home."

Christie looked blank. "Do you remember that?" Evie asked. "The security guard said you were trying to go for a hike outside the compound but could hardly stand, so they brought you home."

Christie flashed an angry look. "I don't know what you are talking about. I haven't tried to go on a hike."

"Let me get you some coffee and breakfast while you try to remember anything you can about yesterday," Evie said.

"Just coffee, please," Christie responded and sat on the couch where Evie had been sleeping.

"How do you take your coffee?" Evie called from the kitchen.

"Black, thank you."

Evie returned with two cups of steaming coffee to find Christie looking perplexed. She handed her a cup, sat down in the recliner across from the couch, and waited.

Christie began, "I remember that two security guards came up to me as I was leaving the day care center and told me that the social worker wanted to see me. They took me to her office, and she was asking about whether or not I was drinking and going to work. She gave me a bottle of water..... I don't remember anything after that. Not a thing!"

"Wow!" Evie said. "Last night you said that you thought they had drugged you."

"I guess that's possible. I still feel kind of foggy."

Brittany began to tune up in the bedroom. First, it was just short protests, and then a full-fledged cry. "It sounds like someone is ready to see her mommy!" Christie said and headed toward the bedroom.

* * *

Sam hesitated but then decided to take his contraband computer to work. "I may have a chance to try it," he thought. He summoned a pod and made his way to the office. "First I'll see if there are any reports about rogue computers accessing the system," he thought. He left the other computer in the bag, for now.

Sam booted up his main computer and pulled up the reports from Thursday. He was scanning them to see if anything mentioned his unauthorized access when his door popped open. Mitch Carter strode in. "Good morning, Hanson!"

Sam jumped to his feet, "Good morning, sir!" He hoped he didn't look as guilty as he felt.

Carter held out a hand, and Sam shook it. "Hanson, we have gotten off to a rough start, I realize, and I thought you might need some good news. I like your idea about writing our own payroll program. The one we are using has been the source of many headaches. I just want you to know that I appreciate your efforts."

Sam noticed Carter scanning his computer screen and almost flinched. "Thank you, sir. We have come up with a much better program. It will cut down on the headaches a lot."

"That sounds great. What are you working on so early in the morning?"

"I am going over the reports from yesterday and last night to see if there are any problems that need my attention," Sam said, feeling his nerves tense.

"Good job! I like to keep on top of things, too. I requested to have your meeting with Carlisle moved up to Monday. I hope that is OK. I want to get this new program moving," Carter said.

"I'm sure we can be ready Monday," Sam responded.

"Have a good day." Carter nodded and walked out as Sam was saying, "Thank you." Sam took a deep breath and sat back down. Feeling a little shaken, he resumed scanning the reports. "Just what I had hoped for," he muttered to himself. He saw no indications of unauthorized access to the system.

* * *

Mitch Carter made his way to the office, taking the elevator. "I'm not sure why, but I still have suspicions about Hanson," he thought. He sat down in his chair and spun around. "Good! No blue jay today!"

Carter leaned back in his chair. The office was dark and quiet. At 7:45am, Mary had not yet arrived. Carter liked this time of day. He could let his mind roam. He liked to think about his business, make plans for how to grow it, and consider the direction his group of A-30 members should steer the country. But today his thoughts went in an all too familiar direction.

He could feel the rage rising as he thought about his kids and how his wife left him. It was eleven years ago, but it still made his blood boil. She had just disappeared one day while he was away at a conference. She had taken the two children, a boy and a girl, and left with no way for him to contact them. Finally, after three months, she permitted him brief talks with the children. She always cut them off before the call could be traced.

"How could they do that to me? I hate them!" Carter muttered as he remembered trying to talk them into coming to live with him. They both said they wanted to stay with their mother. "Children are turncoats! I provided for them, and they abandoned me. I'll find all of you one day, and you'll be sorry!" He shook his head. "I have to get my mind on something else!" The same scenario played over and over and over whenever the memory resurfaced. The children would be twenty-four and twenty-two years old now, but he still thought of them as small. Carter had never been able to see the hole that their loss left in his heart, only the rage that covered it. And the rage still burned hotly.

Carter heard Mary come in. He picked up his phone and snapped, "Get Zeke Starke here as soon as you can."

"Yes, sir," Mary replied. She called Starke, "The boss wants to see you ASAP."

"I'm on my way," Zeke replied.

Zeke walked into Mary's office about three minutes later. Mary tipped her head toward Carter's office door and said softly, "Foul mood!"

Zeke opened the door and walked into the room with its dim lights and cold grays.

Carter was standing, looking out the window over his chess board trying to puzzle things out in his mind. "Zeke, do you ever play chess?" Carter asked.

"I don't seem to have the time or patience for it, sir."

"We're in a chess game right now. And the longer this NOAA thing drags on, the worse position we have. Did you interview the girl?"

"Yes. Daniella interviewed her yesterday evening."

"And?" Carter demanded impatiently.

"And the girl doesn't seem to know anything."

Carter huffed and stalked back to his desk. His mind was reeling. "And the baby?" he asked.

"I don't think the baby knows anything, either."

Carter exploded. Anger shot to his temples. He clenched his fists and barked, "Don't be flippant with me, Starke! You know what I mean! Do we have any more leverage with the baby? We have to get this thing corralled and soon!"

Zeke replied stiffly, but composed, "As you know, we threatened to take her baby away if she didn't improve her work performance and reduce her absences. She missed the day after that, apparently from drinking, and has since been present every day, running the fiber optics extruder with no problems. I don't know if she will make it today after the dose of scopolamine she was given. If she doesn't, that might give us more leverage."

"I don't need to remind you how high the stakes are, Starke. Do you suspect the girl was lying or really doesn't know anything?" Carter asked.

"Daniella's impression was that she had no idea what we were talking about."

"Good grief! Are you sure the drug will keep her from remembering... from suspecting?"

"Daniella assures me that she won't remember anything from the point that the drug took effect."

Carter sat down and massaged his temples as he thought about his next move. "No progress with our other source, either?"

"No. There was one wrinkle in the interrogation of the girl, though," Zeke stated. "When the guards got Christie back to her apartment, the pastor, Sam Hanson, and his wife were there at the door."

Carter shook his head and thought, "Hanson always seems to be in the wrong place at the wrong time." He looked at Zeke and raised his eyebrows to let Zeke know he was waiting for him to continue.

"It appears they were there to talk to Christie about her drinking problem. We know she went to the pastor the day we threatened to take her baby. The security guard told them that Christie had tried to exit the compound with her baby but was too drunk to stand up, much less hike. So, they had brought her and the baby back to the apartment."

"Lies!" Carter barked feeling his frustration soar. "It gets complicated when we start telling lies, Starke. Now we have three more liabilities!" Carter felt a tinge of anxiety, something he wasn't used to. He resented not being in total control. "Do you have any GOOD ideas for what to do next, Starke?"

"I recommend we wait and let time pass. Nothing has surfaced so far, and the program is working as designed. It seems we have the situation contained," Zeke said.

Carter felt his eyes squint and his jaw tighten. "Waiting gives up control, Starke," he spat. "Waiting just lets the time bomb tick down. I want this issue resolved! We know he made a copy of the program. That thing is out there somewhere, and until we have it, it is foolish to rest. Take the baby! See if that will get any answers."

* * *

Evie heard a panicked cry from Christie's bedroom. "Oh my God! What is today?" Christie called.

"It's Friday, Christie," Evie responded. Evie heard rushing coming from the bedroom and went to look.

Christie was throwing a wet diaper toward the pail. "I have to get to work! I can't believe I'm late! They will blame it on drinking!"

Evie saw the panic in Christie's eyes and knew she was right. She pushed in and took over the diapering. "You get changed and ready, Christie."

Christie rushed through getting dressed and flew out the door. Evie looked at Brittany, looked at the door, expecting Christie to come back. "Well, Brittany, I guess it's just you and me." Evie fed Brittany, put her in the stroller, and delivered her to the day care center.

"I'm delivering Brittany for Christie. She was running late today," Evie told the day care attendant.

The attendant scanned Brittany in and said, "Thank you. We'll take good care of her."

The reply seemed automatic, like something the attendant told every mother or father who dropped off a child. But Evie felt angst as she walked back toward home. "Maybe I should have kept Brittany today," she thought.

Chapter 13

The bright crescent moon cradled the dark sphere in the dawn sky as David stepped out of his building early Saturday morning. There was a cool crispness to the air that invigorated David as he walked toward the check point. Bobby Bridges was on duty and smiled as David walked up. "You're out before the sun," Bobby chided.

"The early morning is the best time for a hike. There are more critters stirring around. The light is interesting, and it's cooler, too," David explained.

"Happy trails!" Bobby said as David started across the foot bridge.

"You have a happy Saturday, Bobby," David replied. He hit the trail with purpose, walking briskly as he climbed the mountain. When he began to huff and puff on the switchbacks, he slowed down to catch his breath. It was only then that he heard the familiar song of his little brown bird. David looked up and saw it sitting on the branch of a black gum tree. The little bird eyed him, tilted its head, and then flew on up the trail.

David followed, hoping that the bird was a sign that he would see Viviana today. Reaching the stream, David sat on his usual rock and waited. He heard a crow call off in the distance and smiled. A few minutes later, Viviana pushed through the rhododendron.

"Buenos días, Word Man," Viviana said.

"Good morning to you, too," David replied

"Your bird sings like it is happy to see you."

"It stayed with me all the way up the trail," David replied.

"What you name it?"

"Name it? I don't even know what kind of bird it is!"

"It's a wren, silly Word Man. You know nothing of the forest. It talks a lot. Just like you," Viviana said with a smile.

David felt a flush of emotion at Viviana's teasing. He realized he was just looking at her eyes and finally managed, "A wren. Hmmm. Do you have any ideas for a name?"

"The bird has picked you to watch out for. It is for you to name."

"Picked me to watch out for?"

"Of course. Why else would it be flying with you?"

"Wait, how can a tiny bird like that watch out for me?" David said perplexed.

"It cannot unless you learn to listen," Viviana responded.

Rey squawked as if in agreement, and David noticed he was sitting on the same branch from which he had flown at David on their first meeting. "How do I learn to listen to a bird? I can hear its song, but that doesn't mean I understand what it is saying."

"You listen with the wrong thing. It is a matter of hearing with the heart," Viviana instructed.

"Hearing with the heart," David repeated. "How do I do that?"

"I no can teach you. You have to discover it. It is in here," Viviana said and put her hand over David's heart.

Viviana's hand felt powerful, magical, warm, and David found it almost hard to stand up. As she removed her hand from his chest, a name came unbidden. "Canto! I think I'll call the bird, Canto. Isn't that the Spanish word for song?"

The bird sang a little song, as if in approval. "I think Canto likes the name," Viviana responded.

David walked back toward the rock where his backpack lay. "Are you hungry? I brought food. We could have a picnic!"

"A picnic? What did you bring, Word Man?"

"Egg salad sandwiches and brownies." Viviana's eyes widened ever so slightly. David thought he saw excitement in them.

"You brought a sandwich for me?" Viviana asked.

"Yes. Of course. Would you like one?"

"Yum!" she said.

David pulled out the sandwiches along with two quart-sized sports drink bottles. "These are for you, too," he said.

Viviana's eyes narrowed, and she looked at him for a moment. "You bring me gifts. I think you like me."

David stammered and blushed but found the courage to say, "I think you are right."

Viviana held out her hand. David looked at her hand and looked her in the eye. "The sandwich?" she said.

"Oh, yeah." David handed her a sandwich and watched as she took a bite. Her eyes closed and she seemed enraptured by the taste. He saw the corner of her mouth lift in a smile.

"This is sooooo good!" Viviana said. David quickly looked away as she opened her eyes. "Aren't you going to eat?" Viviana asked.

"Would you like this one, too?" David asked.

"No, silly Word Man. You eat."

"I'm worried that you don't get enough to eat," David said.

"No worry, Word Man. There is plenty to eat all around us. You are the one with problems. I see it in your eyes."

David was surprised. "How can she tell that?" he thought. "There are some things going on back in the compound that aren't good," he said. "They are threatening to take a mother's baby away because she has been drinking and not pulling her weight on the job. I think we have convinced her to stop, though."

"The compound is an evil place. Dark," Viviana responded. "They do have good vegetables, though."

David saw a flash of fear cross Viviana's face. "What do you mean, 'They have good vegetables?'"

Viviana took the last bite of her sandwich and said, "Did you say something about brownies?"

David sensed that the subject was changed and pulled out the brownies. Viviana seemed to relish the brownie as much as the sandwich. She opened the drink and took a swallow. "Ugh! That is awful!"

David laughed. "You don't like sports drinks?"

"It seems slimy!"

"Oh. Well, I thought you could use the bottle for water after you drink it."

Viviana studied the drink bottle.

"It is good and sturdy and has a wide mouth so it will fill easily," David instructed.

"How would I carry it?" Viviana asked.

David felt crestfallen. He hadn't thought of that. He looked around and seized the solution. "How about this?" David asked and held up the backpack.

Viviana smiled and said, "Now that would be useful. You would give that to me?"

"It is yours if you want it!" David said happily.

Viviana smiled and reached tentatively for the backpack. "You are kind, Word Man. Thank you."

"You are welcome!" David said.

"Getting water is not supposed to take all morning," Viviana said. "I must get going."

David watched as she dumped the sports drinks into the stream and filled them with water. "May I ask a question?"

"You ask a lot of questions. Why would this one be any different?" Viviana responded.

"What are you wearing?"

Viviana looked perturbed. "This is deer hide. It is good for dresses."

David thought she sounded almost guilty. "I can't picture you killing a deer," he said.

"The deer came and offered itself. It was old."

David was trying to process what she said. All that came out was, "What?"

"You no understand. That is why you can't hear with your heart. You are meant to be a part of this," She said gesturing to the mountain and trees all around them. "It calls to you. One day, maybe you will hear," she said and stood still as though she were waiting for something.

"Well, I might understand if you told me," David thought, but he didn't say it.

"Remember?" Viviana asked.

"Remember what?"

"You have to leave first."

David didn't want to leave, but he could see in her eyes it was time. Viviana pulled the backpack on. The straps were set for him, and it hung way down. "I think we need to adjust the straps," he said.

"How you do that?"

David walked over and showed her the ends of the shoulder straps. "Pull these, and it will tighten up."

Viviana did and smiled. "That is much better! Thanks!"

"You're welcome." David looked her in the eyes for a moment, looked around to make sure he was not leaving anything, and said, "Bye."

"Bye."

David started walking back toward the compound with his heart heavy. "When you come again?" Viviana called out.

"Wednesday morning?" David called back. "I have church Sunday and meetings Monday and Tuesday."

"What is today?"

David was shocked that she did not know what day of the week it was. "Saturday," he called back.

"I see you then, Word Man. Be careful in that dark place. Don't let it burn your soul."

Chapter 14

Evie spent Saturday morning putting the final touches on her classroom for Monday. Sam stayed home and did some housecleaning and other chores. When Evie came home for lunch, they began talking.

"Sam, I've been thinking," Evie whispered. "What if this apartment is bugged?"

Sam felt a shock go through. "I had not even thought of that!"

"Do you think they could be monitoring our calls?" Evie asked.

"I don't see why they would. As far as I know, we are not suspected of anything. I think we are getting a little paranoid here," Sam replied.

"Sam!" Evie scolded, then whispering, "These people will stop at nothing to get what they want. Christie said that security guards came up to her when she left the day care Thursday afternoon and took her to the 'social worker's' office. She said they were asking her about her drinking and job attendance. They gave her some water, and that is all she remembers. Why would they drug her?"

Despite his doubts, Sam sensed that he should trust Evie's instincts. "All I can think of is that they were interrogating her about something," he whispered back. "But if you are right, then we had better quit talking about this."

"I know!" Evie said a little louder than necessary. "Let's call David and see if he wants to hang out and eat supper tonight."

Sam was confused but knew the look on Evie's face meant that he should agree. "OK. That sounds like fun. I'll call him." Sam shrugged his shoulders and held up both hands, as if to say, "What?"

Evie nodded her head, so Sam pulled out his phone and gave David a call. "Hey, David! It's Sam. Evie and I were wondering if you would like to get together this afternoon and hang out a while. We could go out to eat for supper."

"That sounds like fun. I'll be over in a bit," David said.

Evie was shaking her head, "No."

"Umm, we were actually thinking we would come over to your place today," Sam responded.

After a brief hesitation, David said, "OK. My place is a mess but come on over."

"Great! We'll see you about..." Sam looked, and Evie was holding up three fingers. "Three," Sam finished. Sam hung up and asked, "Did you get your classroom ready?"

"I did. I ended up not putting anything on the walls. I think I'll use the children's work for decorations this year. That made setting up a breeze!"

Sam was surprised. Usually Evie decorated her room to the nth degree with artwork that she hoped would inspire her students.

* * *

At two o'clock Evie piped up and said, "Sam, let's go for a walk before we go to David's."

Sam put down the book he was reading and said, "That sounds like fun. Let's go."

They walked out of the building into the early September heat. Fortunately, the buildings provided some shade as they walked along the sidewalk, listening to the river's soothing sounds as it navigated the rocks on its way. "How are you feeling about this year's classes?" Sam asked Evie.

"You know, Sam, I don't really have much of a feeling one way or the other. I'm afraid I'll just be going through the motions this year. It's weird. It's like the class isn't even a part of my life."

"Well, that's interesting. I had hoped you were looking forward to it," Sam responded.

"My heart is not in it, Sam," Evie said.

"Well, my heart is not into this heat!" Sam said. "Let's go on to David's apartment."

Sam knocked on David's door, and he answered in his usual chipper manner, arm flourishing to invite them in, "Come in! Come in! My fine feathered friends!" David chimed.

"Hey, David! You seem mighty happy today," Evie responded.

"It is a wonderful day!" David said.

"What makes it so wonderful? It's obviously not the weather, because it's miserably hot outside," Sam queried.

"Every day is a wonderful day. 'This is the day that the Lord has made!'" David responded.

Sam saw the discerning look on Evie's face and knew something was coming.

"You went hiking this morning and saw that woman, didn't you," Evie pronounced.

"Yes, I did. And her name is Viviana in case you have forgotten. She actually lives out on the mountain somewhere. She won't let me know where, though. She claims that she survives just fine. I took her a sandwich and a brownie today just in case she was hungry. She seemed to enjoy them," David gushed.

"So, you took her out to dinner!" Sam teased.

"No. No, it wasn't like that," David stammered.

"How does she survive out there? Is she all alone?" Evie asked.

"I hadn't thought of that," David said. "I assume she is all alone. She says that the birds help her survive."

"That's odd," Sam said. "How could birds help?"

"I'm not sure," David said. "But I believe her. She says," and he stopped.

"She says what, David?" Evie asked.

"You will think this is silly, but she says that I have a bird, too. She said that it picked me to watch out for."

"OK, now I think this woman may have a few screws loose," Sam said. "Maybe you had better think twice about going out to see her."

"But she is right!" David countered. "There is a little brown bird-- Viviana called it a wren-- that flies along the trail with me when I'm hiking. It sings as we go."

"You know, I have a bluebird that does that with me!" Evie exclaimed. "I talk to it while I jog!"

"I think we have a bunch of bird brains on the loose here!" Sam teased.

"You are just jealous that you don't have a bird friend!" Evie chided.

"What would we like to do on this hang out Saturday?" David asked.

"Plot and scheme," Sam said.

"I am afraid our apartment may be bugged, so we thought we would come over here, just to be safe," Evie explained.

David's eyes glazed over for a moment as he thought. Then he said, "No, I don't think it could be bugged. We talked about the note and going over to Christie's to hack into the system. If it were bugged, we'd all be in jail by now!"

"You're right, David!" Sam said, feeling a flush of relief. "I guess the more minds, the better!"

"So, what's our next step in 'Operation Arnie'?" David asked making air quotes.

"Operation Arnie?" Sam asked.

"We have to call it something, and he is the one who started it all," David responded.

Evie brought David up to speed on what Christie had told her about her interview with the "social worker." "Christie was late to work yesterday. I didn't even think about setting an alarm to get her up on time. I guess they have one more strike against her."

David started thinking out loud. "OK, so we know something is amiss with Arnie, and they are after Christie. We know that Christie and Arnie were in a relationship. Maybe they are after Christie because they think she knows something about Arnie. Maybe all of this has nothing to do with her drinking problem."

"The question is where can we find information about what's going on?" Sam asked, and the gears in his mind began to spin. He started visualizing the compound, the apartments, office building, factories, and nuclear reactor hoping that something would trigger an idea.

While lost in his pondering, he heard Evie say, "There is something missing."

That set off the spark. "You're right, Evie! There is something missing! The jail!" Sam said with excitement.

"What jail?" Evie asked. "I didn't know there was a jail."

"Me either," David said.

"That is what is missing!" Sam said. "We have no indication that Arnie left. We have no indication that Arnie died. What if they are holding him somewhere?"

"Brilliant!" David chimed. "Should we walk through the compound looking for a jail?"

Sam patted the bag hanging from his shoulder. "That is what this is for," he said reaching to pull out the computer. "I think it's time to hack into security and see if there is mention of a jail or detention center."

"Sam, are you sure that is wise?" Evie asked, and Sam could see the worry in her eyes.

"There was no mention of unauthorized access the last time I hacked in, so I assume the program works. I doubt we'll find a sign that says, 'Arnie Johnson is being held here' if we walk through the compound. I think this is the only way."

Sam was a little nervous, but mostly excited as he booted up the computer. "Let's see what this baby can do!" he said.

Sam sensed Evie and David's tension as he hacked into the system. He located the security files and began looking through the directories for any mention of jail, detention, holding, or Johnson. After about fifteen minutes of searching, he had found that the security office building had two holding cells but nothing about Johnson.

All three of them jumped when Sam's phone rang. Sam answered, "Hello, this is Sam."

"Hi, Sam, this is Jonathan Massey in security. I hate to bother you on a Saturday, but we have identified a breach in the system by an unauthorized computer."

"Thanks for letting me know, Jonathan. I'll be right in."

Sam felt sweat pop out in his hands and the tension built in his nerves. His first instinct was to exit the program and shut his computer, but he caught himself. "I think they caught me," he said. "I had better leave this running for a while, or they could put two and two together and realize that it was me if I shut it off right now."

Evie looked frightened, which added to the pressure Sam was feeling. "I have to go to the office. Give me twenty-five minutes and then click right here to close the program." Sam hovered the cursor over the spot so Evie could see. "I have to go," Sam said gravely. Sam issued an emergency summons for a pod and rushed out the door.

The pod was pulling up to the curb as Sam came out of the door. During the short ride to the office, Sam raced through possibilities. "What am I going to do?" Sam felt near panic when the pod stopped in front of the office building. As Sam hopped out and rushed to the front door, he heard two short whistles coming from a tree in front of the building. Scanning the tree, he saw a small gray bird with a tufted black crown. Sam stopped, and he and the bird eyed each other. That pause was all it took for a plan to crystalize in Sam's mind.

Sam raced into the building and went straight to the surveillance room. Breathing a little hard from his dash to get there, Sam opened the door and said, "What's going on, Jonathan?"

"I can't really tell, CHIT. I got an alert that the system has been breached by an unauthorized computer. But I can't actually find an unauthorized user on the system. I don't see anything after that message. I'm sorry, but I may have spoiled your Saturday for nothing."

"Don't worry about that," Sam responded and leaned toward the monitor. "Can you send me a screen shot of the alert message? I'll go see what I can find from my office."

"Sure thing!" Jonathan said, sounding relieved. "It's on its way."

"Thanks," Sam said and hurried out of the room.

Sam nearly ran to his office. The adrenaline was still pumping. He booted up his computer as quickly as he could. Ignoring the email with the screen shot, Sam went straight into his analytics program and began searching the log in list from today. Sam checked his watch, and he had twelve minutes left till Evie switched off the program.

Sam carried the laptop over to his workstation and booted up his other computer. He pulled up the system analysis and ran through everyone who was currently logged into the system. His eye was drawn to a blank line. One sign on was assigned a time, but no name. "That must be me," he thought.

Sam left that screen up and went back to his laptop. He kept an eye on his watch while he searched for signs of hacking. Then it dawned on him that Jonathan must have overlooked, or just didn't understand, that blank line. He noticed for the first time how tense he felt.

Sam kept popping through files on the laptop while checking his watch and the other computer screen. He was seeing no indication that the system had been hacked, which gave him some relief. At the correct time, the blank line showed that the user was no longer on the system.

Sam ran a quick check to see if he could locate where he had accessed the system. He was able to see that it was accessed from David's apartment building, but that was as far as he could trace it.

"Now what do I do?" Sam thought. He sat back for a moment and tried to compose his story for Jonathan. Sam realized his muscles were in knots. He stretched and tried to relax. Then Sam remembered to do one more check. "Oh man!" he grumbled. He was able to trace the files that his computer accessed. "I don't see any way we can investigate this without getting caught. But, I still have to come up with some resolution for Jonathan." Sam realized he was talking to himself. "I must be really stressed!"

Sam stretched, got up, and walked over to look out his window toward Crow Mountain. The same gray bird that Sam had seen when entering the building was sitting on the window ledge and singing the same song. Sam smiled and said, "Maybe I do have a bird. Hey, fellow! Now what do I tell Jonathan?" Sam watched the bird and decided that the best thing to do was to tell Jonathan the truth, sort of.

Sam made his way back to the surveillance room. "Hey, Jonathan," he said as he walked in.

"Hey, CHIT! What do you think of this thing?"

"It appears to be a fluke," Sam responded. "It seems that someone was already logged in and then logged in again. For some reason, the system didn't recognize the second log in and tagged it as an unauthorized computer. I can't tell which computer it was, only that it came from the management building. It looks like the person read a few files. Nothing was downloaded or anything suspicious done that I could see."

"Thanks for checking that out! The boss doesn't like mysteries. Would you mind sending Zeke Starke a report? It can wait till Monday. I don't think we need to bother him today," Jonathan said.

"Sure, I'll be glad to. I hadn't even thought of that," Sam said. As he started out the door, an idea popped into his head, and he said, "Thanks for being so alert and catching that, Jonathan. It's good to know you are keeping a close eye on things."

"Just doing my job, sir. But thanks."

Sam's heart was heavy, and he felt discouraged as he headed back to David's apartment. His cloaking program worked as far as preventing the system from identifying the computer but still triggered an alert. "How will we ever find out what is going on?" Sam thought as he took the short pod ride back.

While getting out of the pod, Sam's phone rang. "Hey, Dad!" Sam said.

"Hey, Sam! How are you doing?" Sam's dad, Katlian Hanson, said.

"A little frustrated today. I had to go into work for a little while because of a security breach. But other than that, I'm fine. How about you?"

"I'm fine. It's your grandfather I'm calling about. He is in the hospital with a heart attack."

"Oh no! How serious is it?" Sam asked.

"The doctor says that he will be OK, but this may slow him down a bit. He is in the coronary care unit, but they plan to move him out to a regular room tomorrow if he remains stable."

"I need to come and see him," Sam said. "But, I have to be here for a big presentation on Monday. I'll see if I can get off and come up after that." After a little more talk about home and how Evie was doing, Sam hung up. He was feeling heavy, like gravity had intensified, as he walked into David's apartment building.

Chapter 15

Zeke Starke had arranged to have Bobby meet him in his office at 7:45am this bright Monday morning. Bobby arrived promptly, wondering what was going on. He was a little nervous, but he couldn't think of any reason that he would be in trouble. He had never been called to Starke's office before. "I can't imagine what this is about," he thought as he walked down the hallway toward Starke's office. Had Bobby known what was going on, he would have stayed in bed.

The door to Starke's office was open. Bobby stood in the doorway and said, "Good morning, sir."

"Good morning, Bobby! Come on in," Starke replied and got up to close the door behind Bobby. "Please, have a seat." Bobby sat down in the chair to which Starke had pointed, and Starke walked back around his desk.

"We have a major problem, Bobby, and we need your help," Starke began to explain.

Bobby kept silent and waited for Starke to continue.

"Mr. Carter wants to see us this morning to find out if you can help us deal with a situation," Starke said somewhat enigmatically. "We are to meet with him at 0800. Will you be willing to hear him out?"

"Of course," Bobby said, feeling even more jittery than before. He had never even seen Mitch Carter, much less met him.

"Great!" Starke said. "Let's head on up to Carter's office, then."

"Am I allowed to ask what this is about?" Bobby asked.

"We'll fill you in when we meet with Carter," Starke said and ushered Bobby out the door.

Starke opened to door into Mary's office and gestured for Bobby to go in. Following Bobby in, Starke introduced Bobby to Mary. "It is nice to meet you," Bobby said. "I hear you are the one who is really in charge around here."

Mary smiled and said, "That is definitely a false rumor!" Mary looked at Zeke with a tense expression.

"That bad, huh?" Zeke said.

"He's wound tightly this morning. Mind your Ps and Qs," Mary said as she moved to open the door to Carter's office. "Starke and Bridges to see you, sir," Mary announced.

Zeke led Bobby into the office. Bobby wasn't sure what he expected to see in Carter's office, but the cold gray was not it. Bobby felt a cold sense of dread as he took in the surroundings.

"Good morning, sir. This is Bobby Bridges, one of our most loyal and trusted militia men. Bobby, this is Mitch Carter."

"It's nice to meet you, sir," Bobby said and extended his hand. He noticed Carter had a puzzled look on his face. He was watching Starke as he held out his hand to shake Bobby's.

"It is nice to meet you, too, Bridges," Carter said, and smiled at him. "I hate to seem inhospitable, but something has come up that I need to discuss with Zeke alone. Would you mind stepping out and giving us just a minute?"

"Of course," Bobby said and went back to Mary's office, closing the door behind him and feeling totally confused. He tried to hear what was being said in Carter's office. He could tell they were talking and that there was urgency to the tone, but he couldn't hear the words.

"What is he doing here?" Carter said in hushed tones, gesturing toward the outer office.

"He is the man I selected to carry out the mission," Zeke responded.

"What? I thought you would do it," Carter said.

"I don't want this traced back to me," Zeke said. "Besides, what am I going to do with a baby? Bridges has two young children. He will know what to do with the girl."

"Starke, we can't keep the baby here! That won't do at all."

"Well, what do you have in mind then?" Starke asked.

"You like to hunt, don't you? Take the baby out and shoot it!" Carter said coldly and resolutely. "Word would get out quickly if we tried to keep the baby here," Carter went on. "It would have no effect in producing the results we need. They have to think the baby is gone and fear something worse will come."

"What could be worse than that?" Zeke questioned. "There has to be hope of getting the baby back to produce results."

"No one will know that the baby is dead but you and me, Starke. There will be hope of getting it back. It will be at the orphanage, remember?"

"There are no orphanages, Sir." Starke reminded him.

"OK, foster care, whatever! That is beside the point," Carter said with a glare.

Zeke felt the weight of what Carter was suggesting settle in like a large stone in his gut. He felt a little foolish for having assumed that he could place the baby with the Bridges. He felt nauseated at the thought that he would have to kill a baby. He realized he was glaring back at Carter, and Carter was speaking.

"I don't want anyone else involved in this. I need you to handle it. The more people involved the more likely this thing is to unravel and blow up in our faces. You know that as well as I, Starke. If we are going to save this company, we have to find out what Johnson did! This is the only way I know to find out. Nothing else has worked, has it?"

Zeke didn't say a word. After a moment he walked to Carter's door, opened it, and said, "Bobby, it looks like we won't need you after all. Thanks for coming." Zeke closed the door.

"There will be a massive bonus for this, Zeke," Carter said. Zeke felt the office closing in on him. He couldn't believe he was in this situation. He couldn't believe that he could take an order like this. "Why don't I just walk away?" he thought. "Maybe I was in the army too long. I got too used to taking and executing orders, no matter what. How can I do this?" He tried to compose himself as he faced Carter.

"Christie was late to work on Friday, so that can be the impetus for taking the baby. Should we give her the option of resigning?"

"Hmm," Carter said as he thought. "That would get her out of the way, and it is in the contract... Yes. In order to avoid the repercussions of a lawsuit, give her the option to resign or lose the baby."

Zeke turned and walked out of the office without another word. On his way back to his office his mind was reeling. "How can I agree to do such a despicable thing? It is an order. The bonus will be nice. This is ridiculous. I can't do it. But, I have to. I can't walk away from this position. I would be killed myself because I know too much. I don't see any other way. Maybe she will opt to resign."

When Zeke got to his office, he picked up the phone. Daniella Morrison answered, and he said, "It's time. Call in Christie."

* * *

At 8:50am, Sam, Sheila Oaks, and Audrey Jackson assembled outside William Carlisle, III's office. They briefly strategized their presentation before the meeting.

"I really don't think we have anything to worry about," Audrey said. "If Carter is behind this, how can Carlisle not go for it?"

Sam and Sheila were in the process of agreeing when Gerald Bush, Carlisle's assistant, poked his head out and said, "Mr. Carlisle is ready. Please come with me." Sam felt a tinge of excitement as he entered the spacious office, noticing the lavish artwork on the walls, the carved antique desk, and the separate conference room.

"William Carlisle the third," Carlisle said as he extended his hand. "It's a pleasure to meet you."

"Sam Hanson, Chief of IT," Sam said. "And this is Sheila Oaks, IT Sector Head, and Audrey Jackson, head of Human Resources."

"Yes, Audrey and I go way back," Carlisle said. "It is nice to meet you, Sheila." Carlisle directed them to the conference room, where Gerald asked if anyone would like something to drink.

When everyone was settled, Carlisle said, "I hear we are worn out with Solumatics and are ready to take payroll under our own wing."

Sam launched into his prepared speech, detailing the background of the problems they had had and how they proposed to improve the payroll process with the new program. Just as he was getting rolling on the speech, Carlisle held up a hand.

"I see that you are passionate about this, and I appreciate that. I know Audrey wouldn't be here if she didn't believe this was a good idea. So, let me save you some energy and cut to the chase. Will the new program work?"

"I am confident it will work and be a great improvement over what we have now," Sam said.

Sheila spoke up, "We have beta tested the program with no problems being detected, sir."

"Well, who am I to question a crackerjack team like this? If you are in agreement that we proceed, let's dump Solumatics and get this up and running as soon as possible."

"Thank you, sir. We will make that our top priority," Sam said, feeling relieved.

Carlisle stood, held out his hand to Sam, and said, "Congratulations on a great innovation, Sam."

"Thank you, sir," Sam replied.

As Sheila and Audrey stood to leave, Carlisle congratulated them, too. Sam hung back as Sheila and Audrey walked out the door. "Sir, my grandfather was put in the hospital over the weekend with a heart attack. I would like to go up and visit him if that would be permissible."

"By all means, Sam, you should go," Carlisle responded.

"Thank you, sir. I'll see about booking a flight."

"Nonsense, Sam! You are an MC2 executive! How would it look if our company executives flew commercial? People would get the idea we can't afford to take care of our own anymore! We will have one of our pilots fly you in a corporate jet. Not Mitch Carter's jet, mind you, but one of the others."

"Wow!" Sam exclaimed. "Thank you."

Chapter 16

Zeke Starke walked into Daniella Morrison's office at 9:25am feeling stressed. The plan was to have a security detail pick Christie up from work, get the baby, and bring them to the office for the decision. Zeke didn't even say hello when he walked in.

"We hit a snag," Daniella said. "Christie wasn't at work, and the baby isn't at the day care center."

Zeke pulled out his phone and called the surveillance room. "Trevor, can you locate Christie Templeton for me?"

"Just a second, sir," Trevor responded.

Zeke could hear the tapping of keys.

"It appears she is in her apartment," Trevor announced.

"Thank you very much, Trevor," Zeke said and hung up. "She's in her apartment."

"That's where the detail is headed now," Daniella said. "I guess we wait then."

Zeke was too antsy to sit down. The doubts still played in his mind but with less fury. He was beginning to resign himself to what he had to do.

"I don't know what good this is going to do," Daniella said. "I don't think Christie knows anything."

"Carter insists that we have to try," Zeke said.

"You know," Daniella said, "I think he hates children. Maybe that's why this is so important to him."

"He also loves his company and feels threatened with this Johnson thing loose out there."

Daniella's phone rang. "We found her. She is in the apartment and drunk."

"Bring her and the baby," Daniella responded and hung up.

Daniella flipped through papers, and Zeke paced while they waited.

"I'm not in the army anymore. I don't have to do this." The thoughts continued to swirl in Zeke's mind. "But if I don't, I will be too much of a liability to Carter. I could fight my way out of this place. Maybe it's easier to just do it and carry on with my life. Maybe she will opt to resign. I should take one of the Apaches and blow my way out of here! But, then what? I wonder what the bonus will be." Zeke still wasn't sure that he could go through with the despicable task when the security detail entered with Christie and Brittany.

Daniella took over and directed Christie to sit down. Zeke stood off to the side, watching.

"Christie, are you drunk?" Daniella asked.

"What else could I do?" Christie said through her tears. "I knew when I was late Friday you would come for Brittany. You don't have a heart! How can you do this?"

With Christie sobbing, Daniella said softly, but firmly, "Christie, it is obvious that you cannot manage your job or take care of your baby. One of them has to go. It is in your contract that you can resign or give the baby up. I need you to make a choice... now."

"How can I make a choice like that?" Christie spat. "If I resign, we both die. If I give up Brittany, she will live. But I will die without her. That is no choice. You people are monsters!"

"This choice is the consequence of your actions, the choices you have made up to now. I am sorry that you have placed yourself in such a predicament," Daniella said. "If the child has a father who is willing, we could place her with him. Otherwise, she will be placed in foster care. Of course, if you give up Brittany, you will still have to perform your job satisfactorily."

Christie sobbed and sobbed. Finally, she hugged Brittany close, kissed her over and over, and said, "Baby, I can't keep you anymore. You are going to have to live with someone else. It is for your own good."

Daniella slid the papers across her desk toward Christie and said, "You may have the rest of today off."

The sobbing stopped. Christie looked pale and lifeless. She signed the papers, and the security guards escorted her back to her apartment.

"It is a good thing she was drunk," Daniella said. "That might have made it easier."

Zeke felt the anger rise. He felt like striking Daniella. "How could she seem so unaffected?" he thought. Daniella handed him the papers showing that Christie had given up Brittany, and that Brittany was to be transported out of the compound. Without a word, Zeke picked up Brittany's car seat and walked out.

* * *

Sam sent Evie a text message as soon as he got back to the office. "We are set to go to Sitka this afternoon at 4:30... on one of the corporate jets! Can you arrange a substitute?"

Sam dug into preparing to be gone for three days. He sent emails to his sector heads congratulating them on the success with the payroll program and informing them of his trip to Sitka. He instructed Sheila to load the program and test it so it would be ready to go with the next pay cycle, which would begin a week from today.

Sam was excited. He was excited to fly on the corporate jet and excited to see his family. At two o'clock he called it quits and headed home to pack. On the pod ride home, his phone dinged. "I found a substitute and can leave as soon as class is dismissed," Evie texted. Sam was nearly packed when Evie got home.

Evie rushed into the bedroom and started throwing clothes onto the bed. "Fold those," she ordered.

Sam saluted her, said, "Yes, ma'am!" and dutifully began to fold, trying to be as neat as he was capable. They packed in such a rush that they were through by 3:15.

"Let's eat something. I'm starving," Sam said. "I wonder if they will have food on the plane." After rushing through sandwiches, Sam put his work computer and the contraband computer in a bag and hauled their bags to the sidewalk. Just before summoning a pod, Sam had a sinking feeling.

"I wonder if they do a security check before we get on the jet. I think I had better leave my computer here." He ran the computer back upstairs and summoned a pod. Cramming their bags and themselves into the small space, Sam directed it to the jetport.

* * *

Zeke Starke felt numb as he carried Brittany to his truck, which was waiting outside Daniella Morrison's office. Somehow the questioning had ceased. He knew he was going through with the order. "What choice do I have?" he thought. "Besides, money makes the world go around."

Zeke placed Brittany in the back seat of the truck and strapped her seat in. At the checkpoint he presented the papers Daniella had given him and was cleared to leave the compound. Zeke tried to think about what he would do with the bonus as he drove. "I will be a rich man!" he thought. But visions of actually shooting the baby kept creeping into his mind. They made him shudder and feel nauseous. "It has to be done. It is better to die a quick death than a slow and painful one from starvation, which is what would happen if Christie had kept her and left the compound. They are both better off this way."

Zeke played the rationalizations over and over as he drove east away from the compound. He had killed many times while serving as an army ranger. But the men he had killed were always the enemy, and they would have killed him if given a second longer. Then, it was a matter of survival. This was vastly different.

The war between the money and rationalizing the kill began to lose to the angst and nausea. Zeke turned off onto an old dirt road. As soon as he was out of sight of the main road, he pulled over and vomited. Zeke sat back in the truck and wiped his mouth with an old towel. He resisted looking at Brittany. "What am I going to do?"

With the thoughts whirling in his head, Zeke realized that he hadn't heard a sound out of Brittany. He finally glanced back and saw that she was sound asleep. "She looks so peaceful," he thought.

Zeke shook his head and clinched his fists. "I have to pull myself together!" He closed his eyes and breathed deeply and slowly. "This is a mission. I have to accomplish it." Zeke pulled out a map and looked it over. He discovered that he was on an old forest service road that led along the back side of Crow Mountain. "This is as good a place as any," he thought and resumed driving, noting the time on his watch.

Zeke drove slowly, having to put his truck into four-wheel drive for the gullies and boulders. He hoped not to wake the baby. After fifty minutes, Zeke came to the top of a steep hill and stopped. The ground leveled out and there was a small, flat meadow on the right side of the road. Forcing himself to act quickly in order not to fall back into the misery of self-doubt, Zeke left the truck running while he hopped out and opened the back door. Without looking at the baby, Zeke grabbed the car seat and pulled it out of the truck. "I'll get the shovel next."

Surveying the ground, Zeke located a spot that was hidden from the road where he thought he could successfully dig a grave. Setting the car seat down, Zeke walked three steps away and reached for his gun.

"DON'T MOVE!" blasted from behind him, and Zeke jumped. "If you touch your gun, you're a dead man."

Zeke slowly turned his head to see a woman with an arrow trained right at his heart. Her posture and the way she held the weapon told him that she would not miss. He thought, "I had better bide my time and wait for a better opportunity." Zeke lifted his hands above his head and just stood there. He heard a cacophony of crow calls all around him.

"What are you doing, man?" the woman questioned.

Zeke stonewalled with silence, watching for an opportunity to pull his pistol. He slowly turned to face her. The woman was strategically positioned next to a large tree. "She knows what she is doing," Zeke thought. "I was just going to the bathroom," Zeke lied.

"No, you weren't."

"Zeke heard the unwavering resoluteness of her voice. "She knows I'm lying," he thought. He said, "Can a fellow help it if he has to pee?" trying to sound innocent.

"The crows say otherwise."

Zeke realized that there were crows all around him, cawing relentlessly. Looking around, he felt the hair on his neck stand up. "Look, we obviously have a problem here. Let me get the baby, and I will be on my way." Zeke thought, "If she planned to kill me, she would have done it already."

"NO!" she shouted. "You will get back in your truck and drive away. NOW! Keep your hands up and do not reach for your gun."

Zeke walked back to the truck with his hands up.

"When you get in, keep both hands on the wheel and back out of here."

Starting to step into the truck, Zeke had a sudden sense of relief. He thought, "I will do just as she said. I don't have to shoot the baby and can still get the bonus!" After backing for about ten minutes his neck was hurting. He found a spot wide enough to turn around and did. Then he paused and had a thought. He pulled out his gun and fired three shots into the air. "Just in case they can hear that from the compound. Now, I can tell Carter that I disposed of the baby, and no one but me ever has to know." Zeke found himself whistling as he drove back.

Chapter 17

Security did a quick bag check and ushered Sam and Evie onto the corporate jet. Buckling himself into his seat, Sam looked at Evie and grinned. She smiled back. Sam was excited to be flying on such a luxurious plane. The plush leather seats were more like recliners than the airplane seats he had known. A nice wooden table with drink holders filled the gap between Sam and Evie's seats.

"I think I can manage this for a while!" Sam said.

"I can't believe how nice this is!" Evie responded. Sam noticed that she was looking around and taking in all the details.

"It's 1630," the pilot's voice came over the speakers. If you will please fasten your seatbelts, we will be off. We should arrive in Sitka at approximately 1825, Sitka time." As soon as he stopped talking, the engines revved, and the pilot taxied out onto the runway. After a brief pause, the jet accelerated, and they were off.

Sam did the mental calculation to discover that they would be in Sitka at 6:25pm. Sam and Evie both jumped when a stewardess came up behind them and asked if there was anything she could get.

"You startled me," Sam said. "I didn't realize there would be a stewardess."

"Surprise, surprise!" she said with a big smile. "My name is Monica, and I will be serving you. Now, what would you like? We will provide dinner in 2 hours."

Sam and Evie decided to splurge, and both ordered wine.

"I could get used to this!" Sam said and noticed Evie's eyes were a little wide, and she had a worried look. "What is it?"

Evie took a deep breath, let it out slowly, and whispered, "That looks like the woman who was posing as the social worker, Sam."

Sam turned his head slowly, as if to look out the window on the other side, to see if the stewardess might have heard Evie. "We need to be careful about what we say then." Sam whispered. Evie responded with a scowl but didn't say anything.

Evie took Sam's hand and whispered, "It's silly, but do you know what I have been thinking since you said we were going to Sitka?"

"No. What?"

"What if we just stayed there and didn't come back?"

Sam flinched and knew Evie saw it. "We can't stay. We have to come back."

"I know. Your precious job," Evie groaned.

"No." Sam looked around again. "We have, umm, other matters to tend to. Remember?"

Evie's lips tightened. "Why do you always have to be right?" she said.

* * *

The plane arrived in Sitka right on schedule. As the jet banked and turned to line up with the runway, Sam marveled at the way the water snuggled up to the small city. Behind, the still snowcapped mountains reached for the sky. It was a beautiful sight, a welcome sight, home.

Stepping onto the stairs, Sam thanked "Monica" for her service and sighed once he was away from the jet. The flight had been tense. Sam had felt that his every thought was being monitored. Evie looked worn. It had been hard to avoid talking about the MC2 issues.

"I have to stop by the bathroom and freshen up," she said. "I think I have actually been sweating!" Sam called his dad to let him know they had arrived.

Already fueled with supper, Sam and Evie decided to go straight to the hospital. As the taxi pulled up to the front entrance, Sam saw his dad and mom standing outside. Getting out, they took turns embracing and greeting each other.

Sam's dad, Katlian Hanson, who went by Kat, was named for a Tlingit war chief who led a battle against the Russians in 1802. He had streaks of gray, most prominent around the temples, in his jet-black hair. His dark almond eyes blended to laugh lines and shone with what seemed a lifetime of joy. At fifty-six, Kat was tall, thick, and muscular as though he had been cut from the mold of a grizzly bear. He wore his hair long, in a ponytail, in the tradition of his Tlingit people. Releasing his hug on his son, Kat said with a big smile, "It sure is good to see you two! It has been too long!"

Sandra, Sam's mom, was all smiles, too. She held Evie by the arms and surveyed her with serene blue eyes. With her long blond hair pulled back, she seemed too pretty to live in such a rugged country. But her eyes were set with deep strength and peace. Sam drank in the peace and joy he always saw in his parents and felt a tinge of envy.

"You two do the manly thing and carry the bags to the car," Sandra said. "Evie and I will go on up."

Kat slapped his son on the back. "I think we can handle that!" Kat started gathering up bags, and Sam began to protest.

"I can carry some of those, Dad!"

Putting the last of the bags in the trunk of the Jeep Cherokee, Kat said, "You look tense, son. What's troubling you?"

"We have problems at work, I guess," Sam said evasively.

"Ah, work! The bane of our existence! It drains our lives of joy but is a necessary evil. I still have fourteen years to go. I shudder to think how long you have to work till retirement." Kat chuckled and said, "But somehow we will make it."

Sam felt an urge to unload all of what was going on to his dad. But he also felt that he didn't want to involve him in MC2's issues. The less he knew the better. Sam filled the walk up to the room with questions about how his grandfather was doing.

"He seems to be recovering just fine," Kat assured Sam. "The doctor says he may be a little slower than before but should be able to go home in a few days."

Walking into the room, Sam saw his mom straightening the pillows and covers while his grandpa had Evie by the hand.

"My precious Evie! It is always such a joy to see you. Your smile warms an old man's heart!"

With a big smile that could warm anyone's heart, Evie said, "Well, let's keep that heart warm so you can get out of here soon!"

Sam felt the pride that always seemed to swell in his heart when he realized just how much his family loved Evie. He walked over to his grandpa and leaned over for a hug, being careful not to disturb the IV and heart monitor lines.

"Hey, Grandpa! How are you feeling?"

"I feel great! If they would just untie me, I would sneak out of this place! And how are you, Yielxaak?" Sam's grandpa asked, calling Sam by his middle name.

Sam's Grandpa, Skautlelt Hanson, was named for a Tlingit warrior who led an attack on the Russians a few months earlier in 1802 than the warrior for whom he had named his son. He was a wiry seventy-nine-year-old, with long, thinning gray hair. His dark eyes were penetrating and wise. He was still highly active and had been splitting wood when he had his heart attack. Going by the name of Skauty (most pronounced it Scotty) he was the chief of his clan, which was centered just out from Sitka. Skauty was a traditionalist. While most of his people used English names, he chose to use his Tlingit name. He had named his son with a Tlingit first name and English middle name, Katlian Paul, but insisted that he be called Katlian. Over the years, both of their names had shortened to easier versions. Sam's dad had appeased Skauty by giving his son an English first name and Tlingit middle name.

"I'm doing fine," Sam said, "Other than worrying about you!"

"No need for worrying, Yielxaak. Old people get sick and die. It is nature. Let's try to enjoy what we have and not worry." Skauty looked deep into Sam's eyes, and then turned to the others. "Kat, you and Sandra look hungry. Why don't you take Evie and go get something to eat? Yielxaak will visit with me for a while."

While it was said as a question, everyone in the room knew there was no question about it. The chief had spoken, and Kat, Sandra, and Evie dutifully said their goodbyes and left.

"Now, Yielxaak, there is more than worry for an old man in those eyes. There is heaviness in your soul and darkness in your heart, like a bear with cubs when there is no salmon. Will you tell me what is wrong?"

Sam felt his heart stir. All of a sudden he felt the heaviness, the desperation, his grandfather had seen. He pulled the chair close and sat down, trying to compose himself.

"Where to begin?" Sam said. "Wait, how could you tell that so much is going on with me?"

"Yielxaak, you spent so much time fighting to defend yourself as a youngster that you never learned to see with your heart. Your Evie learned that from a young age. But, you still have a long way to go."

"Well, I guess it won't hurt to tell. There is something dark going on at MC2. You know that I was promoted to the Chief of IT. It appears that my predecessor just disappeared. It also appears that he may have tampered with a NOAA program that we are hosting on our computers. Now the company security officers are interrogating my predecessor's fiancée, and we think she was drugged. We don't know if they have my predecessor in jail or have killed him. Something dreadfully wrong is going on, and Evie, our pastor, and I have been trying to uncover it." Sam sighed after he had finished and felt the heaviness lifting.

"Yes, that's a big part of it," Skauty said. "I feel there is something closer to home, too."

"No, I think that's it," Sam said.

"The darkness I see seems closer to your heart than work," Skauty said.

"Good grief!" Sam exclaimed, wondering how everyone he was close to could read him like a book. "OK, Evie and I have been having some... troubles," Sam said. "But things seem to be better now."

"Yielxaak, you have a wife with a beautiful, wise spirit. You must learn to listen to her, trust her. She sees from the heart," and he tapped his chest with his fist.

"Grandpa, I am stressed out. What we are dealing with could be dangerous. I fear for Evie's safety. I fear for my own safety. If they discover we are trying to unearth what is going on, we could end up like my predecessor. Evie suggested we should just stay here and not go back."

"Fear is a helpful emotion, Yielxaak. It warns us to be careful and vigilant. But it is not a signal to stop. Never fail to act because of fear. You are there at this time because you are the ones to do what needs to be done. Life is not worth much if it is not lived with integrity. Trust your heart and follow where it leads."

Sam sat back and let his grandfather's words sink in. With his grandfather's encouragement, Sam began to feel that it was possible to take on the mission. He also began to feel a great warmth for Evie. "You know, Grandpa, you are right. The very first time we entered the MC2 compound, Evie said, 'This is a dark place.' Obviously, she was right. I don't know how, but I am beginning to feel that we can do this."

"Of course, you can! Also remember that mountains are sacred places. We can always look to them for help. This Crow Mountain near you is a special place."

Sam and his grandfather continued to talk until the other three returned. When Evie walked into the room, Sam hopped up, gave Evie a big hug, and whispered, "I love you."

Kat and Sandra gave each other puzzled looks and turned to Skauty. He just grinned.

Chapter 18

At 3:10pm that same Monday, the door to David's office burst open, and a sobbing, staggering Christie appeared. "Do you have a gun? I need a gun!" Christie yelled and fell into the small sofa.

Afraid that he already knew, David asked, "Oh no, Christie! What happened?"

"I'm a terrible person! I can't live anymore!"

Even though she was drunk, David's heart went out to her. "You're not a terrible person, Christie. Now, tell me what is going on."

"Will I go to hell if I kill myself?"

"Christie, pull yourself together. God loves you no matter what. Paul said that there is nothing that can separate us from the love of God. So, quit worrying about hell and tell me, what is wrong?"

"I just sat there and let them do it! I didn't even fight. It seemed like the best choice for Brittany at the time. I don't deserve to live!"

"Did they take Brittany?" David asked for clarity.

"They said I either had to give her up or we both had to leave the compound. I was afraid that we would both starve, so I let them take her. Why am I so weak?"

"That is bad news, Christie. I am so sorry," David empathized. While trying to connect with her in order to support and comfort her, David's mind was racing into problem solving mode, too.

Christie buried her face in her hands and sobbed and sobbed.

"I think that crying is the best thing you can do right now." David placed a box of tissues beside Christie, and thought, "Cry and sober up." He left Christie on the sofa long enough to go for two cups of coffee. When he returned, Christie's sobbing had calmed to just flowing tears.

"I think you need to drink this," David said handing Christie a cup.

Christie dabbed her eyes, blew her nose, and took the coffee shakily. David was afraid she would spill it on the couch at first, but she became steadier.

Christie took a sip of the coffee. Her face scrunched up and she said, "Yuk!"

"What? You don't like my coffee?" David asked.

"It is a bit strong."

David's mind was in high gear. "First I need to get her calmed and sober. Then we need to find a reason to keep living," he thought. He started talking, "Christie, I know that right now you feel hopeless, like there is no point in going on. But let's think a minute. If you take your own life, there is no chance Brittany will ever be able to get back with her mother. I don't think that killing yourself is the best option for her, do you?"

"First I want to shoot that social worker!" Christie spat. "There is no point in my trying to get Brittany back. I think they were looking for the chance to take her away. I think they are trying to force information out of me. Or maybe out of Arnie if he's still alive. This is such an awful mess!"

"But you are Brittany's best hope for a normal life, Christie. We don't know if Arnie is still living. You are Brittany's only hope for having a parent. What we need is a plan on how to get her back, not a plan on how to do you in. Are you with me?"

Christie had choked down half of the cup of coffee and seemed a little clearer. She wiped the last of the tears from her eyes and stared into space for what seemed like a long time. David sat patiently, giving her time to process. He ran options through his mind on how to resolve this crisis. "What can I say that will let her decide she wants to live?" David thought. He realized how tense he was, sitting in his chair with his hands squeezing the arm rests tightly. He took a deep breath and tried to force himself to relax.

Still staring into space, Christie said flatly, "If there is a God, why would he let something like this happen? Isn't God supposed to take care of us?"

"I have come to the conclusion that God is not particularly good at taking care of us. I came to that conclusion a while back when I saw so many men in my platoon blown away on the battlefield. I wrestled with that for a long time, wondering why I was still alive when so many were dead. I refused to believe that somehow God had picked me to spare over the others. I went to seminary to wrestle with that very question. Finally, I decided that God is not in the business of taking care of us. Rather, I think God is in the business of loving us and walking with us through life. I think God hurts with us when something bad happens. I don't think God causes it to happen or that God picks some people to take care of while letting others suffer. Things just happen, and God is in the mess with us. I think that if you will let God, God will help walk you through this mess, too."

Christie slowly focused her eyes on David. She still had an empty expression when she said, "You know, that actually makes sense."

"Christie, if you kill yourself, these evil people win. Will you promise not to do that for me?"

'I don't know if I can promise that," Christie said. "It will be too hard to be alone at my apartment. I just don't know what to do," and fresh tears started rolling down her cheeks.

David started to say that she could sleep at his place but realized that might start too many rumors. "Maybe we can find someone for you to stay with for a few days," he suggested.

"No. No, I don't want that."

"Ok. Will you promise to call me if you start having suicidal thoughts?"

She looked at him for a moment and said, "Yes, I think I can do that."

"And do you mind if I call and just check up on you a couple of times a day for a while?"

"You'd do that for me?"

"Of course, I would do that for you," David assured. "I think you need to focus on what it will take to get Brittany back."

A fresh round of sobs started. Finally, Christie managed, "I don't even know where they have taken her."

David felt he was losing the battle. He couldn't think of anything to say to help Christie come to terms with her loss. It dawned on him that getting Brittany back may be a carrot that Christie could never obtain. But right now, that was all he had with which to try to save Christie's life. David sat and thought while Christie sobbed. Finally, he decided to try engaging Christie in some problem solving.

"Christie, what do you think you would have to do to get Brittany back?"

Christie looked up at David, and he saw anger flash in her eyes. She held that mad look for a moment and then softened. "I guess there are two things: Be perfect at work and never drink," she spat.

"Do you think you can avoid drinking for the rest of today and be on time at work in the morning? Those are the first steps, just the rest of today and tomorrow," David coaxed.

"I don't see any point in it! I don't think they will give her back, anyway," Christie sounded defeated.

"I understand how you can feel that way. But how would you feel if there was a chance to get Brittany back, and you didn't do everything in your power to make that happen?"

"Worse than I already feel," Christie responded. "OK, you win. No more drinking today and I will show up for work in the morning. At least ten minutes early."

"Christie, it's not me that wins. It's you and Brittany!" David said.

David thought he almost saw a smile as Christie stood to walk out of the office. When she was gone, he collapsed in his chair feeling exhausted. He made a mental note to check on Christie later that evening. Then, he found himself thinking about Viviana. He felt like he needed to see her right now. It was an odd feeling. "Why am I thinking about her when there are so many problems here?" While still lost in his thoughts, David discovered he was on his feet with his backpack in his hand. Looking at his watch, he decided that he could make it to the stream and back before dark if he hurried.

* * *

David found himself huffing and puffing as he tried to hurry up the mountain. The little wren joined him and whistled its beautiful song along the way. He arrived at the stream but didn't sit down. He felt anxious. This is not the time of day he usually met Viviana. She might not come. That thought saddened him. He found himself pacing when he heard the crow caw. Then he found himself smiling.

Viviana popped through the rhododendron looking stressed.

"I was hoping you would come," David said.

"Why you come this time of day?" Viviana asked.

"I just had a lady wanting to commit suicide. After talking her through that, I felt... like I wanted to see you," David confessed.

"Well, you picked a fine time to come!" Viviana said. "I have problems of my own."

"What's going on?" David asked feeling concerned.

"I have a baby to take care of."

David could feel the color draining from his face. "What do you mean you have a baby to take care of?"

"Some man brought a baby to the mountain. He was going to kill her. I think he was from your compound because he was dressed in what looked like a militia uniform."

David felt even more stunned. Goose flesh ran up his arms, and he shuddered.

"What's wrong with you?" Viviana asked.

"What is the baby's name?" David asked.

Viviana put her hands on her hips and cocked her head, "How do I know the baby's name?"

"Is she about one year old with brown hair?

"Si, that sounds like her."

"I can't believe they were going to kill her!"

"You know this baby?" Viviana asked.

"Her mom is the one I was just telling you about who was planning to commit suicide!"

"Great!" Viviana exclaimed. "You take the baby back to her!"

"Umm," David was thinking. "I don't think I can do that."

"Why not?"

"They already tried to kill her. They will know if I walk back into the compound with a baby. Who knows what will happen then!" David said. "Wait, where is she?"

"You are getting nosey again," Viviana scowled.

David straightened and listened but heard no cries. "What are you going to feed her?"

"I don't know. What do babies eat?"

"You know, I have no idea. Baby food, I guess."

"I haven't seen any of that out here. We'll make do, somehow. I think I can get milk. I must get back. You can make yourself useful by bringing cloth for diapers next time."

David scrunched his forehead and asked, "How can you get milk?"

"A doe will help," Viviana explained.

David jumped when several crows began cawing all around him. He looked up to see what the ruckus was about. The crows were all bobbing their heads, flicking their wings, and cawing.

"What is that all about?" David asked Viviana. When she didn't answer, he looked back down, and she was gone. The crows filed away by twos and threes. David had seen this routine before, but it always left him unsettled. "How does she do that?" he thought. Not for the first time, he found himself wondering whether or not she had turned into one of the crows.

Chapter 19

At 9:00am on Tuesday morning, a bleary-eyed Daniella walked into Zeke Starke's office.

"It's about time," Zeke said.

"Don't start with me," Daniella cautioned. "We didn't get back until 0430 this morning." Daniella explained. "I'm getting too old for these all-nighters!"

Daniella plopped into the chair in front of Zeke's desk. Daniella Morrison, a forty-four-year-old former CIA operative who specialized in interrogation, was just as no nonsense as Zeke Starke. She was fit and serious about her job. She had come to work for MC2 after being "released" from the CIA. When asked about her release, she would just say, "It's classified." She would never talk about the interrogation that had gone wrong, resulting in the witness' death. Since joining MC2 as the Director of Security Forces, Daniella had been on a mission to prove herself a capable, top-notch person.

Daniella was feeling the stress from the long plane trip, the lack of sleep, and the pressure for getting this disaster over the NOAA program resolved. She took a deep breath and looked Zeke in the eye, "I trust you accomplished your mission yesterday."

Zeke did not flinch and said, "The baby is disposed of as planned."

"I still don't think that was necessary, but Carter would have it no other way. I'm sorry the task fell to you. That must have been hard," Daniella said.

"Well, I'd rather not talk about it. Let's move on to today," Zeke said.

Daniella sensed a conflict in Zeke and assumed it had to do with his distaste for what he had done. "The plane trip wasn't a total waste of time but wasn't extremely helpful either. At one point, the wife said that she would like to stay in Sitka and not come back. The husband responded, and I quote, 'We have umm other matters to tend to. Remember?' Other than that, they talked about the family they were going to visit and read their books."

"What do you make of it?" Zeke asked.

"I believe they are suspicious. They think something is going on, but I don't believe they know what it is. I assume it is based on Johnson's sudden disappearance."

"They may know that Christie Templeton was interrogated," Zeke said.

"What! Why didn't you advise me of this?" Daniella snapped trying to control her irritation.

"They were present when Christie was returned to her apartment after being drugged. She may have said something about the encounter up to the time the drug was administered, but we don't know."

"Good God, Starke! I need to know information like this! It could change the whole scenario!"

"So now you know," Zeke countered.

Daniella realized that he was unflustered by her anger. He was not a man that she could bluster. "I assume we are still interrogating Arnie Johnson today," she said to move matters on.

"Yes," Zeke responded. "He is to think the baby was taken and placed in foster care so that there is hope to get her back."

"I am well aware of the drill, Starke," Daniella fired back still feeling testy.

"What about the Hansons?" Zeke asked.

"Right now, I think they are harmless. They will probably be asking some questions. Other than Christie, I am not aware of any loose threads that they could pull for information. Let's just keep an eye on them. I'll have security monitor their movements and computer activity."

"Do you need more coffee for the interrogation?" Zeke asked.

"That would be great! Thanks," Daniella responded with a smile.

* * *

Daniella mustered her poker face and strode into the interrogation room with authority. She sat down opposite Arnie Johnson, who was handcuffed, and did not say a word.

"You know I'm not going to talk," Johnson said as the silence wore on. "Is there any point in going through this again?"

"There has been a new development," Daniella said and saw the concern cross Johnson's face. She sat silently for a moment to let the concern brew. "We know about your affair with Christie Templeton," she said and paused. "We know about your baby," another pause.

"What do they have to do with this issue?" Johnson asked.

"We suspect you may have told Ms. Templeton of your crime," Daniella said.

"I did not commit a crime!" Johnson barked back. "Leave Christie and Brittany out of this!"

"I'm afraid it is too late for that," Daniella said ominously.

"What do you mean?" Johnson asked, and Daniella noted the tension in his voice.

"Good," she thought and went on. "Ms. Templeton has given us cause to take her baby and place it in foster care."

"You wouldn't dare!" Johnson barked.

Daniella looked at him with a cold glare but said nothing.

"You people are animals! She's just a baby!" Johnson blurted out.

Daniella started to walk out and let Johnson dwell on the loss of his baby for a while but decided that she had him where she wanted him: shocked enough to talk.

"You are the only one that can rectify the situation," Daniella said.

Johnson just shook his head, "I hope you rot in hell!" he said. "Brittany is better off being away from this place, anyway."

Daniella decided to play another card. "Do you know how mothers feel when they lose a baby?"

Johnson just sat and stared at her.

"I dare say that Ms. Templeton will become suicidal over the loss of your baby," Daniella said with an intended threat in her voice.

Johnson continued to stare and grit his teeth. Daniella decided to let him think the threat was to be carried out. She got up and headed to the door.

"Wait," Johnson said.

Daniella turned and looked but put a hand on the doorknob. She waited.

"I copied the original NOAA program on a thumb drive before I made the changes," Johnson confessed.

"We already know you copied it. That is nothing new," Daniella said and pulled the door open.

"Wait, there's more," Johnson pleaded.

Daniella slowly closed the door and walked back, saying nothing. She stood and waited for Johnson to go on, carefully watching his expressions and body language.

"I mailed it to NOAA," Johnson said sounding strained.

Daniella stared him down for a full minute, then barked, "You're lying!" and stormed out of the room.

Chapter 20

On Wednesday morning David anxiously tried to work on preparing for the Bible study but kept watching the clock. Time passed slowly. He was waiting for the store to open so he could buy supplies to take to Viviana. "Maybe another cup of coffee will help," he thought. The coffee seemed to make him antsier, though. Finally, 8:45 arrived, and he headed for the store. He was there when Sylvia, the store manager, unlocked the door.

"Good morning," Sylvia smiled. "My first customer of the day!"

"Hey, Sylvia. I hope you are doing well today," David said.

"Fine as a lizard in the sunshine," she said.

"Great! I need to pick up a few things," David said as he walked on in.

"Help yourself!"

David grabbed a basket and found the baby food. He started puzzling over the different varieties, trying to figure out which to buy. He was deep in thought when Sylvia came up behind him.

"Can I help you?" she said, and David jumped. "Sorry, I didn't mean to startle you. You just looked puzzled. You don't have a baby, do you?"

"No," David tried to think quickly. "I, umm. Sorry, I'm a bit distracted this morning. I am putting together a package for a friend who has a one-year-old," David recovered.

"OK, you want the junior foods then," Sylvia explained.

"Great! Thanks!" David said, relieved. Sylvia moved on, and David began loading his basket with jars of meat sticks, soft vegetables, and fruits. He read a label and realized it was just meat held together with some gum. "Yuk!" he thought. Moving on, he noticed a sippy cup, so he grabbed two of those. "Now for something to use as diapers," David thought.

He made his way to the linens and began to puzzle again.

"I don't know," he thought. "Sheets or throws?" Finally, David decided to get two of each. Walking toward the checkout, he spotted a pair of scissors and tossed them in the basket. "Safety pins!" he thought and hunted those down. "How can Viviana keep Brittany warm?" David went back and got two more throws and tucked them under his arm.

Walking toward the checkout the thought crossed his mind. "How is she going to carry all of this?" He detoured and grabbed a daypack big enough to hold it all. At the checkout, David asked the clerk to put the items in the daypack, and she did. He flinched at the price, but it was all necessary. David slipped on the daypack and spotted energy bars. "Lunch?" he thought and purchased four energy bars and two drinks. These he stuffed in the side pouches.

The daypack was right heavy as he started his trek up the mountain. The sky was crystal clear, and David could see mountains stretching out for miles. Reaching the switchback section of the trail, David began to stress. "What if she doesn't come? It's the wrong time of day." He was dragged out of his thoughts by the sound of Canto singing.

"Good morning, Canto! You sound chipper today," David said to the bird. David began to huff and puff going up the switchbacks. Listening to Canto's song, he slowed down and began to relax. "I should have known there was nothing to worry about. You birds seem to have it all under control," he said to Canto. Canto gave an extra loud chirrup, as if in agreement, and continued his song.

Walking around the bend and coming to the stream, David was surprised to see Viviana already there. Brittany was with her. "Buenos días," Viviana said as David walked up.

"I see you brought Brittany today, and I guess the crows told you I was coming," David said feeling glad to see her.

"You are starting to learn, Word Man. She is starting to walk!" Viviana said sounding distressed and pointing to Brittany, who was sitting on a moss-covered rock and playing with a large sycamore leaf.

"I have to leave her to get food and do what needs doing. How can I keep her safe if she is up and walking?"

David could see that Viviana was stressed about caring for Brittany, and he felt the tension in himself. "Can you lock the door and keep her in the house?"

"Silly Word Man! There is no door to lock! I don't know what to do! Maybe I build a rock wall. That might keep her in," Viviana pondered. "I see you brought a fat backpack today," she said pointing to the bulging daypack.

"I brought you some supplies," David said as it struck him that Brittany was naked from the waist down. "What happened to her pants?"

"She pooped. They are drying. It won't matter if she pees or poops out here," Viviana explained.

Brittany looked up, said, "Mama," and started to cry.

Viviana picked her up and cuddled her close saying, "It's OK baby. I take care of you." Brittany seemed comforted, and the crying stopped. David felt touched watching this scene play out before him. He felt a deep longing and wanted to join in the hug.

"What you have in the pack, Word Man?" Viviana said breaking the spell.

David pulled the pack off and said, "Throws, sheets, baby food, scissors, and safety pins," feeling proud of his provisions. "You can have the backpack, too."

Viviana unzipped the pack and began pulling things out, muttering to herself in Spanish. "Very nice," she finally said and smiled at David. "You are very helpful!" Then she spotted the drinks and energy bars. "What is this?"

"Lunch!" David said with a flourish. "Let's sit down and have a bite."

Viviana put Brittany back down on the rock, and she picked up the leaf again. Viviana sat on the ground close to David, and he enjoyed the closeness. Taking the first bite out of the energy bar, David noticed Brittany staring at him. "Do you think she is hungry?" David said.

"It looks like she wants your bar!" Viviana said and laughed. "I guess I'll feed her, too." Viviana pulled out a jar from the pack. "Green beans," she mused reading the label. She resumed digging through the pack when Brittany began to stand. "Quick! Catch her!" she said.

David jumped up and grabbed Brittany before she fell off of the rock. He sat her down by Viviana.

"Where did you put the spoons?" Viviana asked.

David's face turned red as embarrassment crept up his body. "I'm afraid I didn't think about spoons," he said guiltily.

"Oh well, that's just less to wash," Viviana said and looked around. "I see you were playing with your spoon, Brittany," she said and reached for the sycamore leaf. Viviana bit the stem off, folded the wide part of the leaf into thirds, and stuck it in the jar. Brittany eagerly took the first bite. "I believe this will do nicely," Viviana said.

"You're a genius!" David said. "How did you learn to do that?"

Viviana looked David in the eye for what seemed a long time. "If you look, you see possibilities all around you. That is what the crows do. They are very smart creatures. You have been in the compound too long. Your soul has forgotten its connection with nature."

David felt goose bumps on his arms and sensed that she might be right. "How could I learn that?" he asked.

Viviana thought while feeding Brittany a few bites. "I think it is like learning another language. The best way is to go live there."

David felt amazed by Viviana and was staring into her eyes.

"What?" she asked.

"I'm sorry," David said catching himself. "You seem like superwoman!"

"Silly Word Man," Viviana said and gave Brittany another bite.

David opened Viviana's energy bar and said, "Here, you need to eat, too."

Viviana took a bite in between feeding Brittany and said, "Yum! This is good!"

After Brittany had eaten the whole jar of food and David and Viviana had finished their lunch, Viviana opened a sippy cup and carefully filled it with water from the stream where it ran over a rock. She handed the cup to Brittany, who drank from it like a pro.

"I think she has used one of these before," David said. With lunch finished, David began to feel conflicted. He needed to get back, but Viviana didn't seem to be in any hurry to leave. "Well, I still have time to work on that Bible study later," he thought and settled in to stay a while. Struggling to find something to say, David asked, "Would you like me to help you build that rock wall you were talking about?"

Viviana looked at him and smiled. "You are sneaky, Word Man. I think I can manage that. Don't you have work to do? How do you come out here so much?"

"They think I'm out here studying for inspiration," David said.

"That's a good cover," Viviana responded. "But you didn't bring any books. What they think when you go back without a backpack?"

David felt a shock. He hadn't thought of that. "I don't know. I guess I'll just have to hope that the guard doesn't notice."

Viviana stood and said, "It is time for you to go. I have things to do," she said.

David realized she was right. "At least you are not going to disappear this time," he said.

They said their goodbyes, and David walked back down the trail. He was feeling sad and a bit nervous about encountering the guard at the gate until Canto showed up singing. David found himself whistling along with the bird. When he got to the river, the nervousness crept back in.

Bobby buzzed David through the security gate. David tried to go by Bobby quickly saying, "Thanks a lot!"

"Excuse me David, but you seem to have forgotten something," Bobby said.

"I did?" David said, trying to sound puzzled and preparing himself to look surprised when Bobby pointed it out. The sun was bright and hot, so David didn't have to worry if he began to sweat.

"How about that big, fat backpack?" Bobby asked.

"Oh no!" David said faking surprise. "I left it where I was studying." David looked at his watch as though he were thinking. "I don't have time to go back for it now. Is it going to rain any time soon?"

"There is none in the forecast," Bobby answered. "But if there is food in it, the bears and raccoons will have a field day!"

"I ate the food I took. Maybe it will be OK. I hope I can remember the notes I made for tonight," David said while thinking, "That will be easy since there are no notes!"

"Thanks for pointing that out, Bobby. Maybe I can go back for it tomorrow."

"Have a good day, Pastor," Bobby said.

"You, too," David responded. "I'm getting too good at this lying business," David thought as he walked toward the church.

Chapter 21

It was 11:45pm Wednesday when Evie plopped on the bed of their apartment in the compound, tired from the long trip back from Sitka. Sam put down suitcases and immediately started to unpack.

"I was smart enough to get a substitute for tomorrow," Evie said.

"Well, I don't have a substitute, so I guess I'll have to show up in the morning," Sam grumped.

Evie could hear the tension in his voice. "That was a nice visit with your family, though. I'm glad Grandpa is going to be all right."

"It was nice to see everyone. I was afraid to tell you what Grandpa told me when he sent all of you out that first night," Sam said.

"Oh? What was it?" Evie asked sitting up on the bed, her attention piqued.

"I told him about our suspicions and what has been going on here. He said that fear is a helpful emotion, but that I should never fail to act because of it. He said he thought you and I are here at this time because it is our destiny to do something about the wrong being done. He also said, 'Mountains are sacred places. You can always look to them for help.' I'm not sure what he meant by that last bit."

"Grandpa is a wise man," Evie said feeling proud. "I guess that is what it takes to be chief."

"I wonder what they will do about a chief when Grandpa does pass away," Sam said. "Anyway, tomorrow we have to get back on the trail of Arnie Johnson!"

Evie got up, helped Sam finish unpacking, and herded him to bed. She was still feeling wound up from the trip but yawned as she curled up on the couch with the book she had been reading on the plane. She hoped she would be ready to sleep soon. But she couldn't concentrate on the book. Her mind kept going over their conversations on the plane as she tried to recall whether or not they had said anything that might be incriminating. Daniella Morrison had posed as the stewardess again. "Obviously, they don't realize we know who she is," Evie thought. "Other than that one slip up on the way to Sitka, I think we were OK. And Daniella wasn't close enough to hear those remarks, I hope."

* * *

Evie slept in while Sam got up and went to work. She finally pulled the covers off a little after eight and thought she would have breakfast and coffee. Looking out the window, she saw a beautiful blue sky and morning light filtering through the trees. Quickly changing plans, she pulled on running gear and went for a jog along the river trail. The air was crisp and cool for that time of year, and Evie felt joy as she ran along.

About half a mile out, the bluebird landed on a lamppost singing its song. The bird flew ahead of Evie from post to post. Evie felt a surge of joy to see the bird again. After running with her companion for a few minutes, Evie stopped. The bird stopped, too. Evie held her arm up as she had seen falconers do on TV. The little bird tilted its head, looked her in the eye, and flew to her arm, perching so that it was facing her. Evie's heart nearly exploded with the specialness of this encounter.

The little bird chirruped and flew to the next post. When Evie didn't move, it flew to the ground and began hopping along the trail. Finally, it dawned on Evie, "You want me to follow you!"

She started jogging along, and the bird flew from lamppost to lamppost just ahead of her. When she got to the garden area, Evie saw Christie sitting beside the river. She could see Christie's shoulders heaving up and down and realized she was crying. The bluebird was perched on the nearest pole.

Evie stopped running and said, "Hey, Christie."

Christie didn't respond.

Evie walked up to her and said, "Hey, Christie. What's wrong?"

Christie looked up through wet eyes and didn't seem to recognize Evie.

"I'm Evie. I stayed with you the night after you were drugged."

Christie's lifeless expression didn't change. "They took Brittany away," she said flatly.

Evie's heart skipped a beat and she seemed to go numb. "Oh no! When?"

"Monday."

"Oh Christie! I'm so sorry," Evie said, tears welling up in her own eyes. Evie sat down and put her arm around Christie's shoulders. She just held her for a moment while they both cried. "Is there anything I can do to help?"

"This helps," Christie said and patted Evie's hand. "David thinks that if I will behave, do my job and not drink I can get Brittany back. I just don't know. They are such evil people."

Evie felt a tinge of panic. "Wait, why aren't you at work now?"

"The extruder broke down yesterday, so they told me to take today off. I usually walk out here in the evenings, but I decided to come this morning since I don't have anything to do. I don't even know where Brittany is." The tears started flowing again.

"Well, you have something to do now!" Evie stated. "You are going to come have lunch with me, and we'll see if we can find any possible places Brittany might have been sent."

Evie got up. "I'm going to finish my run, and I'll see you at noon. Apartment 206 in the executive building."

Christie managed an "OK."

Evie said, "Bye," and started running down the trail. The bluebird was there, and she stopped. "Thank you," Evie said to the bird and ran on.

* * *

Back at the apartment, Evie showered and grabbed an energy bar. She began to tidy up when she noticed that maintenance had not come to replace the molding that Sam knocked off the mantel. "Good grief! They haven't fixed that yet!" Evie muttered to herself. "Well I'm tired of waiting."

Evie dug up a hammer and backed the finishing nails out part way. She took the piece over to the mantel and began to put it in place when she noticed something sparkle in the hole where she had found the note. Evie looked closer. It looked like there was a metal object deep in the hole. Evie tried to poke her finger in but couldn't reach it. "Tweezers!" she thought.

Evie tried to fish the thing out of the hole. After three slips, she finally plucked it from its hiding place. Evie gasped, covered her mouth with her hands, and felt her heart start to race. She held in her hand a large thumb drive and knew immediately who had placed it there.

Evie ran to her phone and started to call Sam, then stopped. "What if they are monitoring our calls?" She took two steps toward the computer, thinking of an email, but then felt that was even more dangerous. "I could go by Sam's office," she thought. "But, that might look suspicious, too. I guess I'll just have to wait till he gets home."

Evie felt panicky holding the thumb drive. "What if someone shows up? I have to hide this thing!" Evie stood still and began going through the apartment in her mind, searching for a hiding place. Her mind's eye finally lit on the mantel. "It has been safe so far," she thought. "I'll just put it right back!"

Evie tucked the thumb drive back in the mantel and tacked the piece of molding back in place, being careful not to hammer the nails in all the way.

Nervously, Evie began straightening and cleaning. "It will be a long time till Sam gets home!" she thought. At twelve o'clock, Evie was standing in the spare bedroom looking at her kiln and clay and trying to find inspiration for a project. The doorbell rang, and she jumped. "Oh, no! I forgot that Christie was coming!" Evie hurried to the door.

"Hey, Christie! I'm glad to see you!" Evie said with great energy spurred by the shock of her morning discovery. Evie noted that Christie's eyes were dry, and she seemed composed.

"Thanks for inviting me, Evie," Christie said.

Evie led her to the kitchen, running the possibilities for lunch through her mind. "I have turkey, ham, or peanut butter and jelly for sandwiches, or we could whip up a salad. Which sounds better to you?" Evie asked.

"I'm feeling kind of hungry, so a sandwich sounds good" Christie said. "I haven't been eating much lately."

"I can certainly understand that, with all the stress you have been under," Evie responded. She pulled out the fixings for turkey or ham sandwiches along with chips and pickles. "It is fortunate we are both off today. I'm glad I ran into you this morning," Evie chatted, filling the time. Evie set out plates and drinks, and they sat down at the table to build their sandwiches.

Evie felt tense. She wasn't sure if it was awkwardness with Christie or the stress of knowing what was in her mantel. She decided it was a little of both. She determined not to tell Christie about the thumb drive.

"Wow! You have an amazing apartment," Christie said looking around wide eyed.

"Thanks," Evie responded. "I had no idea it would be this nice. When we were getting ready to move, I actually didn't want to come till I saw the place." After a moment of silence, Evie asked, "What exactly do you do at work, Christie?"

"I operate machines," Christie said. "They somehow heat up and pull the fiber optic tubes into long cables. It's a pretty amazing process, but rather dull when everything is working as it should. I mostly turn on and off buttons and check gauges to make sure everything is as it should be."

Evie realized that they were dancing around the proverbial elephant in the room.

They finished their lunch mostly in silence. Evie sensed that Christie was clinging to the promise she had made to hunt for a possible location for Brittany.

"Shall we boot up the computer, or would you like dessert first?" Evie asked. As she expected, Christie jumped at the chance to get started on the search. Evie started toward the spare bedroom for her computer, then decided she would use Sam's contraband computer, just in case. She veered to the office and brought it back to the table.

Positioning the computer so that both she and Christie could see the screen, Evie logged in with her fingerprint. "I have already searched for orphanages, but didn't find anything," Evie confessed. "So, let's try foster care."

Evie typed "foster care" into the search engine and got back results on how to sign up to be a foster parent, foster parent blogs, and desperate pleas for more foster parents. "None of this looks useful," she mused. "Let's try Virginia foster care."

About five results down, Evie spotted "Virginia Foster Care Registry." Christie grabbed Evie's arm and squeezed as Evie clicked on it. Evie could sense that they were both nervous and excited. When the website popped up, it was just a listing of foster care providers in the state. No children's names.

Evie and Christie sighed at the same time. "Of course, they wouldn't list the children's names on the internet," Evie said. "I shouldn't have gotten so excited. Let's try 'recent foster placements.'"

The computer popped up results from that search that were about the same as her original query. Evie was getting frustrated and looked at Christie. She could see the desperation in her eyes. "We're not having much luck with this," Evie said.

While she was speaking, she heard a tap on the window. The bluebird was bobbing its head and flicking its wings. Evie looked it in the eye and said, "Oh no!" She closed out the search engine, slammed the computer shut and ran it back to the office. As soon as she set it down, there was a knock on the door.

Evie startled at the sound and looked at Christie. Christie looked puzzled as Evie went to the door. "Hello, Ms. Hanson. We're looking for Christie Templeton," said a security guard.

"What do you want with her?" Evie asked.

"Daniella Morrison would like to see her."

Evie's anger flared. "Haven't you people caused her enough problems? Why can't you just leave her alone?" she exploded.

"I'm sorry, ma'am. I'm just doing as I was told," said John, the same man that helped them move.

Christie walked over, looking shaken. "How did you know I was here?"

"Your chip told us, ma'am. When we didn't find you at your apartment, surveillance located you," John explained. "Now, please come with me."

Evie saw fear welling up in Christie. "I'll come with you, Christie," Evie offered.

"I'm afraid that won't be necessary... or allowed," John replied.

The two security guards led Christie off, and Evie closed the door. She shuddered and felt panicky. "What can I do?" she thought to herself. Pacing frantically around the room, Evie noticed the bluebird was still perched at the window.

Evie walked over to the window and said, "Thank you" to the bird for the second time that day. Then she thought, "How did I know that the security guards were coming?"

"Somehow you told me, didn't you," Evie said to the bird. The bird chirruped and flew away.

Chapter 22

Christie walked into Daniella Morrison's office bristling. "Sober, she seems much more of a force to be reckoned with," Daniella thought.

Without sitting down, Christie demanded, "Where is Brittany? I need to know."

"Please sit down, Ms. Templeton," Daniella said in a smooth voice with authority, wresting back control of the interview. Christie obeyed.

"Ms. Templeton," Daniella began, "It is common for parents not to be told the placement of their children. It prevents... interference."

"Why did you bring me here?"

"I wanted to check up on you, see if you are doing OK," Daniella said. She did not find it hard to lie during an interrogation. She had put on a character, almost as if she were an actor and these were lines to be delivered in order to achieve her goal. Daniella noted the incredulity that flashed on Christie's face.

"I am glad to see that you are sober today. I also see that you have reported to work on time, and your supervisor said you have done well, except for today of course."

"They told me not to come in today because the extruder is broken," Christie said defensively.

"Good," Daniella thought. "Yes, I am aware that your machine is down. That is why we asked you to come in today. Since you are off, it wouldn't interfere with your work time," she explained. "I don't want to do anything to jeopardize your chances," Daniella said hoping to give Christie the idea that she was trying to help her get her baby back.

"When can I get Brittany back?" Christie asked.

"You can appreciate our concern for your daughter," Daniella said. "It is not good for a child to grow up with an alcoholic parent. You have also placed yourself in a tenuous position with your employment. Should you lose your job, what chance would your daughter have? Those are two serious strikes against you, Ms. Templeton."

Christie dropped her head and said, "I understand that. I will quit drinking and do my job perfectly. Once you see that, how long?"

"We'll see," Daniella said. "I hope you can do what you just promised. Alcohol is a hard thing to beat, but I am pulling for you. Your first week has been great. Keep up the good work."

Christie started to stand to leave, and Daniella said, "Oh by the way, Arnie seems to have misplaced a thumb drive before he left. It had some important programs he and the IT team were working on for MC2. You haven't seen a thumb drive that you don't recognize as yours, have you?

Daniella saw the anger flash in Christie's eyes, and Christie exploded. "What do you mean Arnie left? He wouldn't just leave without letting me know! We were going to be married!"

"I'm sorry Ms. Templeton. You have had a lot to hit you recently. But do you recall seeing the thumb drive?" Daniella asked.

"I have no idea what you are talking about," Christie spat. "Why do you keep asking me about things Arnie did?"

"Because this is important to your company," Daniella countered. "Do you remember his mentioning a thumb drive or a big program he was working on?"

"Arnie didn't really talk about work with me. I couldn't understand the computer stuff, anyway. Why don't you search my apartment if you don't believe me?"

"Would you mind if I sent a couple of guys over to have a look? We really need to find those programs. If we don't, our IT team will have to start all over," Daniella lied sweetly.

"You might as well," Christie barked. "You seem to do whatever you want anyway."

Daniella adopted a stern face to signal to Christie that she was correct and said, "You may go."

After Christie stomped out of the office, Daniella got on the phone with Zeke Starke. "Captain Starke, it's Daniella."

"Good afternoon, Daniella. How can I help you?" Starke responded.

"I'm just updating you on the Templeton interrogation."

"Oh, you're through already?"

"Yes, it was a breeze. She's easy to manipulate in her current state. I am convinced that she knows nothing of the thumb drive or what Arnie did."

"Really!" Starke responded. "I find it hard to believe that he could pull off a stunt like that without talking about it to the mother of his child!"

"Apparently he did," Daniella responded. "She agreed to let us search her apartment, so I will send two officers over this afternoon. Oh, you should know that we found her with the Hanson woman. They were in Hanson's apartment."

"I wonder what they were up to," Starke said. "Did you check with surveillance about their computer activity?"

"Not yet, Starke! The woman just walked out of my office. I'll call you back in a few minutes."

Daniella checked with the surveillance room. "I need you to check Evie Hanson's computer activity for today," Daniella ordered.

Jonathan Massey pulled up the computer access records. Looking over the log he said, "I don't see any activity today by Ms. Hanson."

"Thanks a lot Massey."

Daniella called Zeke back. "No computer activity today. Apparently Hanson was just being friendly and having Templeton over for lunch."

"Daniella, we just keep spinning our wheels and getting nowhere!" Zeke responded. "We have to retrieve the thumb drive before it gets out! What is the next step?"

Daniella paused and was silent long enough for Zeke to bark, "Well?"

"I'm thinking, Starke! Since she can never get her baby back, Templeton is now a liability with only one resolution. I guess our next move is to offer her life in exchange for Johnson's cooperation."

"What, and let them go if he cooperates?"

"No Starke," Daniella said testily. "They will both have to be terminated. You know that."

Starke paused, and Daniella wondered if he was getting cold feet. She made a mental note to assess his emotional status as well.

"You're right," Starke responded. "They both know too much."

Chapter 23

Sam spent most of his Thursday working on the one bug that his team had not been able to resolve on the new payroll program. He had finally succeeded just in time for the computers to process payroll overnight. The money would be deposited into the workers' company accounts by 9am on Friday.

Sam summoned a pod to take him the short distance to the apartment because he was tired after the trip. He walked into the apartment to find Evie running straight at him.

"Thank God you're finally home!" Evie said in a frantic voice. "You have to see this!" With a quick hug, Evie ran to the spare bedroom. Sam stood there confused.

"What in the world is up with you, Evie?" By then, she was running back into the living area.

"Come on!" Evie was hurrying toward the fireplace.

Sam obeyed, dropping his bag on the couch as he passed by. "What is it?"

Evie was pulling at the molding on the mantel, and it popped off. She whipped out a pair of tweezers from her pocket and pulled something out of the mantel.

"I found this stuffed way back in the hole!" she said and handed him a thumb drive.

"What is it?" Sam asked.

"What is it?" Evie shrieked. "You're the computer guru! It's a thumb drive that Arnie Johnson hid in our mantel!"

Sam felt the shock wave travel from his brain to his toes. He stood there with his mouth open, speechless.

"This is what they are looking for, Sam! This is what they took Brittany for! This is why they are hounding us!" Evie said frantically.

Sam was still trying to process what he was holding in his hand when the words, "took Brittany" sank in.

"What do you mean, 'took Brittany?'"

"While we were in Sitka they took Brittany away from Christie. They didn't even tell her where they were taking her. We used your computer this afternoon to see if we could find where she might be, but we had no luck."

Sam felt like he needed to sit down before he fell down. He walked to the couch and sat, trying to process these two revelations.

"Wow!" was all Sam could say at first. "Did you look at what is on this?"

"No. I just hid it back inside the mantel. Then Christie came for lunch."

"I guess we had better open it and see what's inside," Sam said and stood up from the couch. Sam and Evie walked toward the office, and there was a knock on the door. They both jumped and Evie almost screamed but caught herself. She grabbed the thumb drive, stuffed it back in the mantel, and pushed on the molding swiftly. Evie looked at Sam, and Sam went to the door.

"Welcome back!" David chirruped. "How was the trip?"

Sam was too stunned to say anything. Evie piped up, "Come on in, David. It's good to see you."

"You look like you have seen a ghost, Sam," David said as he came through the door.

"I think I have," Sam said closing the door and locking it.

Evie was pulling the molding back off the mantel. "And here is the ghost," she said as she pulled out the thumb drive."

"What is it?" David asked crossing the room.

"I think Arnie hid this in the mantel. It is what this whole mess is about," Evie explained.

"We were just about to look inside it when you nearly gave me a heart attack," Sam said.

"Sorry about that, Sam. I guess my timing wasn't the greatest, but I have some news you need to hear, too."

"Oh no, not more news!" Sam said.

"Did you know that they took Brittany away from Christie?" Evie asked.

"They didn't just take her away... They were going to kill her!" David explained.

"What?" Evie and Sam said at the same time.

"Viviana caught someone out on the mountain with Brittany, a man with a gun. She is convinced he was going to shoot her. Somehow she stopped him from killing the baby."

"Kill a baby?" Evie said just barely audibly. "Who would do such a thing?"

"Viviana is convinced that it was someone from the militia because of the uniform he was wearing. The truck had the MC2 insignia," David said.

"Arnie is still alive," Evie said.

"What do you mean? How could you know that?" Sam asked.

"I just do!" Evie said. "Why else would they kill Brittany? They are trying to break Arnie and make him talk. They are holding him somewhere in the compound."

Sam knew better than to refute Evie.

"If they have tried to kill once, they will do it again. Let's see what is in this thing!" Sam said. "We may be able to save a life!"

The three gathered around the contraband computer while Sam booted it up. He inserted the thumb drive and opened its list of files. There were two files, one named "Message," and one named "NOAA." With a couple of clicks, Sam pulled up the size of the NOAA file.

"This thing is huge! It must be the whole NOAA program! Let's see what 'Message' says," Sam said and clicked the file open.

All three moved their heads closer to the screen. "If you have found this, then I am either dead or in prison. Mitch Carter forced me to alter the NOAA program after it was installed so that it would not display results over an area near Salty Ford, WV. He wants to hide something that is happening there! I also had to put limits on the analysis of data for global warming predictions. I copied the original program onto this drive. If you run it, it will show what he is trying to hide. If you found this, it also means that Mitch Carter has discovered that I copied the program. Beware!"

"Holy guacamole!" David said. "This sounds serious. Let's run the program and see what's going on."

"I'm afraid I can't," Sam said.

"What do you mean, Sam?" Evie asked.

"The program is way too big to run on a notebook computer. That is why we are letting NOAA use the company computers... That's why we are letting NOAA use the company computers! So that Mitch Carter can cover up whatever he is hiding in West Virginia! What is near Salty Ford?" Sam asked.

"I don't know!" Evie said. "Do a search and see."

Sam punched Salty Ford, WV into the search engine. "It looks like it is another small town bought out by one of the A-30 conglomerates. I can't imagine which one," Sam said facetiously. "It looks like it used to be a coal mining town, but the mines were shut down twenty years ago. It doesn't say why the mines were shut down."

"So, we have an attempted murder of a one-year-old, falsifying a government computer program, imprisoning an employee in a cover up attempt, and who knows what going on in Salty Ford! What an upstanding company!" David said.

"Christie will die, too," Evie said flatly.

"What? Why?" David asked.

"She knows too much," Evie explained. "She knows they took her baby. She knows they are after something Arnie did. They can't risk leaving her alive, knowing she will never rest till she finds out what happened to Brittany. Wait, where is Brittany?"

"Viviana has her. We can tell Christie what happened to Brittany," David said.

"No, we can't." Evie said. "She will do something crazy to get to her."

Sam sat with the gears grinding in his mind, half listening to David and Evie. "We need a plan," he said. "And to make a plan, we need a problem list."

Sam pulled out a piece of paper and put "Problem List" at the top. Talking as he wrote, Sam said, "1. Arnie Johnson: Alive or Dead?" Drawing a diamond around "Alive," Sam drew an arrow and wrote, "Find and Rescue." He drew a square around "Dead," indicating that nothing else was to be done.

"2," Sam said. "Christie: Get out of compound and reunite with Brittany."

"3. Uncover MC2 mystery and expose to NOAA."

"4. Save ourselves."

"Do we have to put 'Save ourselves' last?" David asked.

"Is there anything I've missed that we need to add to the list?" Sam asked, ignoring David's comment.

"If we are shooting for the moon, then maybe we could reunite Arnie and Christie, too," David added.

"That would be icing on the cake," Sam replied. "OK, there are our problems. Now all we need are solutions!"

Sam, Evie, and David looked at each other with somber faces as the daunting nature of what they were proposing began to sink in.

"How are we going to do this? We don't even have any weapons," Sam said in a discouraged tone.

"I have an air rifle," David offered. "I used to shoot in competitions."

"Well, we are all set then," Sam said facetiously. "I think I need nourishment. I'm too hungry to tackle this right now."

Evie and David agreed, and the three of them went to the kitchen to see what they could eat. Evie fished out some chicken strips and put Sam and David to work building a salad. They ate almost in silence as each one was processing what lay ahead of them. Sam felt heavy and stressed but was able to eat his entire meal.

After supper Sam got a pad and pen and wrote "Solutions" on the top. Let's brainstorm ideas for how to attack this problem list," he said.

Three stressed faces looked at each other blankly for a moment. Finally, David said, "I've got nothing."

"I know, let's make a list of what we need to know, of what's missing," Evie said. "That always helps me solve a problem, particularly when I feel stuck."

"That's a good idea, Evie," David said. "It always helps to discover the information that is missing."

Sam realized they were right and shifted his brain from problem solving mode to information gathering mode. "You are right! Having more information might make this seem more possible!" Sam said. "OK, shall we start with Arnie or the thumb drive?"

"Let's start with the thumb drive," David said. "It may be the easiest to crack."

"The thumb drive," Sam muttered. "What do we not know or need to know?" He scratched through "Solutions" on his paper and wrote, "Info Needed."

"We don't know what it says about Salty Ford. We don't know what was changed. We don't know why this is such a big deal to Mitch Carter. Basically, we really don't know anything about the thumb drive," Evie said.

"The only way we can learn what the program says is by running it," Sam said. "I could look at the code and try to find the changes Arnie made, but I still wouldn't know the outputs. Besides, it would take weeks to go through a program that big."

"You can't run it on MC2's computers," Evie said. "They will be watching."

David held up a finger, "We have to get it to someone who can run it, someone outside of MC2!"

Sam smiled, "You're right, David. We don't need more information about the thumb drive. We need to mail it to NOAA. I should make a copy first, just in case."

"Sam! You can't just put that thing in the mail. You know security will be watching for a suspicious package. And I think one addressed to NOAA would count as suspicious!" Evie said.

Sam scratched his head and felt frustrated. "How can we get this to NOAA, then?"

"It's risky, but it might work," Evie said. "What if I make something ceramic to send to Grandpa and hide it in there? We could put instructions in the card for him to mail it to NOAA."

Sam's eyebrows rose with hope, and he looked at David. David nodded his head and said, "I think it could work!"

Sam picked up his pen and Evie barked, "Don't write that on the paper, Sam! What if someone finds it?"

Sam felt a little sheepish and put his pen down. "You're right again. Maybe we should try to keep this in our heads rather than on paper. One problem solved, plus Grandpa's birthday is coming up. Next, let's think about Arnie. What do we need to know?"

"That one is easy," David said. "Everything!"

"We need to know where he is, if he is still alive, and what kind of security is around him," Evie clarified.

"Basically, everything that we have been trying to find out but getting nowhere with," David added.

"That is true," Sam agreed. "So, what can we do differently?" Sam watched as Evie and David, with somber faces, looked at first one thing and then another around the room searching for answers. Sam closed his eyes and tried to think. "How can we locate someone that the company is hiding? Maybe if we try to think like Carter, we could get somewhere," he thought.

"Where would you hide someone if you were Mitch Carter?" Sam asked.

"I would want a place that no one could see," Evie said. "So, no windows."

"It would have to be secure enough that I wouldn't have to worry about Arnie escaping. And I would have to be able to get food to him without raising suspicion," David added.

"You're right!" Sam said. It would have to be in a place where Carter's minions have access to bring food in without anyone wondering what they are doing! What options do no windows and obscure generate?"

"There has to be a jail, at least a room or two, on the compound grounds, doesn't there?" David asked.

"I don't think they would keep him there. I think Carter wants this kept as secret as possible. There are probably just a few of his most trusted security forces involved," Evie said.

Everyone fell back into thought. Sam walked over to the south facing window by the fireplace. Surveying what he could see of the compound, Sam kept noticing the cooling tower for the nuclear power plant.

"Would there be a place in the nuclear plant to keep Arnie?" Sam asked.

"It is certainly out of the way. The only folks who go there are the workers," David said.

"There are plenty of windowless places in it," Evie offered. "Let's make a mental note that the nuclear plant is a good possibility. Any of the factories or warehouses could have rooms. But they are usually busy and might draw attention."

"How about Carter's house? Well, I guess I should say mansion," David said. "I'm sure there are basement areas where someone could be tucked away."

Sam was starting to feel frustrated. "We could list any number of possibilities," he said, "but, we're still missing a big piece of the puzzle. How are we going to find out where Arnie is? We can't just knock on Carter's door and say, 'Do you mind if we search your house for Arnie?'"

A slow smile grew on David's face. "Sure, we can. We could find a time when Carter is not going to be there and go in disguise."

"Disguised as what?" Sam asked.

Silence fell on the group till Evie said, "I know! We could go as mold detectors!"

"Mold detectors?" Sam asked, furrowing his brow.

"We could tell the help that Carter requested an evaluation for mold. That would require that we look in the lowest parts of the house," Evie explained.

"That might be possible," Sam said. "But how would we get there? If we take a pod, it will know who we are. If we walk, we might draw suspicion."

Sam watched as Evie and David's faces grew somber again. The weight of what they were trying to do was sinking in. This would be no easy task. Every step had its risks.

Silence sat on the group till Evie said, "We are going to have to take risks. This can't be done without jeopardizing our safety. Of course, we don't need to be reckless either. We will have to try to think everything through."

"I think my thinker is wearing out tonight. Maybe we should take a break and let the possibilities simmer," David said.

"That's a good idea," Sam agreed and stood up to stretch.

"OK, I have to start copying the thumb drive... I wonder how long that will take! We all have to think over plans about how we are going to do this, and Evie has to figure out what she will make to send to Grandpa," Sam said summing up where they were. "I think it best if we don't tell Christie what is going on until we have to," he added.

David and Evie nodded in agreement and got up, too. They said their goodbyes and David left. Evie looked at Sam, and he thought he saw joy on her face.

"Well, at least we won't be bored any time soon," Evie said with a smile.

Sam walked over and hugged Evie tightly and didn't let go.

"What's wrong, Sam?" Evie asked.

After a moment Sam said, "It scares me to put you in danger like this. Maybe you should go back to Sitka for a while."

"No, Sam. We are in this together. For better or for worse, remember?" Evie said looking into Sam's blue eyes. "Sam, we can do this. I know we can. I can sense it. But we have to do it together."

Sam smiled and felt his heart calm. Evie had a way of making him believe he could do anything.

Chapter 24

Walking in from work Friday evening, Sam felt nervous. Carter was scheduled to be off for another A-30 conference Monday through Wednesday. The time to put their hastily conceived plan into action was crashing in too quickly. Putting his bag down in the office Sam called out, "Evie?"

"I'm in here," she responded.

Sam took a quick glance at his contraband computer. "Still copying," he thought. The computer had been copying the NOAA program onto another thumb drive since last night.

Sam went into the spare bedroom/art room to find Evie tinkering with metal wires and a pair of pliers. The wires flared out from a central box. "What in the world are you doing?" Sam asked.

"Sam, do you think the x-ray will hurt the thumb drive if they scan the crow before they ship it?"

"No, it shouldn't," Sam offered. "Why?"

"I expect that it will be scanned before they let the box ship."

"So, what are you doing?"

"If they scan it, don't you think the thumb drive will stand out? I am making a metal frame to 'support' the crow's wings. If they x-ray it, maybe this will look like framework rather than a thumb drive."

"Evie, you're a genius!" Sam said with a grin.

Evie smiled at him and continued tinkering with the wires. The smile warmed Sam's heart. But something didn't seem right. He watched Evie a minute and realized she intended to put the thumb drive in the middle of the central box.

"Umm, Evie, the thumb drive will survive the x-ray, but I don't think it will fare so well in the kiln," Sam said.

"Silly Sam! I'm going to put it in after I fire the bird. See, I'll leave a hole in the bottom and slide the thumb drive in here," she said pointing to the open end of the cage. "Then, I'll bend this little wire up to keep it from sliding out."

"Are you sure you're not an engineer in disguise?" Sam chided, feeling proud of his wife. Then he had another thought. "But, what if someone looks in the hole?"

"That is why I will plug it with self-hardening clay," Evie explained.

"I checked Carter's schedule today. He will be gone Monday through Wednesday for another of his A-30 conferences." The nervousness crept back in.

"Well that's convenient!" Evie said. "We won't have to wait!"

"I wish I felt as confident about this as you seem to," Sam said.

"Sam, we are doing the right thing. Sometimes you just have to trust that when you are in the right, things will work out." Evie looked up to see her bluebird perched on the windowsill. "See, my bird agrees!"

Sam scratched his head, puzzled by all the bird activity these days. Sam remembered the titmouse that was perched on his window after his confrontation with Carter over the NOAA call. He remembered seeing it when he was trying to decide what to say about being caught hacking into the system.

Evie apparently noticed his deep thoughts and said, "What is it Sam? You look miles away."

"I don't think I told you, but I may have a bird, too." Sam went on to tell her of his encounters with the titmouse. Just as he was finishing, the titmouse landed on the windowsill opposite the bluebird. Sam was aghast at the coincidence.

"Do you mean that bird?" Evie asked.

Sam looked at it amazed. "Yep, that's the one!" he said. "But why would it show up just now?"

"Sometimes you have to quit analyzing and just trust, Sam. These birds obviously know more than we give them credit for."

Sam knew that would be a hard one for him. He was much more comfortable analyzing problems and finding logical solutions than trusting his instincts, or birds, or whatever.

Sam lost himself in his thoughts, and Evie lost herself in working with her wires. They were both drawn back out when the two birds began to appear agitated. Bobbing their heads and flicking their wings, they appeared to be fussing at each other. Sam and Evie were startled out of their skin when they heard a knock at the door.

Recovering, Sam looked at his watch. "It's probably just David," he said and started toward the door.

"I think the birds are trying to tell us otherwise," Evie said.

When Sam opened the door, a man was standing there with a paint bucket, brush, and some tools.

"Hi, I'm Tyler from maintenance. Sorry it took so long, but I'm here to repair your mantel."

"Oh, I had forgotten all about that," Sam recovered. "Umm, come in."

"If now is not a good time, I could come back," Tyler offered.

Sam was conflicted, wondering if he would create suspicion if he asked him to come back. Apparently noticing Sam's hesitation, Tyler said, "It will take me about 5 minutes total."

"Sure, come on in," Sam said and stood aside.

Tyler walked to the mantel. "Oh, I see you have already put it back on."

Evie had pushed it partly on after extracting the thumb drive. Tyler whisked out hammer and punch, popped in the nails, and had it painted over in three minutes.

"Thank you very much," Sam said as he ushered him out the door.

"You are very welcome," Tyler said. "I'm just sorry it took so long. It seems a lot of things have been falling apart lately, and this got put on the back burner."

"No problem," Sam said and closed the door. He looked and saw Evie watching from the art room with big eyes. She ran her hands through her red hair and took a long, slow deep breath.

Sam tried that, too. "OK, that was scary" he said. Evie still looked terrified. "It is good you had that piece of molding stuck up there so he couldn't see the hole Arnie had drilled."

"So, the birds weren't fussing at each other, Sam. They were trying to warn us!" Evie said with amazement in her eyes.

Sam's first response was to say, "No, that's silly." But it dawned on him that Evie might be right. Instead he said, "You may be right."

"Sam, we need to learn to watch for that behavior in our birds. They may be helpful."

"You are right again. I will try to keep my eyes open for the little critter," Sam said. When they went back to the art room, the birds were gone.

"I guess they accomplished their mission," Sam said. "I'm getting hungry. Do you want to go ahead and eat?"

Just as Evie said, "That sounds good," there was another knock at the door. Sam and Evie smiled and said at the same time, "David."

Sam opened the door to find David standing there with a huge suitcase. "Are you going off?" Sam asked.

"I brought costumes!" David said triumphantly as he walked in. "When I was in the army, we used to put on plays for entertainment. For some reason, I kept a lot of the costumes I used."

"Interesting," Sam said. "You are just in time for dinner, too. We were about to come up with something to eat."

"Hey, David!" Evie called from the art room. "Sam, would you mind whipping up dinner while I start throwing the clay?"

"No problem!" Sam called back. "Let's see what we can create, David." Opening the fridge, Sam did a survey. "Oooh, how do you feel about trout?" Sam asked.

"Sounds yummy to me!"

Sam pulled out a bag of spinach to sauté and some instant mashed potatoes. Sam and David chatted while Sam got the fish baking. In the background, they could hear the muffled thuds of Evie slamming the clay onto her table.

"Tell me about this acting career of yours," Sam said.

"When I was stationed in the Middle East, there wasn't much to do. A group of us started putting on skits as a joke. The troops seemed to enjoy them, and we evolved into putting on real plays. I must say, we were quite good," David explained.

"Do you happen to have a mold inspector costume?" Sam asked.

"No, but I have been thinking about it. I think I should dress up in the MC2 shirt, khaki pants and wear my Inspector Clouseau mustache and hat. We did some spoofs on the Pink Panther once."

"Wait, what makes you think you are going into Carter's house?" Sam asked.

"It has to be me, don't you see? You and Evie have to be at work."

Sam started to argue, but realized David was right. He put David to work on the potatoes while he got out a large pan to sauté the spinach.

When dinner was nearly ready, Sam called back to Evie, "It's about time to eat."

Sam heard one last thud, and then Evie said, "I'll be there in a minute."

Sitting down to dinner, David said the blessing.

"David plans to invade Carter's house dressed as the Pink Panther," Sam said as soon as David said, "Amen."

"Are you serious?" Evie laughed.

"I think it will be enough of a costume to hide my identity, but not enough to be suspicious. I made a good Pink Panther, I must say," David responded.

"I could see that," Evie said, "but I think one of us should go. We don't want to put you at risk."

"I already explained to Sam that both of you have to be at work Monday. I can slip away from the office without anyone noticing. Now, what sort of equipment does a mold inspector need?"

"I have no idea," Sam said. "I had not even thought of that."

"Maybe it's a vacuum cleaner type device that sucks up mold samples," David offered. "It could be like the Ghost Busters!"

Evie whipped out her phone and said, "Let's find out how that is done."

"Wait," Sam said, suddenly feeling nervous. "After they sent Morrison on the plane with us, I wouldn't be surprised if they are monitoring our internet activity. Maybe we should use David's phone."

David entered a search into his phone. "It appears petri dishes are left out for a few days for air samples. Scrapings can be taken to determine if it is mold or mildew. Where are we going to get petri dishes?"

Sam, Evie, and David looked at each other a moment with gears turning.

"I bet the science department has some at school. Maybe I could borrow a few," Evie said.

"But how can we get them before Monday?" Sam asked.

"I guess David will have to meet me there super early Monday morning. He can't go in until Carter leaves, anyway," Evie suggested.

"If this works, going back to collect the petri dishes will give us an entry for the rescue," Sam said. "But what if he is not there? We still have to go back to make this look legitimate.

What if Carter is back by then?" Sam was beginning to feel anxious about what they were doing. "I don't know that this is such a good idea."

"We have already talked about this, Sam," Evie said. "We have to do SOMETHING! This is the best idea we have had."

Evie's confidence steeled Sam's nerves. "You're right. I was just losing my cool," Sam said. "OK, let's see those costumes, David."

The three left the table and went to the living area. Sam and Evie sat on the couch and watched as David began pulling out costumes. The first was a southern belle type dress, and Sam and Evie laughed.

"Gone with the Wind," David explained.

The next two were dresses, too. "Umm, David, is there something you need to tell us?" Sam asked.

"With my great figure, I often got cast as the lady," David said, swinging his hips. Pulling out four more costumes, David finally said, "Ah, here it is." He pulled out a cape and hat. In the hat he had tucked a pair of heavy rimmed glasses and a mustache.

David swung on the cape, put the hat and glasses on, and held the mustache in place. "What do you think?"

Evie laughed, and Sam said, "I think it may be a bit hot to be wearing a cape, but the rest is great!" Sam went quiet, deep in thought.

"What is it Sam? You look like something is wrong," Evie said.

"Let's say that David finds Arnie and we are able to get him out of the house before Carter gets back on Wednesday. How are we going to get him out of the compound? They can track his every move in the surveillance room. We can't just put him on a bus and send him out, you know."

Sam watched Evie and David's faces grow somber, again. Silence fell over the room as the three wrestled with Sam's daunting realization. Time seemed to stand still for Sam as he searched his mind for solutions. No one spoke as the minutes ticked by. Sam quit looking inside his mind and started looking around the room. From the couch, his eye caught the side of the aluminum foil box that he had used to line to pan for cooking the fish.

Apparently Evie noticed Sam's eyes light up and asked, "What is it, Sam?"

"Aluminum foil!" Sam said excitedly.

"Aluminum foil? Do you care to explain?" David prompted.

"Aluminum foil might just block the signal being sent from Arnie's chip!" Sam said. "If it works, they won't be able to track him."

"We wrap Arnie in aluminum foil? Don't you think that might be a bit conspicuous?" David pointed out.

"No, we just wrap the foil around Arnie's arm to cover the chip. All we need is a strip of foil and some tape!" Sam explained.

"Brilliant!" Evie said. "I think David should wear a strip when he goes to Carter's mansion, too."

"That sounds good to me," David said. "I would love to be off the radar during this invasion!"

"We're making progress!" Sam said. "Next we have to figure out how to get Arnie out of the compound."

The pondering resumed until David said, "Maybe we could sneak him into the back of a delivery truck that's on its way out of the compound."

Sam smiled feeling hope dawn. "This may just be possible after all," he said. "OK, we have weekend homework. David, you need to learn everything you can about mold, like how to detect it and how to remove it in case they start asking questions. Evie, you have a crow to make and get ready to ship. I have to find out when Carter will be back and see if I can find a schedule of deliveries and shipments. Monday morning, Operation Arnie commences!"

Chapter 25

Birds were chirruping everywhere as David stepped into the cool Saturday summer morning. Sunrise flamed the sky with a beautiful pink as he left the checkpoint and started up the trail. David was excited to see Viviana again. He needed to stay and work on a sermon for tomorrow but found that he simply could not miss a chance to see her. As he walked up the trail, with Canto singing his song, it dawned on David, finally, that he was attracted to Viviana. He no longer thought of her as someone who needed help, but as someone with whom he longed to be.

David remembered how Evie and Sam had seemed to realize his attraction immediately and felt embarrassed. "How can I be the last to know?" he thought. "I wonder if Viviana realizes that I'm attracted to her. Should I tell her?"

Thoughts and feelings mixed and swirled as he got closer to the stream where they always met. "I don't know what to do, Canto," David said to the bird.

Canto cocked his head and looked at David. "I guess you don't either," David said with a laugh.

David got to the stream and sat on his usual rock. He realized that he had brought nothing with him and felt more embarrassment. Thinking quickly, he decided he would ask if she needed anything and bring it back tomorrow. "Or maybe even this afternoon!" he thought.

Canto sat quietly on a small hemlock branch near the stream. David sat quietly, waiting. Viviana did not show up. "OK, let's see if I can think about my sermon for tomorrow," David thought. "No one after lighting a lamp hides it under a jar or puts it under a bed. Well, that's obvious, Jesus. The lamp would either go out or catch the bed on fire. Why would Jesus make such an obvious statement? What does the light represent? I think it is our connection with God. If we are not supposed to hide it, then the light in our souls must be for the sake of other people. God both empowers our lives and uses us to reach out to other people."

David found that he was able to lose himself in his thoughts. He had closed his eyes and kept expanding the sermon, listening to the stream. David jumped when Viviana touched his hand.

"Were you asleep?" she asked.

"Wow! No, I was thinking about a sermon." David felt a little disoriented and wasn't sure how long he had been there. He realized he was smiling big when he said, "How are you?"

"Things are working out, so I'm less stressed," Viviana said while holding Brittany on her hip. David noticed a layer of the throw blanket covered over by a piece of sheet on Brittany's bottom.

"Do the diapers work?"

"Almost. They don't catch all of the pee," Viviana said. "Do you think they have anything like plastic pants at the store?"

"I don't know, but I will look today. Do you want me to bring them back this afternoon?" David asked eagerly.

"You do like to hike, Word Man. No, just next time you come will be fine."

David felt a little disappointed but said, "OK."

Viviana put Brittany down, and she flipped over onto her knees and crawled to a seedling. She pulled off a leaf and held it up toward Viviana.

"Are you hungry, again?" Viviana asked, and Brittany nodded, "Yes."

Viviana pulled off the backpack David had given her and pulled out a sippy cup, a jar of baby food, and a piece of wood that she had fashioned into nearly a spoon shape. As she opened it, Brittany stood and toddled over to her. The jar said, "Beef and gravy," but the food was a bluish purple.

"What is that?" David asked.

"It's blueberries and nuts mixed together. She loves it," Viviana explained. "It helps make the food you brought last longer."

"Do you need more food already?" David asked kicking himself for not bringing more.

"It will run out in three or four more days, I think. She seems to eat a lot!" Viviana said.

"OK, then. I will definitely have to come back tomorrow afternoon. I have church in the morning."

"Oh, so today is Saturday."

It always surprised David that Viviana did not keep up with the days of the week, like the rest of the world. She seemed just to take each day as it came. David felt envious. They were silent for a bit as Viviana fed Brittany.

She handed David the cup and instructed him to get water where it flowed over the rock. He did and handed it back.

As Brittany drank, David said, "I have an exciting day on Monday."

"What is happening Monday, Word Man?"

"Do you remember how I told you about Brittany's mother?"

"Si."

"Well her dad is the reason they were going to kill Brittany. We think they are holding him prisoner and trying to get him to tell where he hid a thumb drive that he stored a program on that MC2 had falsified. We found the thumb drive and now are going to try to rescue him. I'm going to go to the owner's house, where we think they are keeping him, dressed up as a mold inspector. If I find him, we are going to try to get him out," David said feeling excited.

"I think you'll be in jail by Monday afternoon," Viviana said.

"What makes you think that?" David asked feeling crestfallen.

"They have security cameras everywhere. They will see you."

"That's why I'm wearing a disguise," David explained. "Wait, how do you know that there are security cameras everywhere?"

"I just do," Viviana said defensively.

The realization hit David that, if Viviana was right, this might be his last visit with her. "No, I will see her tomorrow," he thought.

Viviana seemed to sense David's tension and asked, "What is the matter?"

"I just realized that if I get arrested I won't be able to see you... I mean I won't be able to bring food and stuff for you," David said.

"So, don't get arrested!" Viviana said and punched David in the arm. She smiled and David felt himself melting in her raven eyes.

"I will do my best to stay out of jail," David said, recovering.

"You will have to act like you know what you are doing. Don't let your eyes shift around, like you are suspicious or scared. Speak with authority. Don't ask if you can come in, state it like there is no choice."

"OK," David said.

"Keep your ears open and listen, don't just look. You will need all your senses. Trust your instincts, too. If you see Canto or one of the crows bobbing their heads and flicking their wings, you know danger is coming. It is time to run," Viviana coached.

"You mean the birds will be there?" David asked.

"Of course, silly Word Man! Have you not noticed?" Viviana chided.

David felt a little more confidence creeping in. "I guess they do seem to always be around," David said.

Viviana put Brittany down and stood and stretched. She pulled out her deer bladder and filled it and both sippy cups at the stream.

"Oh no, does this mean it's time to go?" David asked.

"It is a busy day with lots to do," Viviana said.

David stood up, trying not to let his disappointment show. "I'll be back tomorrow afternoon with food and pants. Is there anything else you need?"

Viviana leaned over and gave David a kiss on the cheek. "That's for good luck on Monday," she said.

David couldn't stop grinning. "Thanks," was all he could say. "I guess I should go on then?" he managed.

"Bye. See you tomorrow," Viviana said and waited for David to walk down the trail.

David's heart seemed aflutter as he walked. "How can something as simple as a peck on the cheek leave me feeling this way?" he wondered.

Chapter 26

Sunday morning dawned with another beautiful sunrise. Sam was already up because he was tired of fighting to sleep. Sitting in his office, he was running over and over the plans they had made trying to find any details they had missed. Sam was pacing when he was startled by Evie's "Good morning!"

"Good morning to you, too," Sam said. "I was thinking of frying some eggs for breakfast. Would you like some?"

"That sounds good, but I want to shower first," Evie said.

"OK, just holler when it is time to start cooking," Sam said. Thankful for the distraction, Sam watched Evie head for the shower and then went to the kitchen to get things ready.

More and more doubts seemed to be creeping into Sam's mind. When Evie arrived at the table, Sam slid the eggs onto plates and a flood of questions slid from his mouth. "What if they call security on David before he ever gets in? What if the aluminum foil doesn't work and surveillance is able to identify him if Carter starts asking questions? What if... I think we should call this off."

Sam and Evie heard a peck on the window and looked over to see the titmouse eyeing Sam. "See, Sam," Evie said. "It is going to be OK. Your bird friend is here to reassure you."

"Are you sure he's not here to tell me to call all of this off?" Sam asked.

"Look at how he is looking at you, Sam. That's not a warning. It's encouragement."

"OK, I guess you are right. I'm getting really worked up this morning worrying about David getting caught."

"I'm nervous, too," Evie confessed. "Maybe church will help calm us down."

"I hope you are right!" Sam said.

After breakfast Sam and Evie dressed and walked along the river trail to church. The church was a white clapboard building with a steeple. It had simple stained-glass windows along the side that reflected the morning sun with gentle hues. The sanctuary was large enough to seat more than two hundred people but was seldom crowded. The front doors, three sets of paneled oak doors with stained glass, faced west and were accessed from the pod road that passed along in front of the apartment buildings.

Sam and Evie took their usual seats, the fifth pew from the front, just to the right of center. The organ prelude was one of Sam's favorites and seemed to calm him. As the service progressed, the choir sang the anthem, and then David got up to preach. Sam was feeling less antsy and tuned in as David began his sermon.

"Can you tell anything about another person by looking at her or his face?" David asked. "If you look, you can usually tell if a person is happy, sad, or angry just by the set of their eyes. That seems pretty amazing to me. What do you think people saw on your face this morning as you came into church? I think Jesus told the parable about not lighting a lamp and putting it under a bushel to help each of us realize that we have something inside us that is meant to be shared with the world around us."

Sam's mind drifted from the sermon to that thing that was inside him. "What is inside me?" Sam thought. "I'm so stressed out this morning, but I can't put a finger on exactly what is bothering me. What is going on in there? I'm... I'm... scared! I am afraid! That's the emotion! I am afraid that David will get caught. But that's not really it." Sam continued to look deeply into his heart. Finally, his heart connected with his mind, and what was really the source of his angst surfaced. "I'm afraid that once we take this next step, there is no turning back. I will lose my dream job. Evie could be in danger."

As these thoughts rose through the mist of Sam's confusion, he suddenly realized that tomorrow would be a turning point in his life, in all three of their lives. "This is a fine time for me to be growing feathers," Sam thought. "That doesn't sound like something to share with the world."

David's voice penetrated Sam's thoughts, and he tuned back into the sermon. David was saying, "To me, the light of the lamp represents God's relationship with each of us. It is the love with which God holds us close, with which God guides us, with which God comforts us. Once we realize that the great love of God resides in our hearts then we know we really have something great to share with the world."

Sam's mind walked back out of the sanctuary and into his inner world. "So, there is supposed to be love in here," he thought. For some reason, the memory of his and Evie's wedding surfaced. Sam remembered, even felt deep in his soul, the overwhelming love he experienced as he watched Evie walk down the aisle. A tear welled up in his eye as he re-experienced that powerful emotion. "Wow! If I could love Evie that much, how much could God love me?"

David's voice came back into focus. "I think the reason Jesus tells us not to hide the light is that God's love is not meant just to make me feel better, but for me to share with people in the world. The love God has placed in your heart, the compassion to reach out and love another person, may be exactly what that person needs in her or his life."

Sam drifted away, again. "All I seem to have is fear, and what good is that to anyone?" What his grandfather had said while they were in Sitka floated into Sam's consciousness: "Fear is a helpful emotion, Yielxaak. It warns us to be careful and vigilant. But it is not a signal to stop. Never fail to act because of fear. You are there at this time because you are the ones to do what needs to be done. Life is not worth much if it is not lived with integrity."

The memory seemed to spark hope in Sam's heart, and he felt goose bumps crawling up his arms. "Grandpa is right! I am afraid, but I cannot let that paralyze me. It may be scary, but whatever is going on here has to be exposed, and innocent people have to be rescued. Maybe this is what God has placed in my heart for this moment: fear and resolve. Operation Arnie will go on. So what if I lose this job? Evie and living with integrity are the important things in my life!"

Sam realized that David was looking at him and tried to tune back into the sermon. "You carry the light of love in your heart," David was saying. "The light of God's love, no less. And that is the most powerful force in the universe! Our mission is to let that light shine in every relationship we have and in everything we do."

When the service was over, David gave the benediction and walked down the aisle to greet people as they left. Sam and Evie worked their way out, shaking David's hand as they walked by.

"Would you like to come for lunch today, David?" Evie asked.

"Thanks, but I have some hiking to do," David said.

"I see," Evie grinned. "I'll see you in the morning then."

Sam and Evie walked out into the warm sunshine and headed home. Evie reached over and took Sam's hand. "That was a good sermon," she said.

"It must have been, but I'm afraid I spent most of the time daydreaming," Sam confessed. "Despite all my doubts and fears, I did come to realize that what we are doing to try to rescue Arnie is part of sharing our inner light with the world. Like Grandpa said, we may have been placed here just for this very purpose. It is still scary, but I realize that we have to press on."

"I'd say that is the sign of a very good sermon!" Evie said and squeezed Sam's hand.

Chapter 27

Evie arrived at school at 6:45am on Monday morning. After putting her things down in her room, she went to the science wing. Monica Oppenheimer was unlocking her door, and Evie called out, "Good morning, Monica!"

"Good morning, Evie. What brings you to this neck of the woods?"

"I need a few petri dishes and was wondering if you had any I could use."

"I don't since I teach chemistry. But I'm sure biology uses them. Let's check the stock room. How many do you need?" Monica asked being helpful.

"I think five or six will be plenty," Evie said hoping she would not have to explain why she needed them.

Monica unlocked the supply room that was between her room and the biology classroom. "Let's see, where would they keep those? Ah! There they are." Monica pulled out a box with six petri dishes and handed them over.

"Perfect!" Evie said with a smile. "Thank you!"

"You're welcome," Monica said. "What does an art teacher plan to do with petri dishes? I can't imagine!"

Evie cringed and hoped Monica didn't notice. She had thought about using the excuse of mixing some special paints, but she could do that in any container. She feared that if she said anything about mold, it would come back to haunt them. So, thinking as quickly as she could, she decided to go with mixing paints.

"I'm mixing some special paint today. Since there is a small amount, these will be perfect for keeping it covered and being able to get the brush in and out," Evie explained. She felt guilty about lying, and it was hard to keep that from shining through.

"Thanks again!" Evie said and headed back to her room, where David was waiting.

"Hey, David!" Evie said. "You look nervous."

"To tell the truth, I am," David said. "But it is show time!"

"Come on to the back," Evie said and led the way to her supply room. She unlocked the door and whisked David in. Shutting the door behind them, Evie said, "Good, you're wearing long sleeves. Quick, take your shirt off."

"What?" David asked.

"Hurry up and take off your shirt!" Evie said.

David started unbuttoning, and Evie could see that he was totally confused. "Remember, we are going to wrap this foil around your arm. Hopefully, it will block the signal," Evie said as she ripped off a long piece of aluminum foil.

"Oh yeah! I had forgotten that!" David said.

Evie cut the foil so that it was about four inches wide. When David got his shirt off, she carefully wrapped the foil around and around his arm, taping it in place.

"If it gets out that you and I were in your supply room with my shirt off, the church folks will have a field day!" David chided.

"Well put it back on then," Evie said. "Here are the petri dishes. Wait! We need a bag so those won't be seen." Evie pulled out a cloth bag she had used earlier and deposited the box in it.

"Remember, you will know that Carter is gone when you hear the jet take off," Evie said.

"I've got it," David responded.

"Now you had better scat before the kids get here," Evie said. When she opened the door, three of her first period students were already there. They giggled as Evie and David walked out of the supply room. Evie said, "Good morning," to the students and walked David out into the hallway.

"It looks like you might have some rumors to deal with, anyway," Evie said to David.

"Yep, it might get a little juicy!" David said.

"Good luck today, David. I will be praying!"

"Thanks, Evie. I'm going to need it, I fear!" David said.

* * *

Zeke Starke walked into Mary's office at precisely 7:55am for his Monday meeting with Carter. "Good morning, Mary."

"Morning, Zeke. Go on in. They are waiting for you."

The "they" registered with Zeke, but he didn't want to ask and let on that anything unusual was going on. Opening the door to Carter's office, Zeke was surprised to see Daniella Morrison standing in front of Carter's desk.

"Good morning, Mr. Carter. Daniella," Zeke said nodding to Daniella as he walked over to the desk. He was tempted to ask what was going on but decided to wait and let it unfold on its own.

Mitch Carter stood and shook Zeke's hand, "Daniella and I were strategizing on ways to get this thing with Arnie Johnson wrapped up," he said. "She is proposing that we threaten to take the woman's life if he won't tell us where the thumb drive is. What do you think of that idea, Zeke?"

"If you make a threat, you have to be willing to follow through on it," Zeke said.

"Daniella seems to think that Christie has to go anyway," Carter responded.

"She knows too much, and like any mother, she will not rest till she finds out what happened to her baby," Daniella said. "We can't let that happen, can we, Zeke?"

"I am hoping that being an alcoholic, Christie will just drink herself into oblivion," Zeke said. "The more killing, the more exposed we all are."

"Zeke, sometimes I wonder if you have lost your appetite for what we need to do here. The only way to protect this company is to find that thumb drive and dispose of the people who know about it. I'm sure taking care of the baby was hard on you, but we have to keep focused on what we are trying to do," Daniella growled.

"Do I look like I have lost my appetite?" Zeke said stiffening and with menace in his voice. "As far as I can tell, Johnson hid the thing, and it will never be seen again. Maybe if we put Johnson some place less comfortable and convince him that he will be there till death, he will consider talking."

"That's an idea, Zeke," Carter said sounding interested. "Why haven't we thought of that before?"

Zeke looked at Daniella and started to say, "Because your interrogator is incompetent," but held his tongue.

"That would have been my next move," Daniella said.

"OK," Carter said. "Let's see what happens if you present Johnson with the threat of the woman's death. In case that doesn't work, be thinking of a nasty little hole where we can stick him."

Carter turned his attention to his computer screen, and Zeke realized that was their cue to go. He walked out of the office fuming and dreading having to coordinate the interrogation with Daniella. He also realized that Daniella was astute at reading people, so he strove to keep his emotions in check.

"My office? Or do you just want to go straight to Johnson?" Zeke asked once they were out in the hall.

"Let's take a moment in your office. I want to pick your brain about strategies," Daniella responded.

Zeke led Daniella back to his office without a word. Unlocking the door, he gestured for her to sit down across from his desk and closed the door.

Daniella did not sit down. "What is up with you?" she said, and Zeke heard the anger in her voice.

Zeke saw Daniella clench one fist and thought, "If it's a fight you want, it's a fight you'll get." He slammed his hands down on the desk, leaned toward Daniella, and towered over her in a threatening way. She did not flinch or back away. "I think we are pushing this thing too far! It is obvious that Johnson is the only one who knows where that thumb drive is, and we have him contained so that he can't tell anyone. Unless you are going to start letting him have visitors, we should be OK! If anyone else knew about it, it would have surfaced by now. I say we take care of Johnson and be done with it."

Daniella bristled, stiffening her spine and running a hand over her curly black hair. "Starke, as long as the thumb drive exists, it is a potential threat to this company. If it is discovered, you could lose your cushy little job! We cannot rest until it is destroyed."

Zeke glared at Daniella, and she glared back. "Apparently Carter agrees with you," Zeke spat. "So now what?"

"I say that we do just as we have planned. First we present Arnie with Christie's pending death. If that doesn't work, then we put him in a hole somewhere for a long time. What I wanted to run by you is how do you think it would work best?"

"How would what work best?" Zeke spat back.

"Would it be more effective just to tell Arnie that Christie will die, bring Christie in, and have her present during the discussion, or actually have him watch her die if he doesn't talk?"

Zeke was silent, and Daniella continued musing, "I guess we could let him see the killing on live stream video as another option."

"You really get off on this kind of thing, don't you?" Zeke said. "As an interrogator, you should realize that a two-step process is the best. First you tell him what is going to happen. If he doesn't talk, then you make him watch. Of course, after he watches her die, there will be little incentive to tell us anything."

"You are right," Daniella said.

Zeke had the uneasy feeling that this had been more of a test than a strategy meeting. He looked at Daniella and said, "Well?"

"OK, let's go," she responded.

Chapter 28

Zeke and Daniella walked out of the office building. As the pod pulled up, Zeke heard the corporate jet's engines roar as it lifted off of the runway. He looked over his shoulder to watch the plane climb into the sky. "He's off to his meeting and leaving us here to do the dirty work," Zeke thought but didn't say it. He suspected Daniella would tell Carter anything negative. They climbed into the pod and made their way to Johnson's holding cell.

Just outside the interrogation room, Zeke said, "I assume you will be doing the talking."

"Of course," Daniella said. "You can throw in comments if you think they will help persuade him."

Zeke fought back the desire to light into Daniella for what felt like arrogance. Knowing that it wouldn't do for the prisoner to hear the interrogators arguing just outside, he kept silent and hoped his angry demeanor would help persuade Johnson that they were serious.

Daniella nodded at the guard, and he unlocked the door. She led the way into the room, Zeke following close behind. The guard locked the door behind them.

"I see you have brought help this time," Arnie said looking at Zeke. "Does that mean it's time for the torture to start?"

"Yes, it does," Daniella said. She sat down and Zeke leaned against the wall trying to look menacing. He noticed that

Arnie kept taking fearful glances at him and thought it must be working.

"Arnie, we don't want this to get any uglier than it already has. But the fact is we will not stop until we have that thumb drive in our possession. How ugly it gets is all up to you."

Arnie sat there in silence.

* * *

David had opened a window in his apartment, listening for Carter's jet to take off. He had decided not to go to the office since it was a longer walk to Carter's house. When he heard the roar, David stood up and stretched. He had to admit that he was nervous.

Walking to the bathroom, he carefully applied the mustache and inspected it. He pulled on the hat and set it at just the right tilt. He put on the thick rimmed glasses last. Eyeing himself in the mirror, he said, "It's show time."

As David was locking the door to his apartment, he realized that he had forgotten the name tag and clipboard he had made up to look more official. He went back into the apartment, hung the lanyard around his neck, and slid the clipboard into the bag with the petri dishes and potato juice solution. With his supplies gathered, David took a deep breath and let it out slowly to calm his nerves.

David began the walk to Carter's house with the sun to his left. It was a warm morning, and he knew it would be hot by the afternoon. He felt a little awkward in his long-sleeved shirt, but it covered the aluminum foil well. He came to the manicured drive that left the entrance road and meandered toward Carter's mansion. The drive was lined with crepe myrtles and dogwood trees in an alternate pattern. The crepe myrtles were at the end of their bloom, their scarlet bundles weighing down the branches.

David continued his walk and could see the mansion nestled in a wooded area. As he walked, he rehearsed what he would say when someone answered the door. Getting closer to the mansion, David marveled and said to himself, "Why would anyone build a house this big for one person?" It was a beautiful home of rockwork and rough sawn timber.

* * *

Daniella glared at Arnie, waiting for him to say something. "OK, I'll bite. What do you mean by, 'How ugly it gets is up to me?'" Arnie asked.

"We have reached the limits of our patience, Arnie Johnson," Daniella said with menace in her voice. "Will you tell us where you hid the thumb drive?"

"I think you already know the answer to that," Arnie said. "No."

"Remember, you are the one forcing us to do this," Daniella replied. "If you will not tell us where the thumb drive is, Christie will die."

"You wouldn't dare!" Arnie spat.

Daniella sat silently. Finally, Zeke said, "Don't underestimate us, Johnson."

Zeke watched and could see Arnie wrestling with what to do. He could see Daniella calculating her every move. Finally, she said, "Well?"

"Well what?" Arnie said, appearing shaken.

"Will you spare Christie's life or have her killed? It's your choice."

Arnie sat like a stone. After a couple more minutes, Daniella stood. "I see you have made your decision. This time tomorrow Christie will be dead. You are the only one who can save her," Daniella explained and walked toward the door. She stopped and said, "Oh, just so you know the truth, Brittany wasn't sent to foster care. She is dead." Zeke flinched and hoped Daniella had not noticed.

* * *

As David approached the front entrance, he heard a door shut and people's voices coming from the right side of the house. David's heart and feet froze. He could hear the voices coming closer. Finally, David's mind kicked in, and he ducked to the left side of the house pretending to inspect for moisture. David watched from the shadow of a large hemlock tree as a man and a woman walked down the drive. "That looks like Zeke Starke," David muttered to himself. He felt a twinge of excitement. "This could be promising!"

David waited till they reached the end of the drive and hopped into a pod. Then he returned to the front door and rang the doorbell. It dawned on David that he could be on camera, so he pulled out the clipboard and scrawled a couple notes. The door opened and a smartly dressed middle aged woman appeared.

"May I help you?"

David was surprised. "I didn't expect this," he thought. "I expected a maid or something." Realizing his hesitation, David launched into his rehearsed spiel.

"Hello, I am Daniel Smith with Sporatics Mold Eradication. Mr. Carter requested a mold assessment of his home. I believe this is the right place," David said trying to sound authoritative.

"I am Joselyn King, house manager. Mr. Carter has said nothing about mold detection. And nothing happens in this house without my authorization," the woman said stiffening her spine and making herself as tall as she could.

Glad he had anticipated having to convince the staff to let him in, David launched into his next spiel.

"I have the paperwork right here that shows that Mr. Mitchell Carter called the office on Wednesday, September the fifth, requesting an evaluation for mold," David said and held out the clipboard for her to see. "I think I did a nice job with the business logo. This thing looks official," he thought.

Joselyn took the clipboard from David and looked it over. "This is highly irregular. Normally, I would be the one setting up something like this. I need to check with him before I can let you in, and he is in a very important meeting all day. I'll take your number and call when we can reschedule," she said.

David started to try playing on her sympathy but decided that playing to her obvious desire to do her job well and please her boss was better. "I understand that Mr. Carter can be a bit short tempered. We wanted to schedule for Thursday, but he insisted that it be done today. All that is involved is placing a few petri dishes in strategic locations and taking some scrape samples if I find anything suspicious. It is your call. We can go ahead and do this and make Mr. Carter happy, or you can risk putting it off and making him angry."

David was pleased to see that she hesitated and appeared to be thinking. He started to say more but decided it was working.

At last she said, "I guess you are right. Come on in, but don't bother anything. We keep this place ship shape."

She stood aside, and David walked into the elaborate marble foyer. He was wowed by the split staircase and ornate furniture. "Wow! So, this is how the other side lives!" he said.

"You will kindly keep from disparaging Mr. Carter for his wealth and do your job," Joselyn said testily.

David looked around the lower walls and floorboards. "Nothing suspicious here. Mold will be more likely on the lower floors. Would you please show me the stairs down?" David said, trying to sound more professional.

"This way," Joselyn said leading David to the kitchen. She opened a door to stairs and said, "I will be in my office over there," and pointed down a short hallway leading from the huge kitchen.

As Joselyn walked away, David started to call out, "Where is the light switch?" but decided he would find it himself. Standing there puzzling, he heard a phone ring. Joselyn hurried into her office.

"Carter mansion, this is Joselyn speaking. How may I help you?"

David stuck his head into the stairwell. When the lights came on, he felt silly. "Motion detectors! I should have known. Far be it from Carter to have to turn on a light switch." Taking his first step down the stairs, he heard Joselyn talking. David paused to listen.

"It is just a man from a mold detection company. Apparently Mr. Carter has gotten worried that there is mold in the mansion."

After a pause, "Well, he has had some coughing lately, so it is possible."

Listening a little longer, David heard, "That will be fine. Better safe than sorry, I say."

David cringed and realized that surveillance must have observed him and called to ask questions. "Better safe than sorry must mean they are sending someone to investigate!" he thought. David wanted to run but decided he it was better to continue with the ruse. "I should have about fifteen minutes to get out of here before they come," he thought, checking his watch he hustled down the stairs.

The stairs dumped David out into what appeared to be a large storage room. Lights continued to come on as he walked, and he saw boxes and boxes of food supplies, propane tanks, cookers, and heaters. "Carter has enough supplies to hunker down for a long time," he thought. He passed a row of twenty-five-gallon water barrels. There was a large garage door straight ahead, apparently for truck deliveries.

Remembering his mission, David pulled out a petri dish, poured some solution in it, and left it on one of the barrels. He continued walking quickly through the room and came out into a hallway. He went right and found a series of rooms equipped with computers and office equipment. One room had communication equipment. They appeared to be shortwave radio and satellite communication devices.

David went the other direction, freezing when he heard muffled music. Continuing toward the music, he saw a door to the outside straight ahead. He came to another hall that turned left and followed the music that way.

At the end of that hall, David located the source of the music. He realized he was sweating, and panic was close. David corralled his emotions and knocked.

A security guard opened the door. "May I help you?"

"I'm Daniel Smith with Sporatics Mold Detection. I am here to test for mold. Do you mind if I inspect these rooms?" David said.

"Yes, I mind!" the guard bristled. "From this point on is off limits per Mr. Carter's orders," he said and slammed the door.

The slam of the door almost covered up the sound of the doorbell. David panicked and ran to the door leading outside. It led from the west side of the mansion toward the woods. The door was unlocked, and he almost ran out when he saw Canto flying straight at him. He was startled but then realized that he would be seen by surveillance if he ran. Shutting the door, he tried to think.

"They know I'm here, so hiding will just look suspicious," he thought. "I can't run, as Canto told me. Options. Options. Options!" He was still trying to figure it out when he heard the door open across the basement. Finally, David sprang into action, dug out a petri dish, set it on the table/umbrella holder by the door, and was pouring solution in it when a security guard came around the corner.

"Mr. Smith, I presume," the security guard said. "I'm Mark Conner with security. We need to verify your identity if you don't mind."

"Sure," David said and held out his name badge.

Mark looked it over and said, "I'm afraid we will need a little more than this."

Just then David heard more footsteps, and a second guard appeared. David recognized the portable chip scanner that this guard was carrying and knew he was caught. He didn't panic. "I have rehearsed this, too," he thought.

"Hi! I'm Mike Chastain, and you appear to be..." the guard said hesitating and looking at the scanner. "Pastor McCutcheon?" The guards looked at each other and looked at David.

"Are you sure?" Mark asked.

"That's what it says," Mike replied, showing Mark the scanner screen.

Another guard appeared at the door and walked in. "No one outside that I see," the third guard said.

"Pastor, you have some explaining to do," Mark said.

"I have been curious about what this mansion looked like since I moved here," David said. "I couldn't resist having a look, so I dreamed up this ruse. I didn't mean any harm."

David could see that Mark wasn't swallowing his story. "You wanted to see the mansion, and you're touring the basement?" Mark queried.

Trying to sound like an awestruck tourist, David said, "I got a glimpse of the upstairs and was planning to go back and say there was evidence of mold down here. That would have given me cause to look around upstairs. I thought that would be more convincing."

"Did you see anyone else down here?" Mark asked.

David's first impulse was to say that he hadn't but realized the other guard could confirm their meeting. "There is a guard in that room," David said pointing, "He told me to go away, so I did."

"Pastor, that story is a bit odd. I'm afraid you will have to come with us," Mark said and nodded to the third guard. He pulled out handcuffs and cuffed David's hands behind his back. The guard frisked David while Mark looked in his bag.

"Nothing but petri dishes and a bottle of something," Mark said. He opened the bottle and sniffed. "It doesn't smell explosive, but we had better analyze it to be sure. Did you put out any more of these dishes?"

"Yes, I did. The solution is potato juice in water. It is harmless," David said.

"We will need you to show us all the dishes you have placed," Mark said. He gestured for David to lead the way. Mike stayed in front while the other two followed David.

David felt petrified. "What am I going to do?" he thought. As he started to turn, he saw Canto perched on a limb near the door. David looked Canto in the eye as he turned to walk.

Chapter 29

It was 3:47pm when Evie stepped out of the school into the hot September sun. She was feeling nervous and wanted to call David immediately but restrained herself. "I can wait till he comes for supper like we had planned," she thought.

As her pod pulled up, her blue bird landed on a lamppost, chirruping wildly, and flicking his wings. Evie watched for a minute, realizing that he was trying to tell her something. "What is it, buddy?" she asked out loud.

Evie intuitively knew that the bird wanted her to follow. She cancelled the pod and walked toward the bird. The school was located between the factories and apartment buildings to make it easier for parents to drop off their children before work. The bluebird led Evie in the direction of the factories. She followed and felt her skin prickle. "This can't be good," she thought.

The bluebird seemed to be in a hurry, so Evie followed quickly, her flats comfortable enough to run in if necessary. The bird continued from lamppost to lamppost. Evie noticed the sign on a small one story building as she passed by that said, "MC2 Security."

"That must be where Daniella Morrison's office is," she thought. Evie continued following the bird. It turned left so that she was walking with the fiber optics plant on her right. She noticed a line of three men walking toward another small building. The bluebird seemed to be heading toward them. As she got closer, she saw something familiar in the frame of the lanky one in the middle.

The bird landed on a lamppost when they were close enough for Evie to see that it was David, and he was handcuffed. He turned and caught her eye, then looked away. Evie cringed and almost burst into tears. Evie's feet seemed glued to the pavement. She just stood and watched as David was led into the small building.

Evie walked slowly past the building and noticed there was no identifying sign. She turned left at the next block, heading downhill toward the living quarters. Evie's heart seemed to skip a beat when she realized that there were bars on the windows. "Oh no! God, how could you let this happen?" Evie complained.

Evie kept walking, not knowing what to do. She realized she was almost pulling her hair as she ran fingers through it. Hearing the familiar chirrup, Evie looked back and realized the bluebird was following her.

"Thank you little bird," she said. "It is bad news, but I needed to know." The bluebird flew and landed on her shoulder. Somehow Evie didn't flinch. She reached up and stroked the bird with one finger. The little bird tilted its head, looked her in the eye, and then flew off. "That little bird has an amazing effect on me," Evie thought, suddenly feeling calmer.

Evie was grateful that her brain had shifted from panic to problem solving mode. She pulled out her phone and started to call Sam but decided that was a bad idea. Sliding the phone back into her purse, she tried to lay out possibilities for what to do next. Her thoughts kept coming back to "What would David want us to do?" She realized that he would tell them to continue on with the mission and not worry about him.

"Silly David," she thought, "Of course we are going to worry about you."

Back in the apartment, Evie decided that finishing the crow would help keep her mind occupied till Sam got home. She walked into the art room feeling nervous. She always felt nervous when it was time to open the kiln, never knowing how the pieces fared through the firing. Evie touched the top of her head then rubbed the top of the kiln before opening it, her good luck ritual. "I hope having the metal and foil in there didn't cause the crow to crack," Evie thought.

Opening the kiln, Evie breathed again. The bird was in one piece and looked exquisite. Evie had had trouble with the clay pushing into the metal cage she had made for the thumb drive, so she wrapped it in aluminum foil to preserve the inner space. Evie grabbed a flashlight and looked up the hole in the bottom of the bird. The foil looked blackened, but the cage was intact. "Yay!" she said with a shiver and a big smile.

Evie set the piece carefully on the table. It was designed to look like the crow was launching from a limb, about to take flight, with wings partially outstretched. Evie had had to work the limb, which served as the base, up the crow's legs to join with the crow's bottom for stability. This also allowed a tunnel for placing the thumb drive in the crow's body.

After finding tweezers and needle nose pliers, Evie ran her hand under the mattress all the way to the middle, locating the original thumb drive. Evie returned to the table, positioned a task light so she could see into the crow's cavity, and carefully worked the thumb drive into its cage. Keeping the bird upside down, Evie took the pliers and bent the wire over the bottom of the cage to keep the thumb drive in place. With this done, Evie set the crow down and clapped her hands. "Yay! It worked!" she said to herself.

Evie was smoothing the self-hardening clay into the hole when she heard Sam coming in. The opening of the door seemed to release the channel of emotions Evie had bottled up since seeing David in cuffs. She jumped up and ran to Sam, tears clouding her eyes. By the time she grabbed Sam in a hug, she was sobbing.

Sam hugged her tightly and said, "What's wrong, Evie?"

Evie continued sobbing. "Oh no! Is it David?" Sam asked. Evie shook her head, yes. Sam just held her till the sobbing slowed, and Evie could talk.

Evie pulled back, rubbed her eyes, and told Sam the story of how the bluebird had led her to see David being taken into a building in handcuffs. "He's in prison, Sam!" Evie said, "With bars and everything! We have to get him out of there! What do you think they will do to him?" Evie was talking rapidly with both her words and her hands. She could see the concern in Sam's eyes but was grateful for his steady calmness. She had enough emotion for several people, and Sam often served as an anchor that let her be free to fly without blowing away.

"Evie, we have to be calm and try to think this through, consider our next steps carefully," Sam said.

Evie was pacing around the room. "I know what David would say. He would say to carry on with the mission and not worry about him! He would tell us to keep trying to find Arnie and get him to safety! But we can't just let David rot in prison!"

* * *

"Daniella Morrison, Head of Security. How may I help you?" Daniella said as she answered her phone.

"Ms. Morrison, this is Mark Conner with security. We have had an incident that I wanted to inform you about."

"Well, go on," Daniella said sounding a little testy this late in the afternoon.

"We caught Pastor David McCutcheon wearing a disguise and going into Carter's mansion. We placed him under arrest, and he is in the holding cell."

"What? Are you serious?" Daniella asked having trouble believing her ears. "Did he take anything?"

"No. He says he just wanted to see inside the house. He had petri dishes that he was putting out with a solution in them. We are having the solution analyzed, but he says it is potato juice."

"Have you ever been on basement guard duty in the mansion, Conner? Do you know what is down there?" Daniella asked.

"No, ma'am, I haven't, and I don't," Conner replied.

"OK, I'm coming over to talk with the good pastor," Daniella said and hung up.

Daniella pulled up a chair outside the bars of David's cell and sat down. "I hear you have been busy breaking and entering this morning," she said.

"Actually, I didn't break anything, ma'am, just entered." David responded.

"We have a smart one," Daniella thought. "Mr. McCutcheon, you are hardly in a position to be making jokes. Do you mind telling me exactly what you were doing in Mr. Carter's home uninvited?"

"Like I told the security guards, I have been curious about what the inside of the mansion looks like ever since coming to MC2. I decided I would pose as a mold detector so I could have a glimpse of such an amazing place."

"Curiosity?" Daniella said. "You know what they say, 'Curiosity killed the cat.'" Daniella just let her last statement hang in the air for a bit. "Now, do you mind telling me why you were really there?"

"I do see the veracity of your proverb, ma'am, and I realize that my plan was ill conceived. I should have had more respect for Mr. Carter, but that is actually why I was there."

"Were you looking for Arnie Johnson?" Daniella snapped making her tone threatening.

"I thought that he left the company to pursue other ventures. Is he in Mr. Carter's house? I never did get to wish him well on his departure."

About that time, Mark Conner walked in. "The analysis is done, and the solution is potato juice. Nothing harmful."

Daniella looked David in the eye and pondered her next move. She thought, "I don't believe a word you are saying, Pastor McCutcheon." But she said, "Your story is ludicrous, but believable. We should prosecute you." She looked at Conner, "You say there was no harm done? He just sat out petri dishes?"

"That is correct, ma'am." Conner answered.

"Pastor today seems to be your lucky day. We are going to let you go, if you promise not to repeat any stunts like this one. Please unlock the cell and let the good pastor go," Daniella said. She stood aside as David walked out.

"Thank you," he said.

Once David was out of the building, Daniella said to Conner, "I want him tracked at all times. Give me a daily report of where he goes, what he does, and to whom he talks."

"Yes, ma'am," Conner said. "I'll inform surveillance right now."

Chapter 30

After the tears had stopped and her arms had quit flailing about, Evie put her hands on her hips, and Sam saw fire in her eyes. "I am going to finish the crow and get it ready to mail right now," she pronounced.

"You are right," Sam said, "We do need to carry on," and followed Evie into the art room. "Let's assume that since David got arrested, Arnie must be in the mansion." Sam watched as Evie finished filling the hole in the bottom of the ceramic piece and smoothed it out. "Umm, did you remember to put the thumb drive in?" Sam asked wincing because he knew it was a stupid question.

Evie flashed her eyes at him and said, "Of course I did!" She propped the crow so that the bottom was up to let the plug dry. "How are we going to storm the castle, break out Arnie, and rescue David without ending up caught ourselves?" Evie asked standing suddenly. "And then what about Christie? She could be in danger, too!"

Sam could see that Evie was getting wound up again, but he didn't have any good answers. "Honestly, Evie, I have no idea. But we will figure it out. We're a great team!"

Evie came over and hugged Sam again and said "You know, I can't believe that just a few weeks ago I thought our marriage was falling apart. Now I can't imagine being without you."

"I know what you mean," Sam said choking up. "I guess all we needed was a major foe to bring us back to our senses."

As Sam said the word "senses," there was a knock on the door. Sam and Evie looked at each other. "Who could that be?" Evie said.

"Let me get it," Sam said feeling anxious. He pulled the door open to see David standing there with a big grin on his face. Sam was speechless. Finally, he recovered enough to say, "Hey, David! Am I glad to see you?" and stepped out into the hall to embrace him. During the embrace, Sam caught motion to his left and noticed a security guard stepping into the shadows. "Come on in, David! I'm glad you could make it for supper," Sam said, ushering David into the apartment.

Just inside the door, Sam held his fingers to his lips as he shut the door. Evie burst into the room and nearly bowled David over with a hug.

"How did you get out?" she said giddily.

Seeing a look of puzzlement come over David, Sam echoed Evie's question, "Yeah, how did you get out?"

"You knew I was arrested?" David asked.

"I saw you being led into that building in handcuffs. I didn't know if we would ever see you again," Evie said.

Sam clapped David on the shoulder, "I knew we would. We were just going to add you to the list of people we need to rescue."

"I attribute my release to my consummate acting skills," David said smiling and taking a bow. "I convinced them that I invented the mold detection ruse as a way to see inside the mansion. Just an overly curious pastor! Apparently I was quite convincing!"

"Umm, I'm afraid the security guard in the hall says otherwise," Sam said.

"What?" David and Evie said.

"There is a security guard following you. My guess is that it wasn't your acting skills that got you released. I think they are following you because you are now a suspect," Sam said.

"What could they suspect me of?" David asked.

"I don't know. Maybe something like trying to spring Arnie Johnson from the mansion? Maybe something like trying to bring down MC2 with that thumb drive?"

Suddenly Evie started looking in David's ears and feeling around his shirt.

"What ARE you doing?" Sam asked.

"Checking to see if they planted a microphone," Evie mouthed silently.

"I think I would have known," David said. Evie appeared to be satisfied and stopped the search.

David looked deflated and said, "So, you don't think it was an academy award performance that got me out?"

"Sorry, David," Sam said.

Evie gestured toward the couch and recliners. "Sit down and tell us about your day. Did you find Arnie?"

Sam, David, and Evie sat down, and David piped up, "I think I found him, but I didn't actually see him. When I first got to the house, I had a close call. Zeke Starke and some woman came out of a basement door. I managed to hide on the other side of the house. When I got to the basement, I heard music. When I found it, I knocked on the door and a guard opened it. He told me that beyond that point is off limits to anyone and slammed the door."

"It sounds like you hit the jackpot!" Sam said.

"The good news is that there is a door into the basement just down the hall from where they are keeping him," David said. "That will make it easier to get back in."

Sam noticed Evie looking tense. "What is it, Evie?"

"Since they are tracking David, we are now on their suspect list, too. We will have to act fast," she said. "Sam, is the other thumb drive well hidden?"

"I taped it underneath the bottom drawer of my desk. How does that sound?"

"I would never find it!" David said. "Should we go after Arnie tonight?"

"We can't take a chance on rescuing Arnie until I mail the thumb drive," Evie pointed out. "And it's too late today. I can't mail it until school is out tomorrow."

"I could mail it in the morning," David offered.

"NO!" Sam and Evie both nearly shouted. "They will be all over you if you try to mail something. We have to let Evie mail it. Or I could mail it at lunch time," Sam said.

"I've been plotting on how to do this," Evie said. "I think I will take the crow in and ask for help wrapping it so that it won't break during shipment. If they see what it is, there may be less suspicion."

"That is brilliant, Evie!" David said. "Then do we go after Arnie tomorrow night?"

"I think we had better wait till Wednesday," Sam said. "We need to make sure the crow leaves the compound before we stir up any more suspicion. Next we need a plan. How are we going to get Arnie away from an armed guard? My fiercest weapon is a computer that I could use to hit him over the head... Hey! That might work!"

"I have that air rifle that I told you about," David said. "It might fool the guard."

"Wait, is it a pump rifle or does it use carbon dioxide cartridges?" Sam asked.

"It uses the cartridges. I have a couple of large tanks that I use to fill them," David said using his hands to demonstrate a tank about eighteen inches long.

Sam felt a tinge of excitement and smiled. "I think I have an idea. How big was the room that guard was in, David?"

"It looked really small, like a closet. Why?"

"What happens when you breathe carbon dioxide?" Sam asked.

"I think you die," David said.

"But you pass out first, right?" Sam said.

"Ah, I see!" Evie and David said.

"What if we use some of your costumes and pose as Arnie's aunts? We could say they told us we could visit Arnie. If we slip the CO_2 tank in a large purse and open it when the guard lets us in, he should pass out after a bit. Then we leave, taking the tank, and he recovers. No harm done in the rescuing of this prisoner," Sam explained.

Evie, David, and Sam looked at each other. Sam could see doubts on Evie's face in the way she crinkled her eyes. "I think we should definitely consider that, but keep thinking, too," Evie said.

"Well, I like it," David said. "Sam and I will make fine looking aunts!"

"Sorry, David, since they are tailing you, I'm afraid it will have to be Evie and me that go," Sam said.

Crestfallen, David said, "I guess you are right. It would be better if I stay on the other side of the compound for this."

Sam jumped up and ran into the office, coming back with the contraband computer. "Let's pull up an aerial view of the compound and plan a route to get Arnie to a place where we can sneak him onto a delivery truck."

Sam was booting up the computer when Evie said, "We are still forgetting an important piece to this puzzle. What about Christie?"

"I don't think she is in any danger," Sam said. "We can figure out what to do with her after we get Arnie safe."

The trio fell silent for a few moments. Sam felt anxious about the plan. So many things could go wrong. But he couldn't think of anything better at the moment.

"I need to take some food to Viviana in the morning," David said.

"No, David, that is too risky. They will be following you," Evie said.

"I guess I'll just have to give them the old army slip," David said smiling. "Besides, I can't let Brittany starve. It seems like Jesus said something about feeding the hungry," he said with another smile.

Sam and Evie looked at each other, "Smitten!" David's smile got bigger.

Chapter 31

At 9am sharp on Tuesday morning, Sylvia unlocked the doors to the store, and David strolled in. He went straight to the baby food and started to load everything they had into his canvas bag. He felt a twinge of guilt when he realized that some of the other parents in the compound might need some for their babies.

"I guess I will just take a few," David thought and returned much of what he had placed in his bag to the shelf. He made sure he had a nice balance of meats, fruits, and vegetables and headed to check out.

David was very aware that his every move was being watched, and his radar was on high alert. Stepping out of the store, he pretended to stretch so he could check for guards. Seeing none, he decided that surveillance was watching him by video. He thought about waving at one of the cameras but decided against it. "I guess it's better that they don't know that I know they are watching me," he thought.

David returned to the church office, placed the food jars, his Bible, and a note pad in his backpack and prepared to begin his hike to Viviana. David tried to decide what to do if he were followed. "More likely, when I am followed," he said to himself. "I wonder how far away from the compound they can track these chips?" He thought about trying the aluminum foil trick again but decided that it would create too much suspicion. With a plan in mind, David headed to the check point.

Bobby was on duty again, and David greeted him warmly. "It's another beautiful morning! How are you, Bobby?"

"I am fine," Bobby replied. "How are you doing? I hear you had a rough day yesterday."

"You heard, huh?" David said feeling ashamed. "I let curiosity get the best of me, I'm afraid," he said sticking to his story.

"That was bold of you!" Bobby said. "I'm afraid I was instructed not to let you leave the compound."

"But my request to leave cleared this morning," David argued.

"Let me check," Bobby said and pecked on his computer. "So, it did! I guess they changed their minds."

"I'm going to try a different trail today, the path less traveled, I guess you could say. Isn't there a trail that leads off up the river?"

"There is. It is about a quarter of a mile north," Bobby explained pointing in that direction.

"Thanks, Bobby," David said as he walked across the footbridge.

David heard the gate buzz as he neared. Walking through it, he turned left, following the river upstream. After about a hundred feet, David decided to turn and wave at Bobby as a cover for checking to see if he was being followed. While waving, he saw two guards approaching the check point. David was tempted to run. Instead, he turned and walked on in the direction he was going. He passed the huge oak tree that leaned out across the river. The tree hid him from view, so he decided to cut into the woods and up the mountain.

"If I head up the mountain and keep going east, I can top the shoulder and regain the trail," David thought. Cutting into the forest, David was surprised to see what looked like a deer trail. He followed it. When it cut back to the left, away from his direction, he turned into the undergrowth and tried to speed up.

After hiking at a ferocious pace for about ten minutes, David stopped suddenly and listened. He didn't hear sounds of anyone behind him. He waited a bit and then thought, "Suckers! I bet they kept following the deer trail."

Satisfied that he had lost them, David was about to take another step when he heard the familiar song of Canto.

"Hello, my fine feathered friend!" David said. "You think I lost them too, huh?" Canto chirruped, flew a little ahead, perched on another branch, and looked back at David. David started to hike in the direction he had been going, but Canto chirruped loudly. David looked at him, and Canto flew a little farther in a direction that was more uphill than where David was headed.

"OK, I'm guessing that you recommend I follow you, is that right?" David asked the bird. "Oh great! Now, I'm talking to birds and expecting them to answer!" David thought.

Canto gave a happy chirrup and flew a little further. "I guess you do know these woods better than I do," David said and followed Canto's lead.

David kept his eye on Canto as he followed him straight up the mountainside. After about twenty minutes, David was huffing and puffing so that he stopped for a rest. "Canto, I need a break," he said out loud and put his hands on his knees, bending over to breathe. Canto flew back to a limb near David and waited.

When David's breathing had calmed he stood up straight and said, "After you, sir," gesturing for Canto to lead the way. The bird led him up the mountain, over the shoulder, and back to the trail that would lead David to his meeting place with Viviana.

When David topped the hill and rounded the last corner, he saw that Viviana was already there, and Brittany was toddling around at her feet. He almost ran up to her for a hug but caught himself.

"What is wrong?" Viviana asked.

"What do you mean, 'What is wrong?'" David asked back.

"The crows are anxious. You look anxious. Something is wrong," Viviana explained.

David noticed for the first time that the crows were squawking a lot. "Well, I did get arrested yesterday," David said.

"What? You got caught!" Viviana said putting her hands to her cheeks.

"I did," David said. "They arrested me, but I convinced them it was just a ruse to see the inside of the mansion. Then they let me go."

Viviana looked up at Rey. "You were followed! They followed you on your hike!"

"How did you know that?" David asked.

As if she didn't hear him, Viviana said, "We have to get out of here," sounding panicked.

"It's OK," David said. "I took a different trail and lost them on the way."

That seemed to calm Viviana, and she said, "Do you realize that they let you go so they could follow you?"

"Yes. Well, Sam, my friend, discovered that last night," David responded.

"Look at Canto," Viviana commanded. "Do you know what he tells you?"

David looked at his little friend. Canto was leaned forward, flicking his wings, but not making a sound. "He looks.... worried?" David said.

"Si! He tries to tell you that danger comes," Viviana explained. "If you survive, you have to learn to listen to him!"

"He did lead me up the mountain and to the trail," David said, trying to show Viviana that he was capable of listening to the bird.

Suddenly raucous crow calls sounded just down the trail. "They come," Viviana said quietly.

"What in the world is going on down there?" David said and stepped out onto the trail for a better look. "I think the crows must be fighting over food." David looked back to Viviana, but she was gone. Brittany was gone, too. David cringed, and the thought hit him that Viviana might have been right.

Walking a few paces down the trail, David could see hands flailing at crows that were dive bombing. Then, he could see two MC2 hats just over the brow of the hill. David ran back to his pack, whipped out his Bible and pad, and pretended he had been sitting there studying. As the guards walked up the trail, David could see that they looked frazzled. The crows had stopped their attack. David noticed a few briars and small branches stuck to the men's clothes.

"Good morning," David said, trying to sound chipper.

The guards just glared at him as they walked by. One muttered back, "Good morning." As they got closer, David felt his nerves tense. He wasn't sure what would happen. The guards just kept walking.

"Have a good hike," David called out, but got no answer. David sat there, not knowing what to do. He looked up and saw Canto scratching himself. Canto looked more relaxed, so David decided he should relax, too. He decided he would act like he was studying. But his mind kept wandering, and mostly he was staring into the stream.

The thought dawned on David, "They are up the trail watching me. I need to sit here long enough to make it look like I am accomplishing something."

After a few more minutes David decided that he was wasting his time. He got up to put the Bible and pad in the backpack. He realized that he had not gotten out a pen and felt silly. He also noticed that the baby food was still in the pack and felt worried. He started to leave it by the stream but realized that the guards would see it. He thought about hiding it farther back but thought, "They are watching me."

David decided just to haul the food back home and try again another day. He pulled on the backpack and stepped onto the trail. A sudden streak of mischief hit him, and he called out over his shoulder, "We can go back, now."

Chapter 32

Evie rushed home after school on Tuesday afternoon determined to get the crow mailed before the shipping office closed. She stood before the crow, her elbow in one hand and her chin on the other, pondering one more time, "Should I go ahead and box it up or let them pack it?"

Evie smiled when a sense of certainty came over her. "My first idea was right. If they see what it is, it will seem less suspicious." She picked up the birthday card she had prepared, complete with instructions for removing the thumb drive and mailing it to NOAA, carefully cradled the crow in her arm, and headed for the shipping office.

Evie's nerves began to tense as she summoned the pod. The early September sun was still plenty warm but not as oppressively hot as it had been. She was glad the apartment building shaded her. When the pod arrived, Evie almost lost her nerve. Realizing it would look suspicious to turn back, she got in and directed the pod to the shipping office.

The shipping office was located just at the beginning of the row of factories on the south side of the compound. It was a large building where all of the factory shipments and deliveries were managed, as well as people's personal mail. The compound, like the rest of the country, was served by Ameridirect, the brainchild of Xavier Harrison who had put the other delivery companies out of business by his shrewd tactics. He had become a member of the A-30.

Evie walked into the building and turned right into the Ameridirect office through a door in the solid glass wall that covered the entire front. She tried to control her nerves and seem casual as she walked up to the counter. "Hey, Graciela," she said recognizing the clerk as a fellow church member. Graciela was a short, just a little plump, Hispanic woman in her mid-twenties with a super warm smile. At church she was usually wrangling three small children, a four-year-old boy and toddler twin girls.

"Oh, hey Evie! It is good to see you," Graciela spouted, all happy and perky. "What brings you in?"

"I have a shipping challenge," Evie replied feeling less nervous since she was dealing with someone she knew. Evie held up the crow so Graciela could see it over the counter.

"This is for Sam's grandfather. His birthday is this Thursday. Do you think there is a way we can ship it without breaking it?"

"Wow! That is beautiful! Where did you find it?" Graciela asked.

"I made it," Evie said proudly. "The crow is important to Sam's people," she said not wanting to go into too much detail. As Evie spoke, the door opened, and a security guard walked in. Evie's heart froze. She barely heard Graciela say, "May I see it?" Evie summoned all of her will to keep from running. She managed to say, "Hey, Bobby," as Bobby Bridges walked up.

Evie looked up and saw Graciela with her hands out. "Oh, sorry. I got distracted by Bobby." She handed the crow over. "I'm really nervous about mailing this. Do you think I should just wait until the next time we travel up there?" Then she thought, "Oh no! What if she says, 'Yes?'?"

"But I do want to get it there for his birthday," Evie added.

"Have you been creating again Evie?" Bobby asked. Graciela held it up for Bobby to see. "You are amazing! I want one of those! You know, you could sell your work," Bobby said excitedly.

Evie's nerves felt calmer as she sensed nothing suspicious. "Thanks, Bobby! I'm afraid it takes too much time for me to make a piece to make selling my work profitable."

Evie noticed Graciela studying the piece. She turned it every way and flipped it upside down. "That is so lifelike!" she said. "Why is this spot on the bottom a different color?"

Thinking quickly Evie said, "I leave a hole in the pieces to help keep them from exploding in the kiln. Then I fill it in with self-hardening clay."

"Well, isn't that clever!" Graciela said.

"Bobby, why don't you go ahead? I'm afraid this may take a while," Evie offered.

"Thanks, Evie!" Bobby said. He stepped up to the counter and offered Graciela a small box. Graciela weighed it, and Bobby paid and left.

"I know just what we can do!" Graciela said and carefully set the crow down on the counter. "I'll be right back.

Graciela came back with a large box, bubble wrap, and packing peanuts. "This is so delicate! How did you get the wings to stand out without drooping down?"

Evie started to say that she had propped them till the piece was fired but realized her opportunity. "I built a metal cage with wires that extend out like the wings, and then molded the clay around that cage."

"Wow! I bet that was tedious," Graciela responded. "Here is what I propose: We wrap the crow in bubble wrap and put it in this box," she said pulling a smaller box out of the large one. "Then we nestle it in the peanuts in the big box. I have sent fragile things this way before, and it has always worked."

Evie smiled and said, "That sounds like a great idea!" She watched as Graciela carefully wrapped the bird in enough bubble wrap to entirely fill the first box. She placed the piece in the box and taped it shut. Evie said, "Oh! I almost forgot that I have a card, too," handing it over the counter.

Graciela placed it right on top of the smaller box. She poured in a layer of peanuts, added the box and card, and then filled it to the brim with more peanuts. Sealing down the top, she handed Evie an address label. "I guess I should have had you filling that out while I was packing," she said.

Graciela weighed the box and frowned. "I'm afraid this will be a little pricey with all of the shipping materials and going all the way to Alaska. How fast do you need it to get there?"

"As soon as you can," Evie said.

"I can overnight it for $127, which will get it there Thursday. Two-day delivery, which would get it there on Friday, would be $64."

"Hmm," Evie said to give the impression she was thinking about the cost. "Well, it is his birthday, and I want it to be there on time. Let's overnight it!"

"You've got it!" Graciela replied and printed out the correct labels, including three that said, "FRAGILE!" "You know, if I can get this to the loading dock by 4:30, it will go out today and be there tomorrow!" Graciela said excitedly.

Evie waved her arm toward the scanner to pay and felt the nervousness resurface. Graciela must have seen it in her face. "Don't worry, Evie. I am perfectly positive that it will get there intact and in all its beauty!"

"You're right," Evie said realizing she had been caught. "You packed it perfectly. All I need to do is trust and not worry. I can't wait for him to see it!" she added truthfully. "Thank you so much, Graciela," Evie said as she turned to leave.

"You're very welcome! See you in church Sunday?" Graciela called back.

"I'm sure you will!" As Evie walked to the door, she spied a security guard across the hall from the entrance to Ameridirect. She noticed that the guard looked away, which set off Evie's radar. She tried to control the sense of panic that raced through her body and walked out of the building like nothing was amiss.

Evie summoned a pod to take her back to the apartment. While she waited, she pretended to be surveying the different factory buildings in the background. When she glanced at the shipping building, she saw that the security guard had moved so that he could see out the front door.

As her pod pulled away, Evie thought she saw the guard on a cell phone. A shiver ran up her spine as she surmised that the guard was calling about the package she had mailed. The pod pulled in front of the apartment building, and the computerized voice said, "Thank you for riding and have a good evening."

Every nerve in Evie's body seemed taut. "They are going to seize the package. We are going to be discovered. What do we do?" Her mind was racing around and around. "I need to calm down. So far everything is OK. Oh, good grief!" Evie paced around the apartment for a few minutes. She felt under the bottom of Sam's desk drawer where he had hidden the other thumb drive to assure herself it was still there. It was. Evie took a deep breath and blew out slowly. "Maybe the best thing to do with this nervous energy is to go for a run," she decided.

Evie stepped out of the apartment building and looked around, not seeing a security guard. She started running along her usual trail by the river, and her bluebird friend joined her. "Hey bird!" Evie said out loud. "If we are going to be such good friends, I need a name for you."

The bluebird chirruped and flew on up ahead. Evie hustled to keep up. "I know, I'll call you Azul. Don't you think that's a pretty name?" The bird paused a moment as if considering, chirruped and flew on to the next lamppost. "Azul it is, then. You seem to be in a hurry today." Evie kept pace with the bird even though she was going faster than her usual speed.

Evie was beginning to huff and puff trying to keep up. "Azul, I think I need to slow down," she managed to get out over several breaths. As they passed the church, Azul veered off the trail to the left and flew up the pod road toward the factories. Evie followed Azul with her eyes and stopped dead in her tracks. Oh no!" she said when she saw two security guards, each holding an arm and pulling Christie along in handcuffs.

Chapter 33

Daniella knocked once and opened the door to Zeke's office. She stepped in brusquely, not waiting to be invited. She was feeling tense since this investigation was dragging on. Daniella was not used to having those whom she interrogated hold out this long. She typically used much more aggressive and effective tactics, but Zeke Starke kept nixing those ideas.

"Daniella," Zeke said as she walked in.

Skipping the greeting, Daniella started right in. "I've sent guards to bring the woman in. She should be apprehended and ready by the time we get to Johnson. The techs are setting up a live feed so Arnie can see what is going on."

"Are you just going to pull up the video, shoot Christie, and be done with it?" Zeke asked.

Daniella noted the patronizing tone. "Don't start in on me, Starke!" she snapped. "I am tired of this dragging on and on. Today we start a different path. Johnson is going to watch a little torture today. If that doesn't convince him, he will experience hell tomorrow. By tomorrow evening, I will have answers!"

Daniella glared at Starke, hoping he would argue with her. "A nice fight might feel good right now," she thought. Daniella's phone rang. She glanced at it and ignored the call, feeling perturbed at the interruption. Starke glared back, and Daniella couldn't read what he was thinking. "Let's go," she said, stomping out of the office.

Daniella had to knock twice to get the guard's attention because his music was so loud. Opening the door, the guard snapped to attention and then fumbled to turn the music down. Daniella gave him a disgusted look as she and Zeke strode into the room where Johnson was being held.

"Good afternoon, at least I think it is afternoon," Arnie said.

Daniella didn't say a word. She set her computer on the table and logged on. The feed into the holding cell was up and running. She spun the computer around, so it faced Arnie. The screen showed Christie in handcuffs seated at a table. Daniella watched as Arnie's face grew pale. "Finally," she thought. Daniella always felt a sense of satisfaction, even enjoyment, when her techniques worked.

Daniella placed a call, saying one word, "Proceed." One of the guards pulled out a rope with a knot on the end and whipped it across Christie's back. She screamed out. The volume was up to make sure Arnie heard. A second blow and a second scream.

Daniella watched Arnie flinch and turn away. A third blow and a third scream. Daniella continued to sit silently, watching Arnie.

When the fourth blow hit, Arnie said, "What do you people want?"

Daniella continued to be silent.

"OK! If you let Christie go, I will take you to the thumb drive. You people are sick!"

"I'm sorry, Johnson. You are not in a position to negotiate," Daniella said and snapped the computer closed. "I want you to think how long it is going to take Christie to die like this. Think about how much she is going to suffer, just because of you."

Daniella stood and walked out the door with Zeke following. She ignored Arnie's pleas and offers to tell. Back outside the mansion, she called and told the guard to stop the beatings. "He'll talk tomorrow," Daniella said to Zeke confidently.

A pod was waiting, and they climbed in. Daniella noticed a voicemail from the call that she had ignored. She frowned as she listened to the message.

"The Hanson woman mailed a package today," she told Zeke as she returned the call.

"Chuck, here," The guard said.

Daniella said, "This is Daniella Morrison, Chuck. What was in the package?"

"It looked like a ceramic bird," he responded.

"What do you mean it looked like a ceramic bird? Don't you have the package?"

"No. ma'am," the security guard responded. "I called to see if you wanted me to intercept it and was waiting for your order."

"Yes! Intercept it, you idiot! And bring it straight to my office. Wait, have them scan it first and then bring it to my office" Daniella barked.

Turning to Zeke, Daniella said, "Good grief! The imbecile! We may have something!"

"Or," Zeke said calmly, "we may just have someone's birthday present." It was a cold, silent ride till Zeke got out at his building.

It was 4:55pm when Daniella sat down in her office chair relishing the progress of the day. She looked over a few things on her computer as she waited for the security guard to appear with the package. After a couple of minutes her phone rang.

"Daniella Morrison here."

"Hey, Ms. Morrison, this is Chuck again. I'm afraid the package has already left the compound."

"What?" Daniella nearly screamed.

"The clerk said that Ms. Hanson mailed the package overnight, and she was able to get it on today's truck."

Daniella composed herself and said, "Thank you, Chuck. That will be all for now, but we will continue surveillance on the Hansons."

"So, you think you're clever, do you?" Daniella thought. "We'll see about that!" She grabbed her phone and called Chuck back. "See if you can get the address to which that package was sent, Chuck."

"Yes, ma'am," he responded.

Daniella called Zeke Starke next. "The package has already been shipped. I'm afraid our Ms. Hanson was clever enough to ship it just in time to get it on the truck. I need a detail set and ready to go intercept that package. Chuck is retrieving the address right now."

"Daniella, I think you have lost control. We can't storm someone's home and demand a package," Zeke countered.

"You're right. That is why we have to intercept it at the Ameridirect office before it is on its way to the home, Starke. Get the team ready."

"I don't think Ameridirect will take too kindly to this," Starke countered.

"They will if I get Mr. Carter involved," Daniella said. "You get the team and transport ready. I'll handle the details. And Starke?"

"Yes, Daniella?"

"Don't drag your feet on this. I want that team ready to go ASAP!" and she hung up the phone.

Chapter 34

Sam opened the door to the apartment to find a sobbing Evie. He tensed but ran to hold her. Fearing her response, Sam asked, "What's wrong?"

"They arrested Christie," she said between sobs. "Azul led me up the river to show me."

Sam felt like crying himself but held Evie until she calmed down. "Another setback! Wait, who is Azul?"

"Azul is what I named my bluebird. He wanted to show me what was happening to Christie, so he led me, making me run faster than I usually do."

"So, what you are saying is that you went for a jog, this bird hustled you along, and you got there in time to see Christie being arrested?" Sam asked for clarification, feeling a bit confused. Evie nodded her head in agreement.

"Evie, I know these birds seem to be pretty smart, but do you really think it could do that?"

Sam's heart nearly stopped with the cold glare Evie gave him. "All right, I guess I should know better than that by now," he said.

"Sam, what are they going to do with Arnie and Christie? Why would they arrest her?"

There was a knock at the door. Sam jumped, and Evie screamed and put a hand over her mouth.

"I'd say we are a bit tense!" Sam said as he went to answer the door. It was David looking serious. "Come in," Sam said and closed the door quickly. Sam saw David's concern register when he saw that Evie had been crying.

"What's wrong?" David asked.

Evie relayed the story of how Azul had led her to discover Christie's arrest.

"Wow!" David said. "I'm beginning to believe these birds know more that we do."

Sam almost said something, but stopped himself, learning a lesson from his previous doubt about the bird. This thought did pass his mind, "I wonder if they are losing it?"

David told the tale of his journey up the mountain, how Canto had led him to the trail, and how the crows had distracted the guards long enough for Viviana to disappear.

"Are..." slipped out before Sam stopped himself, not finishing the "you sure about the birds" part. He realized Evie and David were looking at him, waiting for him to finish. The only way Sam could think to finish the sentence was, "Are we going to eat supper?"

"Sam!" Evie scolded. "How can you think of food at a time like this?"

"Well, we usually do eat when David comes over, and I'm sure there is a security guard outside wondering what we are up to," Sam recovered.

"You're right," David said. "We do need to stick to as regular a routine as possible. Have I really come over to eat that much?"

"Yes!" Sam and Evie said at the same time. Evie popped some potatoes in the microwave, instructed Sam to open green beans, and pulled out frozen hamburger patties to cook.

"Now what do we do?" Evie asked.

"I wish people would stop being arrested," Sam said. "It is quite worrisome, and it complicates matters too much."

"We have to play the hand we are dealt," David said.

Sam scrunched up his face, "A poker image?"

"Right now, we are very much in a game of chance," David said.

"You are right," Sam responded. "A new variable to add to the equation," Sam said trailing off into thought. Sam realized David and Evie were watching as the gears of his mind turned. "OK, let's brainstorm reasons for them to arrest Christie."

"Drinking at work?" Evie offered.

"No, I don't think so," David responded. "When I spoke to her after church Sunday, she said she was off the alcohol entirely."

"So far, she seems to be a pawn in the game," Sam said. "They have used her to try to get to Arnie before, so maybe that's what is happening again."

Sam saw Evie's eyes widen and her mouth dropped open. "If they were going to kill the baby, do you think she is next?"

"That would certainly be a way of putting pressure on Arnie to talk," David added.

Silence fell over the threesome as they tried to process this realization. Finally, David said, "I can't think of a more plausible scenario."

"So, do we change plans and go after Christie?" Evie asked. "We can't just let them kill her!"

"No, we can't," Sam said. "But I still think Arnie is the key. If we can get Arnie out of here, they will have no reason to kill Christie."

Sam saw a spark of hope in Evie's eyes, then her face shadowed again. "By this time, they may think Christie knows too much. It may be too late for her," she said sadly.

Heaviness sank their hearts as they finished their dinner. Finally, Sam said, "'Operation Arnie' happens tomorrow morning."

"Why not tonight?" Evie asked.

"By the time we get our act together, I'm afraid it will look too suspicious for two old aunts to be showing up for visitation," Sam said. "To the costumes!"

Sam pulled the bag of costumes from a niche beside the recliner. Trying to sound chipper, he handed the bag to David and said, "What would you recommend, sir?"

David plundered through the suitcase and pulled out the southern belle costume he had used for Scarlett in their "Gone with the Wind" spoof. He found another dress that he had worn in "A Midsummer Night's Dream." "I'm afraid you are a bit full figured for this one, Sam," he said handing Scarlett's dress to Evie. "But this one should do nicely for you."

Sam and Evie held the dresses up, and Sam said, "Perfect! Now, how do we get the carbon dioxide tank?"

"Hmmm," David said. "The tanks are at the church..."

"At the church?" Evie said, looking perplexed.

"Yeah, sometimes I shoot at trees across the river when I'm having trouble concentrating," David explained. "It's still light. You could come back with me to the church on the pretext of... I've got nothing."

"We could pick up the altar cloth that needs repairing!" Evie said excitedly.

"Perfect, Evie!" Sam responded.

David opened his mouth to speak then smiled and pointed at Evie, "She's clever! Very clever! And you can roll the tank up in the cloth so no one will see it!"

David led the way as they left the apartment. He looked left and right and then opened the door to the stairwell. "Dinner was delicious. We are going to the church to get an altar cloth that Evie has graciously offered to repair. Do you care to come along with us?" David called out to the security guard who was lurking behind the door.

Chapter 35

As the darkness of night was just beginning to surrender to the predawn light, David slipped out of his apartment with his food-laden backpack. He tried to walk casually to the check point, assuming that he would be followed.

"Another sunrise hike?" Bobby asked as David walked up to the little room at the check point.

"I do enjoy the mountain early in the morning. There are a lot of birds out and about," David said. As if he had heard David, Canto lighted on the top of the room housing Bobby and let out a beautiful song. "See what I mean," David said and smiled at the bird.

David looked around and said, "I guess my buddies will show up soon to follow me."

"I imagine so," Bobby said. "Do you know why they are still following you?"

"I guess it takes a while to get off the naughty list," David said.

Bobby chuckled, "You are probably right. Have a good hike."

David crossed the river and followed his usual trail up and over the shoulder of the mountain without looking back. As soon as he was out of sight of the check point, he started to jog. After a quarter of a mile of uphill jogging, David was totally out of breath.

"OK, maybe this wasn't such a good idea," he thought. He stopped to catch his breath but felt driven to push on. Before he had recovered, he set off at a fast walking pace. "I have to get far enough ahead to hand off the food to Viviana and let her get away before they catch up," he thought, pushing himself to keep going.

After a few more minutes, David seemed to have found a pace that he could sustain. Only then did he realize that Canto was keeping pace with him. "You sound chipper today," David managed to say. He realized that if Canto wasn't sounding an alarm, then he must be staying ahead of the guards.

David kept pushing himself. He was nearly spent when he topped the hill and could see the rhododendron grove. "She's not here!" he gasped, feeling shock and disappointment. "What can I do with the food?" he thought, trying to come up with a quick solution. Taking a few more steps, he saw a rhododendron branch move, and the familiar deer skin dress and jet-black hair appeared out of the thicket.

David hurried up to Viviana, unzipped the pack she wore without taking it off her back and poured the food in.

"Why are you in such a hurry?" Viviana asked.

"I'm sure I'm being followed," David said between gasps for breaths. "I don't know how far behind me they are. You have to go!"

Viviana turned around slowly, smiling a big smile. David forgot how tired he was as he looked into her raven eyes.

"You are a kind man," Viviana said stepping forward and wrapping David in a bear hug.

David felt tears welling up in his eyes. He had never felt anything so wonderful. He returned the hug and felt at home. Then panic returned and he shook himself loose. "You have to go!" he said, wiping a tear away.

"Silly Word Man, didn't you listen to Canto?"

"I did listen. He seemed to be satisfied that I was staying far enough ahead of the guards."

Viviana pointed to the sky where a lone buzzard was circling.

"What?" David asked confused.

"The buzzard watches the guards. Apparently they were too lazy to climb the mountain, so they sit and wait till you come back down," Viviana explained.

David gasped and sat down on the usual rock. "Well, I guess it was good exercise!"

They laughed.

* * *

Sam and Evie were up at 6am on Wednesday morning. Over breakfast they discussed their plan for the day. "I think we should show up about 9am, Sam," Evie said. "That would give two little old ladies time to have gotten up, dressed, and be ready for the day. You did remember to tell them you would be off today, right?"

"I did. Do you think we can really pull this off?" Sam asked nervously. He noticed Evie's green eyes narrow the way they always did when she thought intensely.

"I have no idea, Sam, but I do know that we have to try. I feel like lives are at stake here. We have to try. Besides, I can't wait to see you in that dress and all made up!"

"Made up! Are you talking makeup? Nobody said anything about makeup!" Sam said feeling almost panicked at the thought.

"You don't think a southern lady would go see her nephew in prison without being properly made up, do you? Besides, you're going to need some work if you want to pass as a lady."

Sam just said, "Humph," and finished his breakfast.

Evie hopped up and pulled out the dresses. Unfolding them, she was surprised to find slips and bras folded inside. "David is a prepared soul! Everything we need is right here!"

Sam double checked the carbon dioxide tank. The gauge registered nearly full. He twisted the valve open and heard a hissing sound. "That can't be good," he called out to Evie. "Could you hear the hissing from over there?"

"I could, Sam. But David said the guard played his music loudly. We will just have to hope that covers the sound."

"I hope we don't have a different guard today, one who is into meditation!" Sam said. "I think we are flying on a wing and a prayer!"

Evie walked over and gave Sam a hug. "I'm nervous, too. I hope all we need is a wing and a prayer."

Evie's hug helped calm Sam's nerves and steel his resolve. "OK, now for the dress?"

"No, no," Evie said. "Makeup first so we don't drop any on the dress." Evie led Sam to the bathroom and sat him down at the dressing table where she kept her makeup. She realized that she needed him to face her, so she had him turn sideways. "Foundation first," she said.

Sam couldn't help himself. As Evie brought the foundation toward his face, he winced and pulled back.

"It's not going to hurt, Sam!" Evie said. "Sit still!"

Sam willed himself to sit still during the process. The foundation felt gooey going on but kind of soothing. He didn't admit that out loud. When Evie finished, he glanced in the mirror. His face was a slightly different color. "It looks smooth as a baby's bottom," he said and started to get up.

"Sit back down, madam," Evie said. "We've only just begun." Next, Evie pulled out a small stick with a blob of color on the end. "We'll add a little brown eyeshadow to go with your earth toned dress."

Sam began to squirm when he realized Evie was coming for his eye. "I'm not sure I can handle this."

"Hush and be still, you big baby," Evie responded, not relenting. The eyeshadow applied, she pulled out her eyeliner.

"Now what?" Sam complained.

"Umm. I think I'll quit while we're ahead," Evie said and put the eyeliner back. "What do you think?"

Looking in the mirror, Sam was surprised and a bit embarrassed at how feminine he looked. "I'm quite a looker!" he said.

"Yes, you are," Evie said. "Just wait till you get the lipstick on! Now hop up. It's my turn."

Sam groaned and got up. While Evie was applying her makeup, Sam searched through bags and purses to find one that would hold the CO_2 tank.

"I set a bag out by the costumes, Sam," Evie called out.

"Got it!" Sam said, feeling somewhat annoyed that Evie was thinking ahead of him, as usual. Of course, the bag was perfect, an oversized medium brown purse exactly right for the tank and matching his outfit, too. Sam experimented with placing the tank in the bag and still being able to operate the valve. He went through the steps of opening and closing the valve five times to be sure he could do it without looking in the purse.

Evie emerged from the bathroom looking much older. "How did you do that?"

"Just a little color here and there," she said.

Evie whipped off two pieces of aluminum foil, and they covered each other's ID chip. "David seemed to think this worked until they were right next to him with the portable scanner. Now let's get you into that dress," she said.

Evie guided Sam through the bra, stuffing it with paper towels, the slip, and then the dress. She stepped back and took a look. "Oh dear, I didn't think of that," she said.

"Didn't think of what?" Sam said surveying his dress. "It looks good to me."

"Your hairy ankles are showing, dear."

"Oops! Should I shave them?" Sam asked, willing to do anything to improve their chance of success.

Evie dug through David's suitcase and pulled out a pair of old lady shoes. "Good! You are the type of lady who wears socks," and handed Sam the shoes.

While he grabbed socks, Evie wriggled into her crinoline petticoat and pulled the emerald green dress over her head. After some bending and tugging, she spun around so that the skirt flared out even more. "Would you please button me in the back?" she asked Sam.

Sam just sat there, mesmerized by her beauty and the way the dress brought out her green eyes.

"Sam!" Evie cajoled, flashing a smile.

Sam slid out of his reverie and got up to button her dress. "You look absolutely gorgeous!" he said.

"Uh-huh. I noticed you looking me over. We do have a mission to accomplish, you know."

"I do know that. But afterwards I get to unbutton the dress."

Evie gave him a quick kiss and said, "We'll see."

Sam looked at his watch. "9:07," he said. "We're right on time for two old ladies!" Sam felt his nerves tightening up again.

Apparently Evie read the tension on his face. "Are you OK?"

"Do you really think we can do this?" Sam said.

"Sam, we have to. We have rehearsed the plan, and we are as ready as we can be. Arnie's life may be in our hands. Now let's get your wig on."

"Wow! I am a looker, for an older lady. OK. Let Operation Arnie commence," Sam said and pulled out his phone to summon a pod.

* * *

"Today is the day, Starke!" Daniella gushed over the phone. "I can feel it in the air!"

"I'm glad you enjoy your job, Daniella," Zeke responded.

"I'll pick you up at 8:45am. We'll have a nice present for Mr. Carter when he gets back this afternoon." Daniella hung up feeling resentful that she had to share what she was sure would be a triumph with Zeke Starke. She wished she could handle the interrogation herself but knew that would be breaking protocol.

So, she summoned a pod and directed it to the main office building, where Starke was waiting.

Getting out at Carter's mansion, Daniella stretched and smiled at Zeke. She felt like an elite runner ready to perform in the Olympics. She noticed Zeke's dark expression. "Don't look so sour, Starke. Everything we have been working toward these few weeks is about to come to fruition. September twelfth will go down in MC2 history! Yet, only you, Carter and I will ever know about it."

"Let's get this over with. What horrors do you have in mind for today?"

"You just sit back and enjoy the ride, Starke," Daniella said darkly.

Daniella was pleased to see Arnie looking haggard and worried. She saw him glance down at her computer and surmised what he was thinking. "I see you are eager to watch more of what you saw yesterday, Mr. Johnson. She is still alive, I assure you. I didn't want you to miss the brutal end. Human beings can suffer so long. Sometimes I wonder why they bother to hold on that hard. I guess we value our miserable little lives."

Daniella sat down at the table and opened her computer. Zeke positioned himself behind her and leaned against the wall. Daniella noted that he intentionally put himself where he could not see the torture.

"You know the rules, Mr. Johnson. You are in charge of how much your beloved suffers. Tell us where the thumb drive is, and we won't even need to get started. Hold out, and Ms. Templeton's pain and misery will go on and on." She pulled out her phone and dialed, not waiting for a response from Arnie. "Proceed," she said.

Daniella watched Arnie's face, and knew he was seeing Christie being placed in a chair with her arms stretched over a table. A guard would handcuff each hand to a table leg on the opposite side. "In case you are wondering, we sit the victim down so that she won't fall down as the torture proceeds. It allows it to drag on longer. It makes the suffering more intense."

Daniella waited till she heard Christie's first scream and saw Arnie look away. She got up, walked around the table, and whispered in Arnie's ear, "My favorite part is the look of desperation on the victim's face right before they pass out." When Daniella saw the tears stream down Johnson's face, she knew the time was close.

"OK, I'll talk," Arnie blurted out.

Daniella returned to her seat without a word.

"Aren't you going to tell them to stop?" Arnie asked.

"You haven't told me anything, yet" she replied in her coldest voice. Another blow landed and Christie screamed again.

"I hid the thumb drive in the mantel," Arnie said in a rush.

Daniella continued to sit there silently.

"I've told you what you want. Now call off the torture."

"Details, Mr. Johnson. I need details."

"I drilled a hole in the right side of the mantel, put the thumb drive in there, and replaced the molding."

"You are talking about the apartment where you lived before deciding to move in here?"

"Yes."

Daniella felt smug. She sat and watched Johnson's face while one more blow landed on Christie's back. "What do you think, Starke?"

"Let's check out his story," Zeke replied. "We can find out soon enough whether or not he is telling the truth."

Daniella slowly reached for her phone and started to dial. Stopping she said, "Johnson, you can't imagine what is going to happen if you are lying."

Arnie hung his head and said, "I'm not lying. Please tell them to stop!"

Daniella pushed call on her phone, "You may return the prisoner to her cell." She stood and glared at Arnie for a few seconds. "Thank you very much Mr. Johnson. We will let you know if your story proves to be true. And woe to you and Christie if you are lying."

With that, Daniella stomped out of the room. "Let's go get our prize!" she said and rubbed her hands together like a child.

"What if the door is locked?" Zeke asked.

"Starke, you are so negative. Locked doors have never been a problem for me," Daniella said, patting her purse. "Why is the pod late?" she said and put in another summons.

Chapter 36

Sam and Evie took the elevator down to the lobby. Sam was trying to learn to walk in a dress. It felt strange. When Sam stepped through the automatic door, he was greeted with a flurry of gray right in his face. He jumped back inside and instinctively held out a hand to stop Evie. "What was that?" Sam could hear what sounded a bit like a squirrel fussing.

Evie looked at Sam like he was losing his mind. "Sam, it's too late to get the jitters. Come on," she demanded. As Evie stepped out, Azul dive bombed. Their pod was waiting right in front of them.

"That was Azul! What is he doing? Let's try again," Evie said and started out the door. Sam was right by her side, and they were greeted by the feathers of Azul and the tufted titmouse flapping furiously right in their faces. They both jumped back inside the door where they seemed to be safe.

"Wait!" Sam hollered and started to run as he saw their pod pull off. The birds quit dive bombing, and Sam looked back at Evie feeling totally flustered. "Now you decide to leave me alone," Sam said, scolding the bird that sat in a small maple tree just outside the building. He walked back to Evie. "The attack seems to be over."

Evie tentatively stepped out of the building. She saw Azul sitting peacefully in the same tree as the titmouse.

"Do you care to explain that?" Sam asked.

"I have no idea, Sam, but I'm sure they had a good reason. It seems they didn't want us to get in that pod."

"Now what do we do? Walk?" Sam asked. Evie didn't respond, and Sam saw that she was looking at Azul.

After a moment Evie said, "I think we summon another pod. And Sam, try to remember that you are supposed to behave like Aunt Lucy."

Evie pulled out her phone and summoned another pod. Sam felt even more irritated that she could seem so calm when problems arose.

"Remember Sam, these birds are on our side. They seem to know more than we do about what is going on around here. We have to trust them."

"Trust!" Sam spat and then remembered to try to be ladylike. Summoning his falsetto voice, he said, "I will try to do just that, Lilly, dear" and directed Evie back inside to wait for the next pod. "Let's get out of camera view," he said.

When the pod arrived, they got in with no bird attacks. On the way to the mansion, they passed another pod going in the opposite direction. Sam cringed, "Zeke Starke and Daniella Morrison were in that pod!" he said. They finished the ride in silence, each lost in thoughts about the upcoming attempt to rescue Arnie.

* * *

The pod pulled in front of the executive apartment building, and Zeke and Daniella got out. They located the Hansons' apartment, which was locked. Daniella dug through her purse and pulled out a thin black case. "I always keep this with me just in case," she said and proceeded to pick the lock.

They entered the apartment, and Daniella began looking over the mantel and fireplace. "I thought he said he drilled a hole." She caught Zeke shaking his head out of the corner of her eye and watched as he walked over, grasped the molding on the side of the mantel and pulled it off with his bare hands.

"There's your hole," he said.

Daniella turned on the flashlight on her phone and searched the hole. "There is nothing in here. It's not here!" she said. "He lied to us!" she nearly screamed. "It's time to quit playing with them and beat the truth out of them!"

"Don't get your panties in a wad, Morrison," Zeke said calmly. "The hole is here, so it looks like Johnson was telling the truth. Apparently someone found the thumb drive," he said as he laid the molding on the mantel and began to stroll around the apartment. "It wasn't found before the Hansons moved in, so I'm betting they are the ones who found it. Morrison, where would you hide a thumb drive that you thought might be dangerous?"

"I don't know," Morrison humphed. "Maybe under a mattress or taped to the bottom of a drawer." She didn't like Zeke's smug tone.

"Let's have a look around. It may be here after all," Zeke said. "You check the bedroom, and I'll have a look in here," and he walked into Sam's office. "Don't make a mess, Daniella. We don't want them to know we have been here!"

"Like that molding ripped off the mantel won't give it away," Daniella called back with venom in her voice.

Daniella walked into the bedroom muttering curses. She ran her hand under the mattress from both sides fumbled through drawers and felt the underside of each drawer. She was moving to the closet when she heard, "Found it!"

Daniella hurried to the office to find Zeke holding up a thumb drive. "It was taped under the desk drawer," he said.

Daniella smiled an evil triumphant smile. "Good thinking, Starke," she said though she hated to admit it.

"Here is your precious thumb drive," Zeke said handing it over.

"Don't be condescending to me Starke! Let's go analyze this and make sure it is what we are looking for. It may just be porn that he is hiding from his wife." Daniella led the way outside and stepped into the waiting pod.

"You go ahead," Zeke said. "I think I'll walk."

* * *

Getting out at the mansion, Sam pointed to the right side, "The door should be around there according to David." They walked downhill along a well-groomed path with fine gravel. The path led them to a door that seemed right. Sam peeked in the window but couldn't see anything because of the reflection on the glass. He tried the doorknob, and it was unlocked. Movement in his periphery caught his attention, and he looked quickly to the right. Azul and the titmouse landed on a branch without making a sound.

Sam ushered Evie in, trying to carry his bag over his shoulder like she did. There was a door at the end of the hall. As they got closer, they could hear muffled music. "This must be it," Evie whispered. Sam gave her a thumb up, and she knocked.

A security guard opened the door, and his look grew serious as he took in Evie and Sam. With one hand on his gun, he pulled an earphone out with the other, and the music grew much louder. "May I help you?" he said.

"I do hope we have found the right place," Evie said, taking the lead to not risk raising suspicion with Sam's voice. "That nice man, Zeke Starke, said we could visit our nephew here. We haven't seen him in ever so long and were just devastated to find that he is in jail. Whatever he did, I'm going to give him a good ear twisting!" Evie continued pouring on the southern charm.

"Who are you?" the guard asked, stiffening.

"We are Arnie's aunts. I'm Lilly, and this is Lucy. May we see our nephew, please?"

"I'm sorry, I will have to check with my superiors first."

"Yes, yes," Evie said. "Do call Mr. Starke and tell him that we have arrived safe and sound. He is an old family friend, and I'm sure will want to know."

The guard started to pull out his phone but hesitated. Evie's charm seemed to be working. "When did you talk to Captain Starke?"

"We saw him yesterday evening when we arrived. He took us to dinner. He is looking fit, is he not?"

The guard seemed to be weighing his options. Apparently he decided against calling. "OK, you can see him for a few minutes."

"Thank you! You are a fine young man. I bet you will go far with this company," Evie said and stepped into the tiny room. She turned to the guard and said, "Do you need to frisk us or anything?"

Sam cringed wondering why she would say such a thing.

"No, that won't be necessary, but I probably do need to get you to leave your purses out here," the guard responded.

Sam's jaw almost dropped open when he realized how successfully Evie had manipulated the guard. "I wonder if she can do that with me," flew through his mind. Sam carefully opened the valve on the CO2 tank as he placed his purse on the floor. Evie sat hers right next to it. The guard had popped the earphone back in his ear and unlocked the door to Arnie's room. He stepped against the wall so Sam and Evie could squeeze by.

Evie led the way in. Despite the bewildered look on Arnie's face, Evie started prattling, "My dear Arnie! It is so nice to see you. How long have you been locked up here? What did you do to get yourself in such a predicament? You know, I have a good mind to twist your ear for this! I hope they are feeding you. You look awfully skinny!"

The guard closed the door sometime during Evie's performance. When Evie stopped, Sam said, "Arnie, we are going to try to get you out of here."

"Who are you people?" Arnie asked.

"We're your aunts. I'm Lilly and this is Lucy," Evie said.

"Actually, I'm Sam Hanson. I used to be one of your sector heads. And this is my wife, Evie."

Arnie cocked his head and studied Sam's face. He didn't look convinced.

"Look, we found the thumb drive that you hid in the mantel and have mailed it to NOAA," Sam said.

"We're afraid they mean to kill you to keep this from getting out," Evie added.

Arnie looked crushed. "I'm afraid I told them where I hid it this morning. They were torturing Christie, and that's the only way I could get it to stop."

"Well, they won't find it," Sam said. "But they will be back after you!"

"How long do you think it will take, Sam?" Evie asked.

"How long will what take?" Arnie questioned.

"I don't know. Let me have a peek," Sam said. He slowly cracked the door and saw the guard sitting in his chair playing air drums.

"Not yet," Sam said. "We set off a carbon dioxide tank in that room. We hope, the guard will pass out soon," he told Arnie.

"And if he doesn't?" Arnie said with angst in his voice.

"Then I guess he will suffer a CO2 tank to the head," Sam said.

A nervous silence fell over the room. They could hear the muffled music through the door. After a few moments, Evie said, "We plan to take you through the woods and to the shipping station. We'll hide until we can find a truck that is pulling out and try to get you on it."

"I can't leave Christie!" Arnie said.

"I think once you are gone, Christie will be OK. She doesn't know anything, and they won't have any reason to harm her," Sam rationalized, trying to convince Arnie to cooperate.

"They have already killed Brittany! What makes you think Christie will be safe?" Arnie spewed, becoming agitated.

"Actually, Brittany is safe on Crow Mountain. It's a long story, and I'll fill you in when we're out of here. They will be able to track your ID chip until you are out of the compound. So," and Sam stopped.

"What is it, Sam?" Evie asked.

"I forgot to pack the aluminum foil! Did you pack it?"

"No, but I knew I might need this," Evie said. She pulled up her skirt and petticoats and pulled an X-acto knife out of her panty hose.

"What are you going to do with that?" Sam asked.

"Arnie, we have to cut out your ID chip. I have some bandages in my purse. Hold out your arm," Evie said.

Arnie looked at Sam pleadingly. Sam shrugged his shoulders and said, "She is always right."

Arnie held up his arm and closed his eyes.

"This will be just like carving in clay," Evie said. "No worries." She felt the chip under the skin and made a cut. It wasn't deep enough, so she cut again. Arnie muffled his groan with a hand over his mouth. Evie pinched the flesh around the chip, and it popped out and landed on the floor. She pulled a couple of tissues out of her dress pocket, gave one to Arnie to catch the blood, and wiped off the chip with the other.

Suddenly the music got louder. All three looked at each other with wide eyes. Sam eased the door open and saw the guard lying on the floor. One earphone had popped out. "He's out. I can't believe that actually worked!"

Sam quietly closed the door back and whispered, "We have to get out of the room quickly, so we don't pass out, too." He held a finger to his lips and eased out the door. Sam grabbed both purses, shut off the CO2, and opened the second door. Looking back, he saw Evie bent over, fiddling with the guard's shirt pocket.

Reading the guard's name tag, Evie said quietly, "Ben Moore, I sure hope you wake up." She stood, and she and Arnie followed Sam out the door.

Closing the door behind them, Sam asked, "What were you doing with his pocket?"

"I slipped the ID chip in there so it would look like Arnie is wherever the guard is."

"Sometimes your cleverness is plumb scary!" Sam said.

"Hand me my purse," Evie responded and pulled out a bandage. Arnie moved the soaked tissue from his wound and Evie applied the bandage.

"Well, let's go. Out the door and to the left," Sam directed. Sam opened the exterior door and froze.

"What is it, Sam," Evie asked.

"Zeke Starke is walking toward us. I'm sure he has seen us."

"Our ruse has worked so far. Try to act normal and just carry on," Evie said. Evie pushed past Sam, whose feet seemed to be glued to the ground. "Come on and smile," she demanded quietly and started walking out the path toward Starke.

Sam slipped his hand inside Arnie's arm and tried to act like a loving aunt. He smiled at Arnie and said, "It is so good to see you. Arnie, have you lost weight? You don't look like you have been eating well," Sam squeaked out in his best falsetto. Sam noticed a look of surprised confusion on Starke's face as they approached.

Zeke Starke stopped in the middle of the path, blocking their way. Evie said, "Good morning, sir," and proceeded as if she were going to walk right past him.

"Excuse me, ma'am," Starke said. "I believe you have a prisoner of mine."

"Oh yes," Evie said and held out her hand. "I'm Lilly, Arnie's aunt. That nice young man said that we could take him for a walk and visit for a little while. We promised to bring him back."

"It's nice to meet you, ma'am," Zeke responded, "but I'm afraid that I need Mr. Johnson to come with me. He has an appointment to keep."

"Arnie! You didn't say anything about an appointment!" Evie feigned anger. "But, we have traveled all the way from South Carolina and have just gotten here. Can't we at least visit for a few minutes?"

Sam realized he was hardly breathing, and nearly gasped when he saw anger flash across Starke's face. "I'm afraid that will be impossible," Starke said sternly and took Johnson by the arm. "I need you to come with me, now."

Arnie jerked his arm away and started running for the woods. Zeke pulled his gun, but then ran after Arnie. Zeke tackled Arnie and put him in handcuffs. Sam watched as the color drained from Evie's face. He thought she was going to faint, then realized he felt the same way. They looked at each other wide eyed and speechless.

Finally, Evie stomped out across the yard, "How dare you treat my nephew like that!"

Zeke Starke stood Arnie up and glared first at Evie and then at Sam. "I don't know who you people are or how you broke Mr. Johnson out of his cell. But I suggest you leave immediately, or you will find yourself in handcuffs, too," Starke said menacingly.

Sam and Evie stood frozen, not knowing what to do. Zeke Starke pulled out his phone. "Do I need to call security?" he asked with the phone in one hand and his pistol in the other. Sam didn't need to be asked again. "Come on, Lilly. This is a fine welcome," he said as he turned and walked up the path toward the driveway. Sam sensed Evie hesitating behind him but felt relief when he heard the gravel crunching under her feet. Sam pulled out his phone and summoned a pod.

"What are you doing?" Evie whispered as she caught up.

"I'm living to fight another day," Sam responded.

"We can't just leave Arnie with that monster!"

"What else can we do? Charge him with our purses?" Sam said, feeling Evie's frustration.

"If we get close enough, you could hit him over the head with the tank," Evie suggested.

"In case you didn't notice, he stayed just out of reach the whole time. I'm afraid he knows what he is doing," Sam said. "Let's go home, regroup, and come up with another plan."

The pod pulled up as they got to the end of the driveway. Sam opened the door and instinctively stood aside for Evie to get in. It dawned on him that Lucy probably wouldn't have done that, and he hoped that Starke hadn't noticed.

Chapter 37

Bursting into their apartment, Evie shrieked, "What if we are too late? What if Starke is taking Arnie to kill him right now?" Sam was feeling panicked, too, but tried to keep himself calm so he could think.

"Azul was there. Why didn't he warn us that Starke was coming?" Evie continued.

"Maybe they are in cahoots with Starke. Anyway, Arnie said that they were torturing Christie. If Starke was taking Arnie to start torturing him and we can figure out where that is, then maybe we can save both of them." Sam was looking for hope to show on Evie's face, but what he saw was shock. "What, Evie? What is it?"

Evie was looking around the living area. "Someone has been here! Things aren't like we left them! Sam, they searched our apartment!"

"What makes you think..." Sam stopped in mid-sentence when he saw the molding piece on the mantel. He felt the shock, too. "You are right." Sam ran to the desk and felt under the drawer. To be sure, he got down on his knees and looked under it. "It's gone! They found the thumb drive!" he said as he looked into Evie's worried face.

Sam tried to stand up but was pulled right back down. He tried his other foot but was stuck. "OK, how do I get up with this dress on?" He was relieved to see Evie laugh.

"Silly Sam, you do need some lessons. First you have to pull the dress up just enough to be clear of your feet without revealing anything you don't want the public to see," Evie said.

"I have a lot to learn if I'm going to make it as a lady," Sam said and finally managed to get on his feet. "This changes everything," Sam said as he realized the seriousness of what they had just discovered. "We are no longer operating under their radar, Evie. We will be prime targets!"

* * *

It was 8:15am when Skauty Hanson was surprised by a knock on his door. Leaving his beloved coffee behind, he went to the door and opened it to find a package. Willing his early morning joints to bend, he picked up the package to see that it was from Evie and felt a warm smile. "That girl is so good to me! She always remembers my birthday," he thought as he took the package back to the table. Taking a sip of coffee, he whipped out his hunting knife.

"I don't see any need to wait till tomorrow," he thought as he sliced through the packing tape. Fishing through the peanuts he found the card that was written in Evie's fluid cursive with its left-handed slant. Skauty sat down as he read through the birthday wish, which was followed by an apology for asking him to do something potentially dangerous. Reading through Evie's precise instructions regarding extracting the thumb drive and sending it to NOAA as soon as possible, Skauty found himself smiling again. "They are doing the right thing," he thought. "I am proud." Then darker thoughts entered, "I hope they are OK. If this is as serious as it seems, I had better get this mailed quickly. Someone will be after it!"

Skauty quickly pulled out the second box, spilling peanuts on the table and floor. He opened it, pulled out a wad of bubble wrap, and peeled that off. He was amazed at what unfolded into his hands. "Wow! That is beautiful, Evie!" he said to himself. He carefully set the bird on the table and reread the instructions in the card. He picked the bird up and scrutinized the bottom. "Yep, there it is," he said to himself when he identified the circle of self-hardening clay. He dug the circle out with his pocketknife and then fetched a flashlight and needle nose pliers.

As he was bending the wire to release the thumb drive, Skauty heard a car door slam, followed by two others. "Good grief! They are here already!" he thought. Skauty quickly shook the crow, and the thumb drive slid out. He bent the wire back into place, slipped the thumb drive into his pocket, and was scooping the clay pieces into the trash when the knock came.

Skauty decided to act like an old man and shuffled slowly to the door. Glancing back, he noticed the card. "It won't do to let them find that," he thought, and went back, folded the card, and stuffed it into his back pocket. Finally getting to the door, he opened it and said, "Good morning, gentlemen!"

There were three men clothed in MC2 security guard attire, all armed. Lamar, the leader, a tall, wiry African American man with a close-cropped beard spoke up, "We are looking for Sk..., Sk..., Mr. Hanson," he said struggling with Skauty's first name and finally giving up.

"I am certainly a Mr. Hanson," Skauty said. "And judging by your sputtering, I am the one you seek. Call me Skauty. Won't you come in?"

"Thank you, Mr. Hanson," Lamar said and the three of them entered the house. "There was a package sent to you by Evie Hanson that we believe has material that was stolen from MC2. I need to see the package," Lamar said assertively.

"You mean this?" Skauty said and shuffled slowly over to the crow. "It is beautiful, is it not? But I don't think it was stolen. You see, Evie is an artist, and she made this for my birthday," he said trying to sound excited.

"May I see it?" Lamar asked. Taking the crow, he turned it over. "I need a flashlight" he said, and one of the other guards, Stanley, handed him one with it turned on.

While Lamar searched inside the crow, Skauty sat down in the kitchen chair in the corner. "You don't mind if an old man has a seat, do you?"

Lamar glared at Skauty, "What about these wires. Was there anything in this little cage?"

"Let me see that," Skauty said, pretending he was looking inside the crow for the first time. "Evie is a very clever girl. I'm guessing it is a framework to support the wings."

"Let me be more direct. Mr. Hanson, did you find a thumb drive in this package?"

"I assure you that I found no thumbs in there," Skauty said.

"Not a thumb! A thumb drive!" Lamar barked.

"I'm not sure what that is, but all I found in this box was the crow, bubble wrap, and these blasted peanuts that I've managed to scatter everywhere. You gentlemen wouldn't be kind to an old man and get those off the floor, would you?" Skauty said unruffled by Lamar's tone.

One of the guards, Jerry, bent down and began picking them up. "Thank you so much," Skauty said.

Lamar felt through the bubble wrap and dug through the peanuts. Finally, he dumped the whole box of peanuts, and Jerry let out an obscenity. "Where is the card, Mr. Hanson?" Lamar asked patiently.

"You know, I was wondering that, too," Skauty said thinking quickly again. "It is not like her to forget a card. Maybe she mailed it separately. Or, maybe she put my grandson in charge of the card, and he forgot!" he said holding up a finger as if that must be the answer.

"When did this package arrive?" Lamar demanded.

"Just long enough for me to get it open before you people so rudely showed up. I haven't even had a good chance to admire it yet."

Lamar looked around the room carefully while Jerry finished gathering peanuts. "I am afraid that we are going to have to confiscate your crow," he said.

"No, I am afraid you are not," Skauty said. As Lamar reached for the crow, Skauty pulled the twelve-gauge, double-barreled shotgun from his lap. He had taken advantage of the dumping of the peanuts to slip it out of the corner. "You have seen that what you are looking for is not here. Now you people will kindly put up your hands and exit my home." Skauty stood and aimed the gun carefully at Lamar's chest.

Lamar hesitated and glared at Skauty. The other two guards put up their hands.

"It's your call, son," Skauty said.

Lamar turned and walked out the door with the other guards following. Skauty followed to the front step. As they were getting into their car, he called out, "Have a good day, gentlemen. But please don't bother to come back."

* * *

Daniella hopped out of the pod clutching the thumb drive and smiling like she had won the lottery. She hurried into her office and popped the thumb drive into her laptop. She told the computer to open it, but all she got was a screen saying the file was not readable. Her spirits somewhat dampened, she called the security computer specialist. "Shannon, I need you in my office, now."

"Yes Ma'am," Shannon replied. "I'll be there as soon as I can."

Shannon O'Shields, a tall, skinny, gangly brunette with big brown eyes, who seemed to be all arms and legs, flew into Daniella's office. "What is the trouble, Ms. Morrison?" she said, alarmed by the call.

Daniella stood up and hesitated. Shannon had arrived so quickly that she had not had time to decide how she would approach explaining what she needed done. She started, "Ms. O'Shields, I need for you to analyze this thumb drive." Then the thought appeared that seemed right. "I believe it has stolen intellectual property on it. I tried to look at it on my laptop, but I couldn't open it. I need you to see what is on it and let me know as soon as possible."

"Yes, ma'am," Shannon said.

"That means that you are to stop anything you are currently working on and address this. That also means that you are not to discuss this with anyone but me. Am I clear?"

"Yes, ma'am," Shannon said.

Daniella thought she was going to salute. She handed Shannon the thumb drive and watched her turn to leave. "Oh, Shannon? One more thought. Can you tell if the files have been copied from another source?"

"Do you mean like whether or not this is the original file?"

"No, I mean if the files on this thumb drive were copied from another thumb drive," Daniella said realizing that there could be more than one copy of the program.

"Ms. Morrison, thumb drive files are all copies saved from a computer. But I can tell you the date this was saved if that helps," Shannon offered.

Daniella thought for a moment while Shannon waited. "Yes, that will be helpful. Please call me as soon as you know anything."

"Yes, ma'am," Shannon said as she hustled out the door and back to her office down the hall.

Daniella sat down to plan her next move. "Assuming we have the thumb drive," she thought, "We also need to contain the Hansons or at least find out what they know. Then there is that pastor, too." While Daniella tried to decide how far-ranging her clean up would have to be, the phone rang.

"Daniella Morrison here."

"Hello, Ms. Morrison. This is Ben Moore. I am posted on guard at the mansion today, and I need to report that the prisoner is missing," he said sounding a bit groggy.

"What! What do you mean the prisoner is missing? Have you been drinking?"

"No, ma'am. The last I remember is that two of Johnson's aunts came to visit him. The next thing I know, I woke up on the floor and Johnson was gone."

"Hold on a minute," Daniella said. She opened a new line and called surveillance. "I need you to locate Arnie Johnson immediately," she ordered. Daniella waited and could hear keys clicking.

"He is in Mr. Carter's mansion, ma'am," Trevor responded.

"Thank you," Daniella said and hung up. She called up John, who was in charge of assignments today. "John, I need you to send a detail down to Carter's mansion. Ben Moore called and said that Johnson is missing, but surveillance says that he is there. Moore sounds like he has been drinking. Please check it out."

"Yes, ma'am," John responded.

Switching back to Moore's line, Daniella said, "Moore, I am sending a team to help you locate Johnson. Surveillance locates him in the mansion. I want you to position yourself in the driveway and watch to see if he tries to get out."

"Yes, ma'am."

Daniella hung up the phone. "Why can't things just go the way they are supposed to!" she said out loud. She quickly tucked away her frustration and got back into command mode. "What do I need to know right now?" she thought. She called surveillance back, "I need you to pull up security footage of the mansion from this morning. I have a report that two women came in the west side door. See if you can find them and send me a picture."

"Yes, ma'am," Trevor said.

"Thank you, and I need this ASAP," Daniella said and hung up. Daniella thought about calling Zeke Starke but decided he would just add to her irritation. "I can handle this better without him," she thought.

Daniella's phone rang, and she picked up, "Daniella Morrison."

"Ms. Morrison, this is Shannon. The thumb drive contains a program from NOAA. I guess it's not our intellectual property, after all. The file was created on this drive on September 7."

"Thank you for being so quick with your analysis, Shannon. Please return the thumb drive to me now."

"I'm on my way," Shannon said.

"September 7 was after Johnson was in custody," Daniella thought. Daniella's instincts had been telling her that the Hansons and Pastor McCutcheon were involved in this somehow. "I think it is time we bring them in," she decided and called John back.

"John, I believe that Sam and Evie Hanson and David McCutcheon are involved in a plot to steal company intellectual property. I want them arrested and brought in immediately."

"Yes, ma'am. I will address that myself."

As soon as she hung up the phone, it rang again. "My, this is a busy morning," she said to herself. Answering the phone, she said, "Daniella Morrison."

"Ms. Morrison, this is Lamar with the detail in Sitka."

"Hello, Lamar. What do you have to report?"

"We found Evie Hanson's package after it had been delivered to the grandfather. We found nothing but a ceramic crow that was the grandfather's birthday present."

"No thumb drive? Did you search the house and the grandfather?" Daniella asked.

"No, ma'am. We weren't exactly warmly welcomed."

"Lamar, you had three armed men against one old man. Couldn't you exert a little persuasion?"

"Not when that old man had a double-barreled shotgun pointed at my chest, ma'am," Lamar retorted. "He surprised us with it when I tried to confiscate the crow."

"Interesting. Lamar, I want you and your men to stay in Sitka till you hear from me."

"What should we do?"

"I don't know! Go sightseeing or something." Daniella barked and hung up the phone.

* * *

After Daniella Morrison's call, John called three of the security guards on duty and asked them to report to his office immediately. Then he called the surveillance room.

"Surveillance, Trevor speaking."

"Hi Trevor, this is John. I need the locations of Sam Hanson, Evie Hanson, and David McCutcheon, please."

"Sure thing, John," Trevor said and punched in Sam's name. "What is going on? I haven't ever had this many requests to locate people."

"Morrison says that there is a plot to steal intellectual property from MC2. That's all I know," John responded.

"It looks like both Hansons are in their apartment and McCutcheon is at the church, where a good pastor should be," Trevor said.

"Thanks Trevor," John said.

Chapter 38

Sam felt his guts tighten and the anxiety rise after saying that he and Evie would now be considered targets. "What do we do now?" he asked as much to himself as Evie.

"What about David? They might decide to take him back into custody rather than just following him. We have to warn him!"

Evie instinctively pulled out her phone, but Sam said, "No, don't call. If they consider us suspects, then I'm sure they will be monitoring our... everything! We need a plan, and we need it fast!"

"They know that two women came to the mansion, so they will be able to see what we look like on the surveillance videos. We need new costumes. I just hope the aluminum foil prevented them from detecting our chips!" Evie said.

Evie ran to David's suitcase and started rummaging through. She found an old beard and hat and threw them toward Sam.

"I could be a hillbilly!" Sam said.

"Get out of the dress and start putting on... Wait, do you still have those overalls from that square dance we went to?"

"I think so, let me check," Sam said and hustled to his closet.

Evie rummaged a little more, then picked up the wig that Sam had discarded on the floor, "Maybe we could be Ma and Pa Kettle!" she called out to Sam.

"Wouldn't it be better if we went out as Butch Cassidy and the Sundance Kid?"

"Sam don't talk like that! I don't like the way that ended," Evie scolded as she hurried to her closet.

Sam appeared in overalls, a red checkered shirt, and hiking boots. "What do you think?" he said.

"I think you had better get that make up off!" Evie laughed. "Go get my cold cream and rub it all over your face."

"Can't I just wash it off?" Sam pleaded.

"That will take too long. Hurry, Sam!"

Evie put on her overalls, worked her thick red hair into the smallest bun she could manage, and put on the wig Sam had been wearing. "Ick!" came from the bathroom. "Suck it up, Sam, and get that stuff off!"

Sam came back looking like his old self, donned the beard and hat, and did a little tap dance. "What do you think, now?"

Evie linked her arm in his and pulled him to face the mirror. "I think we make great hillbillies!"

Sam said, "There is a problem, though," and took off. He returned with both of their sunglasses and handed Evie hers. They put them on and looked back at the mirror. "We do hillbilly with style!" Sam said and smiled. He watched as Evie's mouth took on a serious turn.

"How long do you think we have before they come after us?" Evie said.

"Not long enough," Sam said. "I think we had better grab anything we are taking and make a run for it!" Sam grabbed a backpack and began stuffing it with his contraband computer, a jacket, a change of underwear, all the energy bars in the pantry, and some water.

As Sam passed by the bedroom, he noticed Evie still looking in the mirror. "Quit admiring your lovely self and get ready!"

"Sam, nobody in the compound dresses like this. We are going to stick out like sore thumbs. I think we need to change into regular clothes," Evie said and began stripping off the overalls.

"You are right, again!" Sam said and ran back to change into jeans, keeping the same shirt. Evie had pulled on a smart looking pair of cargo pants and was sliding her X-acto knife into one of the pockets. Sam noticed that Evie had a nearly full backpack on the bed. He was surprised because he thought she had been looking in the mirror the whole time. "Are we ready?" Sam asked.

"Not yet. There is one more thing we have to do," Evie said.

"Use the bathroom?" Sam asked.

"Well, that too. Sam, we have to cut out our ID chips." Evie pulled out the X-acto knife, and Sam felt himself go pale.

"I don't know if I can," Sam said.

"Oh, hush and give me your arm," Evie said. Sam closed his eyes and looked away as Evie sliced into his flesh. She cut through far enough on her first cut and popped out the chip. "That wasn't so bad, was it?" Evie asked.

"That's easy for you to say!"

After bandaging the wound, Evie presented Sam the knife. Sam tentatively took the knife and said, "This is the part I don't think I can do." Evie held up her arm, and Sam felt squeamish. He reached toward Evie's arm with the knife while pulling his head away.

"Sam! You have to look at what you are doing! Oh, give me the knife!" Evie took the knife, twisted around to reach her arm, and made the cut. "Ouch!" she said and popped out the chip.

Sam took the chip and wiped off the blood. "What shall we do with these?" He looked around as Evie was bandaging her arm. "I know," Sam said and stuffed the chips under the mattress to the very center.

As Sam walked back into the living area, he heard a tap on the window. He and Evie looked over to see Azul pecking rapidly. "We have to go now!" Evie said. They grabbed their bags and rushed out the door.

Sam said, "Let's take the stairs to speed things up," and down they went. As they were walking across the lobby, four security guards passed through the front doors to the elevator. Though his nerves were tense, Sam tried to act nonchalant as he walked toward the door. One of the guards looked over, and Sam nodded, "Good afternoon," he said. The guard responded with, "Have a good day."

Outside the apartment building, Sam could see that Evie looked shaken. "They were coming after us!" she said.

"Wow! That was close!" Sam responded.

"We have to get to David!" Evie said urgently and turned as if to run. Sam grabbed her by the arm. "Ouch!" she said. "That's where the chip was!"

"Sorry! Evie, we have to walk like we are just out for an afternoon stroll, so we don't draw attention to ourselves."

"You are right. I'll try to control myself." She looped her hand in Sam's arm and said, "Let's go for a stroll, dear."

* * *

John knocked on the Hansons' door with three other guards standing to the side. He waited a few seconds and knocked again. After a few seconds, one of the other guards reached over and pushed the doorbell. "Maybe that will work," he said.

"I don't trust doorbells. You never know if they ring," John responded. They waited again, but no one answered.

John pulled out his phone and called surveillance.

"Surveillance, this is Trevor."

"Hey, Trevor. Would you please pull up the location of the Hansons again?" John asked.

After a moment, Trevor said, "I show them as being in the apartment, John."

"That's odd. We are at the apartment but aren't getting anyone to the door. Are you sure they are here?"

"Well, I may have overstated the case. I can actually only tell that they are in the building, not which apartment they are in. I can tell you that they are on the southern end of the building, but not which floor. Maybe they are visiting neighbors," Trevor offered.

"Thanks, Trevor," John said and hung up. He considered the situation for a moment and made a decision. "We are going in."

The guards drew their weapons, and John pulled out his master key. With everyone in position, he unlocked the door and pushed it open quickly. The guards filled the room and spread out searching each room and closet. It took only seconds to determine that no one was in the apartment.

John stood and pondered the situation. "Did you search each closet?"

"Yes, sir," the guards responded.

"Under the bed?"

"Yes, sir."

"OK, let's try the apartments above and below this one. Corey, take Ronnie and go downstairs. Brenda and I will try upstairs."

* * *

Daniella leaned back in her office chair to think. It seemed that all the pieces were coming together, but something still nagged at her brain. Her breath caught as the realization landed with a thud. "Shannon said the file was created on the seventh. Created and not saved?" Daniella picked up the phone and dialed Shannon in a hurry.

"Good afternoon. Shannon O'Shields here."

"Shannon, you said the file was created on that drive on the seventh. Did you mean saved?"

"No, ma'am. That was the initial date the file was placed on the thumb drive."

"What does that mean?"

"It most likely means that the file was copied onto this thumb drive on that date," Shannon explained.

"I see. Thank you, Shannon," Daniella said feeling far away. Hanging up the phone, Daniella now felt for certain that there was another thumb drive out there. She let out a string of obscenities and then realized that she needed to let Starke know what was going on. "But first I'm going to have Christie brought over for one last chat," she thought.

Daniella called over to the holding center.

"Detention. This is Paul speaking."

"Paul, I need you to bring Christie Templeton over to my office for a few minutes," Daniella ordered.

"I'm sorry, ma'am, but I cannot do that."

"What do you mean, you cannot do that?" Daniella spat.

"Captain Starke picked up the prisoner about a half hour ago," Paul explained.

Daniella exploded with anger but managed to remain civil to Paul, "Thank you very much." She dialed up Starke.

"Hello, Daniella."

"Starke, where are my prisoners?" Daniella barked.

"They are with me, Daniella," Starke said calmly.

"And where are you?"

"I'm at the helipad."

"Starke, tell me what is going on," Daniella demanded.

"You have your precious thumb drive, so I am finishing the mission. You wouldn't want me to do it in the compound, would you? We are going for a helicopter ride," Zeke explained.

"Hold off on that, Starke," Daniella said realizing that she was giving orders to her boss. "We still need the prisoners. The thumb drive is a copy, so the original is still out there somewhere. Bring them back to detention, and we will see if we can get to the bottom of this one last time."

"I'm afraid it is too late for more interrogation, Daniella," Starke said and hung up.

Daniella slammed her fist on the desk and cursed some more. Daniella jumped when her phone rang.

"Daniella Morrison," she said in a rage.

"Ma'am, this is John. We have been unable to locate the Hansons. Trevor says that they are in the apartment building, but we have searched their apartment and checked with the neighbors, who deny having seen them."

"Are you sure? Did you search the neighbors' apartments?"

"No, Ma'am, we didn't."

"Well, don't just stand there! Get back to those apartments and search! This is urgent, John!" Daniella barked.

Chapter 39

As he and Evie walked along the river toward the church, Sam had to fight every step not to run. He could almost feel the guards coming back out of the apartment building looking for them. "It won't take them long to find out we are not there, Evie," Sam said with strain in his voice.

Evie looked back. "I don't see them yet."

"Do you think we should run?" Sam asked.

"No, you were right, Sam. Not only do we have to avoid the guards, we have to avoid drawing attention from the surveillance monitors."

Sam felt the blood draining from his face at the realization of just how exposed they were. "The first thing they will do when they discover we are gone is have surveillance watching the monitors for us. I hope we won't trigger any facial recognition, but they will be able to go back and see who came out of the apartment building. I wish we could hurry!"

The walk to the church was one of the hardest things Sam had ever done. Every nerve was on hyper alert, but he had to walk like he was out for a stroll. He could see on Evie's face that she was struggling, too. When they finally stepped into the church, Sam took a deep breath and wasn't sure he had breathed at all the whole walk.

They hurried to David's office, and Sam didn't bother to knock. Bursting in on David, they found him standing and staring out the window. He turned with a baffled look on his face.

"Hello. May I help you?" David asked.

"David it's us, Sam and Evie," Sam said.

"Oh! I do see a resemblance, now."

"We have some bad news," Sam said. Before he could continue, the sound of a helicopter taking off and flying close by drowned him out. Sam saw Evie's eyes open wide with fear.

"Oh no! They are sending up a helicopter to search!" Evie said loud enough to be heard over the roar.

The three remained quiet, listening. The helicopter seemed to be leaving the compound, though, and continued flying away.

"David, they searched our apartment and found the thumb drive. We saw guards coming into our building as we were leaving. They are after us!" Evie said in a rush.

"Wait, back up a bit. What happened with Arnie?" David asked.

"The plan worked perfectly," Sam said, "Right up to the part where Zeke Starke was walking down the path when we came out of the house. I'm afraid he took him. David, I'm sure that now they will be after you, too. We have to get out of here!"

Sam watched with bewilderment as David grew a big smile on his face. "Those are the best words I have heard in a long time! I am tired of being followed everywhere I go. Let's do it!"

"Not so fast," Evie said. "There are a couple of things we have to take care of first."

"We need a way to disguise you enough that facial recognition won't identify you," Sam explained.

"And we have to cut out your ID chip," Evie added.

"Well, I will miss the convenience of that thing, but you are right," David responded.

Evie pulled out her X-acto knife. David didn't flinch and held up his arm for her to go to work. With the chip popped out and bandage in place, "What do I do with this puppy?" David said eyeing the chip.

"We left ours under the mattress," Sam said.

David smiled again, "What if I flush it down the toilet?"

Sam and Evie looked at each other and laughed. "That's actually a great idea!" Sam said. "You will either totally disappear, or they will chase you to sewage treatment!"

"Bon voyage!" David said as he flushed the chip. "Now for a disguise." David went rummaging through a closet and pulled out a box. "My Moses costume for church plays," he explained.

David pulled out a long white beard and pulled it on. He stuck bushy white eyebrows on in front of the mirror and then turned, "Ta da! What do you think?" The beard hung all the way to David's waist.

Evie scrunched up her eyebrows, "I'm afraid that is a bit much. We want to blend in," she said. "Could we give the beard a trim?"

David pulled scissors out of his desk and handed them over, "Make me gorgeous!"

Evie trimmed up the beard so that it was common looking.

"I recommend a hat and sunglasses, too," Sam said. "We don't want to take any chances."

David pulled out a fishing hat from the closet, sunglasses from the desk, and said, "Wait a minute." Walking back to the closet, he pulled out his Moses staff. "Now I think I'm ready!"

"Yep! I think that will do!" Sam said.

"You look like an old man ready to go fishing," Evie added.

"I have a fishing pole here, too. Should I get it?"

"No, I think it would be in the way," Sam said.

"OK. Now what?" David asked. "Keeping with the fishing theme, we could cross the river and try to get over the fence. That is the quickest way out."

"True, but then what would we do? Besides, I'm sure they watch the perimeter more than anything," Sam said. "I think it is best if we stick with the original plan and try to sneak a ride on a delivery truck."

* * *

Daniella's phone rang, again. "Daniella Morrison. And I hope this is good news!"

"It's Mark Conner, Ms. Morrison. We have searched the mansion but have not found Johnson. Surveillance says that he is still here, though."

"That's interesting," Daniella said and fell silent pondering.

She was thinking Starke might have been lying about having Johnson when Conner said, "Ma'am? Are you still there?"

"Yes, Conner I'm here. I was just trying to process what to do next. Have you searched all of the closets, under beds, and outside under bushes?"

"I'm sorry, but I'm afraid we weren't that thorough. It didn't seem right to go through Mr. Carter's house like that."

"Mr. Carter will be very appreciative if you apprehend Arnie Johnson, so get back in there and search every square inch!" Daniella demanded. "I want Johnson apprehended!" Daniella's phone beeped with another call coming in. "I have to go," she said and switched to the new call.

Recognizing the number, Daniella answered with, "Did you find them, John?"

"No, ma'am, they are not here."

"How can people just be disappearing on me?"

"I don't know, ma'am," John responded.

"I was actually talking to myself, John. Did you search just outside the building?"

"Not yet, but we will do that right now."

"Do that quickly and then go after David McCutcheon," Daniella ordered.

"Do you really want me to arrest the pastor?" John said timidly.

"Yes, I want you to arrest the pastor! And preferably today, John! Get moving!" Daniella nearly screamed and hung up. Daniella's computer pinged with an email showing the picture of two women coming up to Carter's mansion. Trevor's email explained that this was the clearest picture he could isolate.

Daniella called him immediately, "Trevor, I want your surveillance team to keep a look out for these two women. Watch the whole compound until I tell you otherwise. Call in more help if you need it."

"Yes, ma'am," Trevor said.

Daniella started to feel control coming back into her hands. "You can't hide forever, my little Hansons!" she said out loud. "Let's get back on the trail of that thumb drive," she said realizing that she was talking to herself. Daniella called Lamar back.

"Lamar, I am more certain than ever that the thumb drive we are after was in that package. Go back and search the house. Use whatever force you need to get in."

"We'll do our best, ma'am," Lamar responded.

"Your best isn't good enough, Lamar. I expect results!"

* * *

"We don't have time to linger, gentlemen," Evie prompted.

David walked over to a window that looked out in the direction of Sam and Evie's apartment building. "I don't see any guards on their way."

"Let's go then," Sam said feeling his nerves getting edgy again. Sam led the way as they walked out into the afternoon sun. "I say we take the shortest route to factory row and then head for the shipping and receiving station."

"Agreed," said David. "Maybe it will be shift change and we can get lost in a crowd. This way will get us there the quickest," and David led the way on a path leading west along where the gardens began.

Evie noticed a commotion in a tree up ahead. As they got close enough, she realized it was Azul, the tufted titmouse, and a little brown bird all flying from the tree and returning. "Look at that!" Evie said. "I think they are telling us to hurry!"

"Hey, Canto!" David called out toward the bird. "Canto is the little brown wren," David explained.

"Sam, you really have to give your bird a name," Evie was saying when she noticed four security guards coming from behind the closest apartment building. "Oh no! It looks like we have company," she said in an urgent whisper. Evie's feet seemed to freeze to the ground.

"Keep going," Sam urged giving Evie a gentle push. They kept walking, trying to sneak glances back at the guards. "They seem to be headed toward the church."

"But they have seen us! I saw one looking this way," David said.

"Just keep walking like we are admiring the gardens," Sam said. The three kept walking, and Sam noticed that they were speeding up. "Let's try to keep at a casual pace," he said while every nerve in his body wanted to run as fast as he could. When the guards entered the church, they could no longer help themselves and began walking quickly toward the factories.

* * *

Daniella Morrison let out a long stream of curses when John called to say that there was no one in the church and that they still had not found the Hansons. "Hold on a minute," she barked at John. Putting him on hold, she called Trevor. "I need the locations of the Hansons and David McCutcheon again."

Without a pause, Trevor said, "The Hansons are still in their apartment building, and it appears that Pastor McCutcheon is traveling south along the river trail. Right now, he is in front of the middle workers' building."

"Thank you, Trevor. But how did you do that so quickly?"

"Since these people seem to be of interest, I have kept them on the screen."

"Good job!" Daniella said, thinking, "At least one person around here has good sense." She switched back to John. "John, where are you now!"

"Right in front of the church."

"You should be able to see McCutcheon walking along the river trail heading south from there."

John looked and replied, "I don't see anyone on the trail, ma'am."

"Surveillance shows him..." Daniella stopped in mid-sentence and began cursing again as she realized what was happening. "John, I think they may have cut out their ID chips!"

"That would explain why they are not where we think they are," John responded. "We did see three people walking away from the church as we approached, if that is of any import."

"You idiot! You imbecile! And you are still standing there? Send one guard down the river trail to look for McCutcheon. The rest of you get after those three people!" Daniella screamed and hung up. Daniella called Trevor, "I need a picture of the three people who walked out of the church just a few minutes ago. I am betting you cannot identify them by chips."

"Yes, ma'am. I'll send it over right away."

Daniella got up and paced around her room with her heart racing and anger flaring. "Hurry up, Trevor!" she said out loud. Daniella cringed when she heard the sound of a jet engine coming in for a landing. "Just what I need! Carter is back! Maybe he'll want a quiet evening and not check in till morning."

Daniella's computer pinged, and it was the picture Trevor had sent. Daniella looked over the picture, memorizing every detail. Then she sent the picture out to her entire security staff with an urgent message: "All points alert: Apprehend these three people immediately! They are wanted for intellectual property theft."

Daniella called Trevor back. "Cancel the watch for those two women. I believe they have changed costumes. I want you to direct your energy to locating the three people on that picture you just sent. And I want them found now!"

Daniella tapped her finger on the desk trying to settle on one last decision. "Yes, I think it's time," she thought. Picking up the phone, she called John.

"Hey, John. I think we need a sniper posted on the roof of shipping and receiving. Would you handle that for me?"

Chapter 40

As Sam, Evie, and David approached the first factory building, Evie said, "You know, it is not going to take long for the guards to put zero and three together and figure out that since no one was in the church, the three they saw leaving might be us."

"You are right, Evie," Sam said. "I've been thinking the same thing."

"What about this pavilion up here?" David asked.

"What about it?" Sam said, feeling stressed.

"We could duck in here and watch to see if they come after us," David suggested.

Sam couldn't help himself and looked back to see if they were being followed. "I don't see anyone yet. Let's try it."

The three of them hustled under a pavilion meant for processing vegetables from the garden. It had an enclosed restroom area and a lot of worktables. David started for the cover of the restrooms, but Sam said, "No. If they catch us in there we are doomed. Come on." Sam hurried around the back of the structure, and David and Evie followed.

As soon as they were in place, Sam stooped low and peeked around the corner, looking under the tables. "They are coming," he whispered. "Three of them." Sam tensed. He knew he didn't need to say it but whispered anyway, "Keep quiet."

"Is everyone's phone off?" Evie asked, barely audible.

Both David and Sam pulled theirs out, turned off the volume and powered them down. "Good thinking, Evie," David said. "What about yours?"

"I turned mine off before we left our apartment," Evie said.

Sam felt sheepish. Once again he was lagging behind his amazing wife.

They could hear the guards talking now. "They must be heading for the factories," Brenda said.

John responded, "Ronnie, check that vegetable pavilion. Make sure they aren't hiding in the bathrooms. Daniella is mad at us already, and I don't want to give her cause for more ranting and raving!"

Sam watched as Ronnie peeled off from the group and started toward the pavilion. Sam motioned for Evie and David to move to the far corner of the restroom wall, farthest from the direction in which Ronnie was coming. David stepped around Sam so that he was in front and pointed at his staff. Sam understood that David had the only weapon available.

* * *

Clouds had rolled in, and a light snow began to fall, the first of the season. Skauty looked out his back window at the wondrous scene that led up a pasture to high mountains. It was a scene he could stand and look at all day long. But, he knew he didn't have time for lingering. Skauty grabbed his phone and called his son.

"Hey, Dad! What's up?" Kat said.

"I need you to meet me at the Ameridirect office immediately," Skauty said.

"What do you mean? I have a sightseeing flight that leaves at 10:30 this morning.

"It's urgent, Son. Just trust me and meet me there," Skauty said and hung up before his son could ask any more questions.

Skauty taped down the box that had contained the crow, scrawled the address of NOAA that Evie had written in the card, and headed toward the door. "They will be back soon," he thought. As he turned to close his front door, Skauty noticed the crow. "They aren't going to get my present, though!" he thought and went back for it. He set it in the larger box with the peanuts and brought it with him.

Stepping out into the biting air, Skauty surveyed the clouds and the flurries of snow. "This won't amount to much," he said to himself. Stowing the two boxes in the back seat, Skauty climbed into his Jeep Cherokee and drove to the Ameridirect office.

Kat pulled in right behind Skauty and got out in a rush. "What is so all-fired important that I have to be late for a sightseeing flight?" Kat asked, clearly irritated.

Skauty pulled the thumb drive out of his pocket and said, "This," and handed it to Kat.

"Dad, do you care to explain?" Kat asked.

"Evie just mailed it to me. She says it contains evidence of some sort of MC2 corporate shenanigans that NOAA needs to know about. She wanted me to mail it to them," Skauty explained.

"And you called me here for that? Dad, I'm sure you can mail a package on your own."

"There is a bit of a complication," Skauty added. "An armed security detail showed up at my house this morning looking for the thumb drive."

"What? How did they not get it from you?"

"Apparently they didn't like the look of my twelve-gauge," Skauty said and smiled. "Anyway, I'm sure they will be back. I'm going to mail this empty box to make them think it is gone, and you are going to keep that thumb drive until they are gone. Then we can mail it, see? Oh, and I want you to hold this for safe keeping, too. It's what Evie hid the thumb drive in. Be careful with my crow."

Kat looked perplexed. "Are Sam and Evie OK?"

"I don't know. I haven't talked to them," Skauty responded.

Kat pulled out his phone and called Sam. It went straight to voicemail.

Skauty studied Kat's face and could see indecision. "It will be OK. Just take these with you until the security team is gone."

"Dad, this must be really big for them to send a team after it. I think I had better fly this to NOAA myself. It is too risky to send it by Ameridirect. Where is NOAA, anyway?" Kat asked.

"Here's the address," Skauty said showing him the box. "Oh, and you had better take this, too," he added handing Kat the card from Evie.

Kat glanced over the card and looked worried. "Keep trying to get Sam and Evie. I'll cancel the sightseeing flight because of snow and head out as soon as I can get the flight plan approved."

"Thanks, son," Skauty said.

"You be careful, Dad. They may mean business when they come back."

Skauty entered the Ameridirect office, mailed the empty box, and drove back to his house. Approaching the house on the smooth, graveled road, Skauty noticed a car parked on the side about a quarter of a mile past his house. "They're back," he thought. Parking his Cherokee, he slid his Remington .44 Magnum pistol out of the glove box and tucked it in the waist of his pants at his back.

Skauty walked into the house, "Welcome back, gentlemen. But I thought I asked you not to return."

Lamar walked out of the kitchen holding Skauty's shotgun. "We needed to have a better look around," he said. "Where have you been?"

"I ran down to the Ameridirect office to mail a package," Skauty said with a smile on his face. "I told you not to bother coming back. I hate to see you wasting your time here while the object of your search is on its way to NOAA. What will your supervisor say?"

Lamar glared at Skauty, and Skauty could see the muscles in his jaw clinching. It dawned on Skauty that he probably needed to keep them there long enough for Kat to be off, so he said, "I am glad to see that you people are kind enough to search without throwing things everywhere. Please continue looking so you can satisfy yourself that it is not here." Skauty sat down on his couch, then got up, picked up his unfinished coffee from the table, and warmed it in the microwave.

Sitting down that the kitchen table, he took a sip, "Ah, that's good coffee. You know, you are fortunate to be here for our first snow of the season. I don't expect it to amount to much, though."

Lamar stood in front of Skauty. Angrily, he said, "Old man, don't be flippant with me. What you don't realize is that we have the authority to confiscate that package from Ameridirect. It will never make it to its destination."

Skauty heard the familiar sound of Kat's bush plane in the air and smiled at Lamar. "Well, aren't you just the cat's meow! All authoritative and everything." Looking at his watch, Skauty added, "I believe the truck that package is on is leaving even as we speak."

Skauty thoroughly enjoyed the panicked look on Lamar's face. Lamar ordered his men to stop searching and they headed for the door.

"You will remember to put down my shotgun before you leave," Skauty said.

Lamar looked down at the gun as he was about to step out the door. "I think I will keep this for all of the trouble you have caused me." When he looked back up at Skauty, his jeer turned to fear when he saw the barrel of Skauty's .44 Magnum.

"That would not be very neighborly of you, son. You will set the gun by the door and exit without reaching for your revolver. Do you understand?" Skauty said with force.

Lamar put the gun down and walked out the door. On his way down the steps, he could hear Skauty laughing.

* * *

Sam, Evie, and David held their breath as they heard the guard's footsteps coming closer. David started to inch forward, and Sam held him back. The door to the bathroom opened and closed. The second bathroom door opened and closed. Sam turned and faced the other direction from David in case the guard came that way. He felt sweat on his temples. Listening as closely as possible, Sam heard the guard's footsteps receding.

"All clear," Ronnie said to John.

Sam breathed a sigh of relief and looked at his watch. He sat down and leaned against the wall. "I think we need to wait at least ten minutes before we leave to be sure they are far enough ahead," he whispered. Evie and David sat down, too.

It was a long ten minutes. Sam looked at his watch every few seconds at first, then began to wait longer periods. Finally, he whispered, "Should we change our route and go back by the river trail?"

"That is wide open," David pointed out. "We could go along the path behind the apartment buildings. That would put us two blocks east of the guards' route."

"I don't know about you, but I can't stand sitting here much longer. I feel like a sitting duck," Sam said.

"I think your first thought was wise," Evie said. "We need to let the full ten minutes pass."

"That will be three more long minutes!" Sam whispered. The second that Sam's watch told him the ten minutes were up, he said, "Let's go."

Sam peeked out around the corner of the bathroom. Seeing nothing, he slunk along the wall to the front corner. With his heart beating rapidly, Sam looked around that corner. "No guards in sight," he said.

Sam led the way back downhill toward the apartment buildings. David and Evie came along side so that they looked like three friends out for a walk. As they turned up the road behind the first apartment building they heard a ruckus.

"Perfect!" Evie said. "School is out!"

Sam felt hopeful as he watched groups of children, parents, and babysitters flowing onto the playgrounds. "We shouldn't stand out in this crowd," he said. Trying not to hurry, Sam walked on.

"What if someone wants us to stop and chat?" Evie asked.

"Even worse, what if someone recognizes us?" David added.

"Let's cross our fingers and trust our disguises," Sam said. "I don't think we have any other good choice right now."

They proceeded through the fray. Sam felt on high alert, scanning the crowd for familiar faces or security guards. He had to will his feet to keep walking when he saw the familiar black cargo pants and fiery red MC2 security shirt.

"Don't panic, but there is a security guard up ahead," Sam whispered.

"I see him. That is the guard that is always posted here after school," Evie said. "I don't think he is after us."

"Let's stick with the plan and just coolly walk on by," Sam said.

Sam tried to keep an eye on the guard without being noticed. He saw a little girl run up to the guard and grab him by the knee. The guard looked down, smiled at the girl, and pulled something out of a bag over his shoulder. The girl trotted off, and all of a sudden the guard was swarmed with children.

"Aw, he's giving out candy," David said. "Can we get some?"

"I'm afraid your sweet tooth will have to wait, David," Sam said.

With the guard fully occupied, Sam, Evie and David breezed past the playgrounds and on to the back of their apartment building. Sam started to relax a bit, feeling that they had made it past one great danger. Sam eyed the large sugar maple with benches built at its base.

"Let's have a seat on those benches and plot our next move," Sam said.

"I think you are beginning to think like a bird, Sam," Evie said pointing to the same maple tree where Canto, Azul, and the titmouse were perched. "You really do need to give your friend a name," Evie reminded.

Taking seats in the shade of the maple, Evie asked, "Do we go by the pod road or take the footpath between the office building and the warehouse?"

"I think we should take the footpath," David said. "There is tree cover along the way."

Both Evie and David noticed that Sam was deep in thought. "Well?" they said at the same time.

"Wingston!" Sam said.

"Wingston?" Evie asked. "Sam, are you getting too stressed?"

"No. I think I'll name my bird Wingston," he said.

"That's quite catchy!" David said.

Sam looked up at the titmouse and said, "Hello, Wingston! I'm Sam."

The titmouse flicked its wings and let out a pleasant chirrup. Wingston and Azul then flew to an oak tree just off the back corner of the office building. Canto flew in the opposite direction.

"Where do you think you are going, Canto?" David called after the wren. "Do you think Canto wants us to split up?"

"I don't think so," Evie said. "He didn't seem to want you to follow."

"Maybe it's his break time," David said, and Sam and Evie chuckled.

"Shall we follow the birds?" Sam asked as he stood up, knowing the answer already.

Sam, Evie, and David walked across the pod road and followed the footpath between the office building and warehouse, the small gravel crunching noisily under their feet. Going west, shipping and receiving was just on the other side of the warehouse.

The footpath put them out across the street from the front doors of the warehouse. Sam led the way as they crossed the road and turned right to skirt along the front of the large building.

He paused at the corner and looked at David and Evie, "Do we just walk in through the front door when we get there?"

"We could go around through a loading dock, but we would be spotted for sure," David said. "I think we just walk in like we own the place and then hunt a place to hide until we can hop a truck."

Evie nodded her head in agreement with David. Sam took a deep breath, let it out slowly, and walked around the corner of the warehouse. The shipping and receiving building was straight ahead.

"I hope Graciela is not on duty at Ameridirect," Evie said.

Walking on, Sam noticed movement on the roof. He stopped and held his hand out automatically, like a parent who hits the brakes on a car. Before Sam understood what he was seeing, he heard an ear-piercing screech. Sam watched as a bird, flying incredibly fast, dive-bombed a man on the roof of shipping and receiving, hitting him right in the face with its talons. The man flipped over backwards, and Sam saw the silhouette of a rifle barrel against the sky.

Slowly, it dawned on Sam that what he had seen was a sniper taking aim at him.

"Sniper!" Sam managed to squeak out, watching as the man began to sit back up.

"Run!" David shouted and took off around the building with Sam and Evie following.

"Over there!" Evie yelled, running across the road.

"Evie! Wait!" Sam called realizing she was heading back into the line of sight of the sniper. Then Sam saw why Evie had run that way. Wingston and Azul flew down into a large drainage culvert under the delivery road. "Come on, David," he said as he ran to follow Evie.

Sam watched as Evie ducked and scampered along the culvert. He came in right behind her. David was so close that he almost ran into Sam. They worked their way to the middle of the culvert.

Catching his breath, David said, "Is this what it means when they say, 'Your life is in the gutter?'"

Sam and Evie looked at David as if he were nuts. They couldn't help themselves and burst out laughing.

"Well, that was definitely unexpected," Sam said.

"It looks like they have upped the ante," David said. "I think they have decided we are better off dead than alive!"

"I wonder if they have more than one sniper," Sam said.

"I don't want to go looking," David said.

Sam could see that Evie looked worried. "Now what do we do?" she asked. "Should we stay here till it gets dark?"

"I think that is risky," David said. "It is possible the sniper saw us."

"Or surveillance might have picked us up. Anyway, they apparently know our general vicinity," Sam said. "I think it's time to see what is going on a little more closely," he said and pulled off his backpack.

Sam got out his computer and logged into the system, not even bothering to hack. He worked into the security files and found an email from Morrison that was sent to every security team member. "They have put out an all-points bulletin on us, complete with a picture of us exiting the church," Sam said.

"So much for our disguises," David said. "There is no way we can get out of here, now!"

"Don't be such a pessimistic pastor," Sam said and began typing.

"What are you doing," Evie asked.

"I'm issuing a new order to stand down on the search. The criminals are apprehended," Sam said with a smile on his face. "It will look as though it came from Cruella de Vil herself," he added and punched send. "That ought to fix it!" Sam said and held up a hand for high fives.

"Brilliant!" David said. "Maybe my life won't end in the gutter after all."

A sense of relief flowed over the group. "Let's hang out in our comfy little home for a while so that the new order gets around. Then we can try getting to our ride out of here," Sam said. Sam logged off the computer and closed it down to conserve battery power.

Chapter 41

Sam checked his watch. "It's 3:42," he said. "How long should we wait?"

"I'd give it a good hour to let everyone get back to normal activities," David said.

"That's a long wait, but you are probably right," Sam said. "Anyone for a picnic?" he asked and fished in his backpack for energy bars and water.

"You must have been a Boy Scout," David said.

They ate and drank and plotted. Sam tried to hurry time up, but it just crawled. Finally, he said, "I'm not sure I can stand this much longer!"

"I know what you mean," Evie said. "Do you think we could go now?"

"It's been only thirty-four minutes," Sam said eyeing his watch.

As he was speaking, Wingston and Azul landed in the culvert with them.

"They seem calm," Evie said. "I think it's time to get out of the gutter!"

"I still think we need to wait," David said. "And where is Canto? Have I been deserted?"

Sam looked at the birds and looked at David. "Don't you think we should trust the birds?" he said.

"They are just sitting there, though. That might mean they want us to stay put," David said.

As if understanding him, Wingston flew out and came back. Azul did the same thing.

"I guess that answers your question," Evie said. "It is time to move."

David peeked out, looking first at the roof where the sniper had been. There was a tree in the way, so he could see nothing. Looking around, he saw no security guards.

"Wait here a minute," David said. He slipped out of the culvert and went to the base of the tree. Looking around the trunk, he saw that the roof was empty. David went back to the culvert. "It looks all clear," he said and started to go back out.

"Wait," said Evie. "I think it's time to ditch the beards and wig. That is what they are looking for."

"Good idea, Evie," Sam said. They shed their fake hair and hats, leaving them in the culvert, but kept their sunglasses.

David looked again before stepping out of the culvert. "No one in sight," he said. They began retracing their steps toward the shipping and receiving building.

* * *

Daniella was pacing her office like a caged tiger. "How long can it take to find three people in a compound this size!" she said with exasperation. Being unable to stand waiting another minute, Daniella called Trevor in surveillance.

"Surveillance, this is Trevor speaking."

"What is going on, Trevor? Why haven't you located these criminals?" Daniella spat. "Have you seen them at all?"

"Yes, ma'am. We last saw them alongside the warehouse. A sniper was about to take a shot when apparently a falcon mistook him for prey and attacked."

"Well, where are they now?"

"I don't know. We stood down on the search and have resumed normal operations."

"What do you mean, you stood down the search? Did I not order you to put all resources toward apprehending them?"

Daniella screamed into the phone, feeling her blood pressure rise.

"You did, ma'am. Then, we got your second order about forty minutes ago to stand down the search. You said the criminals were in custody," Trevor responded.

Daniella slammed her phone on the desk and opened her email. Seeing the email to which Trevor had referred, she banged both fists on her desk, "Hanson did this!" She picked her phone back up, "Trevor, Hanson must have logged into the system and sent out a fraudulent email. Resume the search with everyone and every resource you have. And do not stop unless you talk to me personally. Do you understand me?"

"Yes, ma'am!" Trevor said.

Hanging up from Trevor, Daniella called John, "John, where are you?"

"I'm back in my office, ma'am," John responded.

"I assume you called off the search, too."

"Yes, ma'am, just like you ordered."

"That order was issued by Hanson! You should know better than to stop a search of this magnitude without checking with me personally!" Daniella barked, enjoying releasing her rage.

"I did think it was rather odd that they were apprehended without me knowing about it," John said.

"I need you to set up a perimeter around shipping and receiving. They seem to think they can get on a truck headed out of the compound there."

"I'm on it, ma'am!" John responded.

Daniella fired off another email calling for all security personnel to resume searching for the three criminals in the picture she had sent earlier.

Daniella's phone rang. It was Mitch Carter. She groaned as she pushed the answer button. "Welcome back, Mr. Carter," she said trying to sound cheerful.

"Hello, Daniella. I trust things are going well with our project," Carter said. "I have been trying to reach Starke, but he is not answering his phone."

"Starke took an Apache to dispose of the prisoners, sir. He probably can't hear his phone," Daniella explained hoping that would satisfy Carter.

"Well, that is good news!" Carter said. "I assume that means we have the thumb drive?"

"We have a thumb drive," Daniella said. "We have since discovered that it is a copy. I believe Sam Hanson has the original, and we are in the process of bringing him in," Daniella said trying to make things sound more in control than they were."

"Are you sure it's a good idea to remove the first prisoners before we have this thing resolved?"

"I tried to tell Starke the same thing, but he blew me off. He said it was time." Daniella said trying not to let her anger show.

"Keep me apprised of what is happening, Morrison. I will be at home the rest of the evening and in the office in the morning."

"Yes, sir. I will," Daniella said glad that the conversation was over.

Daniella stood up and found herself pacing again. "I am surrounded by imbeciles!" she thought. That thought was followed by another that made Daniella smile, "I am the only one here who has experience in hunting down targets!"

Daniella set her phone to silent and pulled her 9mm revolver from her purse. "I'll show Hanson how this game is really played," she said and walked quickly out of her office toward shipping and receiving.

* * *

Sam, Evie, and David walked silently, each fearing that Sam's email might not have worked, but not wanting to say it out loud. When they were back in the shade of the warehouse, David broke the silence, "They are looking for three people traveling together. I think we will have a better chance if we split up. Between that and not having our artificial hair, we should have a good chance of getting into shipping and receiving without being noticed."

Sam felt the sting of worry, "I don't want to leave Evie."

"I think David is right," Evie said. "Let's split up to get inside shipping and receiving. We can meet in the lobby as if we just happened to see each other there."

"OK," Sam said. "I guess I'm out numbered."

"I'll go first," David said, "Just in case the sniper is still there."

"I can't let you do that!" Sam said.

"Yes, you can," David responded. "Like you said, you don't want to leave Evie. It's better that I take the chance."

"And for diversity's sake, I will go around the other side of the warehouse," Evie said.

"That's a good idea!" David said. "Let's space ourselves apart by two minutes."

Sam and Evie followed David to the corner of the warehouse. Sam realized how tense he was and tried to relax. The thought of his friend stepping out into the line of fire was a noose around his heart. David looked back, pointed to his watch, and stepped around the corner.

Sam grabbed Evie's hand and held his breath. No shot was fired. David didn't fly back around the corner. Letting out a long breath, Sam whispered, "He must be OK."

Sam and Evie walked to the other side of the warehouse for a tense two-minute wait. Sam grabbed Evie and hugged her when it was time. "Be careful!" he whispered.

Evie hugged him back. "No worries, Sam. I have my little friend with me," she said pointing to Azul sitting on a branch nearby. Releasing Sam, Evie started her walk toward the building.

Left alone, it was all Sam could do not to run and catch up with Evie. He almost peeked around the corner to assure himself that she was all right but forced himself not to. When the long two minutes were finally up, he decided to follow Evie's path, just in case.

All seemed calm as Sam made his way along the warehouse building. A tractor-trailer rolled by on its way toward shipping and receiving. Sam crossed the road and turned right. Just as he was turning to go into the front doors, Sam noticed movement. The front door of the security building was opening, and the last person Sam wanted to see stepped out: Daniella Morrison.

Sam quelled the urge to run and managed to walk into the building. He hurried over to where David and Evie were standing. "Daniella Morrison is coming!"

"Let's not stand here like a welcoming committee! Forward, Ho!" David said. He started to take a step, then stopped. "Madam, which door will you select, shipping or receiving?"

"I'll take shipping, thank you, because I want to be shipped out of this place!" Evie responded.

The trio walked toward the shipping department. "Remember, we go in like we own this place," Sam said.

David opened the door labeled "Shipping," and they stepped into a cavernous space filled with huge rolls of wire, giant pallets of transformers, and everything else one could need to build or maintain an energy grid. There were aisles between the pallets wide enough for a huge forklift to maneuver, but otherwise the room seemed full.

Sam couldn't see where the trucks were loaded because the pallets were too high, but he could tell the direction because of the sunlight coming through the open bays. Sam tried to mime that they needed to get close to the bays where trucks were loaded. David and Evie shrugged their shoulders, so Sam gave up and whispered, "We need to get near the bays but still be hidden."

David pointed to the back of the building and started that way.

"But that's the wrong way," Sam whispered.

David drew a map on his palm that showed he planned to follow the perimeter of the supplies until they were in position. Sam and Evie gave thumbs up and followed David, keeping Evie in the middle. Just as Sam was about to turn the corner at the back of the room, he heard a door open.

When they reached the opposite corner, they heard Daniella's voice coming from somewhere in the middle of the room, "I know you are here, Hanson, with that sweet little wife of yours."

Sam, Evie, and David froze, and Sam felt his blood congealing in his veins.

After a pause, Daniella went on, "It would be a shame to let your wife be hurt by your selfish actions, Hanson." Another pause and then, "Pastor McCutcheon, I believe you are here, too. Will you let Ms. Hanson be harmed?"

Sam realized that during the pauses, Daniella was listening to see if she could locate them. He looked at David, and David was shaking his head and finger. Sam knew that he meant that giving themselves up was not going to help matters.

Evie made her fingers walk on her palm and pointed to the far corner of the room. Sam and David nodded their heads, acknowledging that they understood Daniella was moving in that direction.

David peeked around the roll of wire and scooted across the next aisle. Sam and Evie followed.

"We have guards all around the building. You cannot escape," Daniella roared.

Sam could tell that she was at the very back of the building, so he made a motion for them to move forward. David pointed to his eyes and then pointed two fingers toward the back of the building. Sam took Evie's hand and looked backwards while they moved. They were two thirds of the way toward the loading bay when Daniella stepped into their aisle at the back corner.

"Run!" Sam yelled.

David immediately turned right into another aisle, ran for four aisles, and turned left toward the bays. He stepped right and pulled Evie along with him. Sam followed.

"Hanson, this is all just a misunderstanding," Daniella said.

"I don't think I misunderstood the sniper, Morrison," Sam hollered back, then pushed Evie and David to move, pointing in the direction of the door from which they had entered. He assumed Daniella would keep moving toward the bays. They stopped and listened.

"Calling off the search was a clever move, Hanson," Daniella said.

David moved his hand across his neck, telling Sam to quit responding. David pointed that Daniella was moving back toward the entrance door, too. Sam pointed toward the bays, and all three began walking quietly that way. David made a left, crossed over two aisles, and turned right toward the bays again.

They reached the end of the aisles, and there was an empty space between them and the bays. Apparently a truck had recently been loaded and was still parked at the bay on the far right. Sam pointed to the truck, but its trailer doors were closed. "Let's make a run for the truck. We can either get out behind it or jump in the cab," Sam whispered. David and Evie nodded agreement.

David peeked out and did not see anyone, so he motioned to Sam and Evie to follow. They walked as quickly as they could and still remain reasonably quiet. When they were halfway to the truck, Daniella Morrison stepped out from the corner of the pallet that was located along the aisle that led to the entrance door. Her revolver was aimed at Sam.

"That's better. I'm glad you decided to turn yourselves in like good little children. I see you have shed your disguises. You don't even need to put your hands up, but I will ask you to drop your stick, Pastor McCutcheon," Daniella said oozing contempt. "Did you silly people really think you could outsmart me?"

Sam stepped in front of Evie to protect her.

"I'm afraid you lost the chance to protect your little wife, Hanson," Daniella said with a cruel tone that she seemed to enjoy. With her gun still aimed at Sam, Daniella pulled out her phone. "Let me call some escorts for you, and we will go make ourselves more comfortable," Daniella said.

When she moved her gun hand to start to dial, David started to run toward her. "No, no, no, McCutcheon!" Daniella barked with authority and trained the gun on him. "You don't want me to kill you before we've had a chance to talk, now do you?"

David stopped. Sam felt hopeless and dropped his head. Evie stepped out from behind him, "Morrison, do you mind telling us what this is about? Why are you hunting us?"

"Hunting is a good word, Evie. I do enjoy a good hunt, but this one is over. You know exactly what this is about. Don't play dumb with me! One of you has something that I plan to retrieve before this is all over... and you are all dead!"

Sam watched as a cruel smile came over Daniella. All he could think of was to say, "I have the thumb drive. If you will let Evie and David go, I will take you to it. They know nothing about it."

Daniella burst out laughing and laughed long. She stopped suddenly, and her face was hard as stone. "Too late, Hanson," and Daniella went back to her phone.

Chapter 42

Within seconds of Daniella's call, six guards converged on the scene. "Take them to the holding cells," Daniella ordered. Three guards pulled their weapons, and the other three took a prisoner by the arm. They frisked them and marched them down the metal steps outside the bay. Sam noticed that the keys were in the truck as they walked down.

With one guard holding an arm, one guard behind each prisoner with a gun drawn, and Daniella in the rear, they marched toward the detention center, which was across the street and one block north. Sam's mind was racing, trying to think of something to do when he heard raucous crow calls. Looking up, Sam saw what appeared to be at least a hundred crows flying everywhere and calling to each other. He looked back at Evie, and she shrugged her shoulders.

The guards roughly shoved their prisoners across the road. The loud cawing stopped suddenly, leaving an eerie silence. In an instant, a whole battalion of crows descended at full speed on the group. They dive-bombed the guards and Daniella, clawing at their eyes and pecking at their heads. The guards began flailing at the crows. One guard's gun went off, and a crow went down. The crows kept coming.

Sam was stunned. Finally, the reality of what was happening set in, and he said, "Run! This way!"

Sam ran back toward the truck with the keys in it. Evie and David followed. Suddenly, Azul dive bombed Evie. "Quit,

Azul!" The bird flew at her, again. "Wait! The truck is a trap!" Evie called out. "This way!"

Evie ran west between the transformer and fiber optics factories, following Azul, and stopped at the back of the transformer factory. Sam and David caught up.

"The keys were in that truck!" Sam said a little more angrily than he intended to.

"Azul warned me not to go that way!" Evie said.

"You have to admit, the birds have been right so far, Sam," David said. "What an attack they launched!"

"Yes, the crows were awesome," Sam said. "But why would they do that?"

"Maybe they don't like bullies," David said.

"Guys, we are still on the run here!" Evie said. "What's our next move?"

"We can't pretend that they don't know we are here!" David said.

Sam looked around, searching for solutions. Spotting the helipad, he asked, "David, do you know how to fly a helicopter?"

"A buddy let me take the controls once during my army days, but I wouldn't say I could fly one," David answered.

"That may be our best bet," Sam said.

"Sam, are you crazy?" David responded. "I'm not even sure how to start the thing!"

"Well, I hope you can figure it out in a hurry!" Sam said. "Let's go."

David shrugged his shoulders, and he and Evie followed Sam. Azul lighted on the ground, held out one wing, and hopped as if he was hurt.

"What's wrong, Azul?" Evie said and walked toward the bird. It just kept hopping away in the opposite direction from where they were heading.

Evie stopped, "Guys, I think Azul is trying to tell us something."

Sam and David stopped. David observed Azul's hopping and said, "Some birds will do that when they are trying to draw a predator away from its nest."

"I think Azul is trying to draw us away from the predator!" Evie said.

The next sound they heard was an Apache being moved out of the hanger.

"Uh oh! Time to go!" David said. "I say we follow Azul."

The trio began moving in the direction Azul was hopping, which was along the backside of the transformer factory away from the helipad. As they walked, Azul suddenly flew. Evie said, "Run!" They ran and ducked around the corner of the transformer factory, in between it and the wire factory. David sprinted ahead, then grabbed Evie's arm and pulled her into the crepe myrtles that decorated the side of the building. Up ahead was the street where the crows had rescued them.

"I think we are fairly safe from eyes on the ground or by camera here," David said. "We need to regroup and come up with a plan."

* * *

Daniella realized that she was still flailing her arms, but the crows were gone. She stopped and moved her hair out of her face.

One of the guards spoke up, "What is with these birds?"

Daniella looked around but did not see her prey. She pulled her phone out of her pocket and called Trevor. "Tell me you were following us out of the shipping bay and walking toward detention."

"Yes, ma'am!" Trevor said. "I saw the whole thing. That was an incredible bird attack!"

"Where are the prisoners, now?"

"I don't exactly know, ma'am."

"Trevor, I don't have time for games! What are you talking about? Did you track the prisoners' movements or not?"

"I was tracking them, ma'am. They ran west, behind the fiber optics factory."

"Are you trying to tell me that you lost them?" Daniella yelled.

"Ma'am, it appears that crows have landed on every one of our cameras. They are blocking my vision. All I can see is black feathers."

"Trevor, figure out a way to get the system functioning again! And I mean immediately!" Daniella hung up, not waiting for a reply.

She called John. "I need a pilot to meet me at the helipad. The surveillance system is being blocked by crows."

"I'll send a pilot immediately," John replied.

"And John, send someone around to shoot those blasted crows off the cameras!" Daniella hung up.

"I'm going up in a chopper to hunt. You three go back to shipping and receiving. Make sure you check that truck I had parked with its battery disconnected. You three go behind the fiber optics factory and track north. If you find them and they run, shoot to kill," Daniella gave the guards a serious look, then lit out for the helipad.

* * *

"Hey, Sam, is that a surveillance camera?" Evie asked pointing to the corner of the wire factory. "The thing with a crow sitting on it?"

Following Evie's finger, Sam said, "It is! And look at that! The crow is sitting right on it."

"It's blocking the view of the camera," David said, amazed.

Sam inched eastward along the side of the transformer factory till he reached the corner. Peeking around, he saw another camera outfitted with a crow. Calling back to the others, Sam said, "Hey guys, it looks like the crows are covering all the cameras. I think it's safe for us to move."

"But where are we going?" David asked.

"Since they seem to be focused on shipping and receiving, I think we should go the other way. Aren't there woods on past the gardens?" Sam asked.

"I think so," David said. "But the only way out in that direction is through a fence with razor wire."

"We need something that will cut through the wire," Sam said. "Maybe there are some tools in the garden pavilion."

"We could pass through the store and buy some wire cutters," David offered.

"That would be an idea, but we cut our chips out, remember guys?" Evie pointed out.

"Let's try the pavilion," Sam said. "Come on."

As soon as they stepped around the corner of the building, they heard the sound of a helicopter taking off not far behind them.

"Quick, back under the trees," David said, running back under the cover of the crepe myrtles. Evie followed, and Sam dived in just as the helicopter cleared the building.

"That was a bit too close," Sam said.

"The school!" Evie said. "When the helicopter is out of sight, we could take cover inside."

Sam found himself holding his breath again as the helicopter seemed to take forever circling around the factory buildings before moving on toward shipping and receiving.

"Now!" David said, and the three ran to the school building. Sam felt very exposed as they ran down the sidewalk beside the playground to the back door. Looking to his right, he could see the helicopter slowly moving away from them. Then it started to bank to the right.

"It's turning around! Hurry!" Sam called out.

David tugged at the door. "It's locked!"

Evie was already digging in her backpack. "It's always locked," she said as she pulled out her electronic key fob. Reaching around David, she held it to the door.

David tugged again. "It's still locked!"

"I must have pulled the fob away too quickly!" Evie said.

"Any time now, the helicopter is headed this way!" Sam said. He felt like a cornered rat with a cat looking right at him.

Evie held the fob to the door again. "Pull now!" she said to David. The door swung open, and David literally pushed Evie and Sam inside before running in himself.

The school seemed very dark until Sam remembered that he was wearing his sunglasses. Pulling them off, he heard footsteps coming down the hall up ahead and to the left. Sam's eyes flew open wide, and he looked at Evie.

"It's probably the janitor," she whispered. "Let me go see."

Evie walked to the corner and turned in the direction of the sound. "Hey, Heather! You are just the person I am looking for! Do you know if we have any wire cutters here? I am doing an art project with wires that need to be cut to the right length."

Heather, a large, sturdy woman in her late forties, responded, "Sure," and pulled out her needle nose pliers. "You can borrow these."

Assessing the pliers, Evie said, "My wires are right thick. I'm not sure I can cut them with these."

"Oh, you need the real wire cutters! They have some of those in the shop class. I'm sure Mr. Castleberry wouldn't mind if you borrowed them. Just make sure you leave him a note! He is mighty particular about his tools."

"Thanks so much!" Evie said coaxing a smile out of her stress.

Sam breathed another sigh of relief.

"Come on you two," Evie called out. "Heather says we can find them in the shop class."

Sam looked surprised, then realized that Heather was headed in his direction. He motioned for David to come on, and they walked around the corner like they knew what they were doing.

"Hey," Sam and David said.

"We're with Evie," Sam added.

"I gathered that," Heather responded. "Y'all have a good afternoon."

"You, too!" Sam replied and followed Evie and David.

Evie led them to the shop classroom. "What are we looking for, guys?"

David and Sam spread out looking through cabinets and closets.

"Now that's what I'm talking about!" said David as he pulled bolt cutters out of a cabinet. "This should do the trick nicely!"

"Great! Now all we have to do is get there without being spotted!" Sam said feeling hopeless.

"Sam, we have made it this far," Evie consoled. "We will make it the rest of the way. I know we will."

"We don't get any extra points for standing around," David said. "Let's move!"

Sam started back the way they had come, but Evie said, "Let's go out the front door. It will put us farther from our suspected location. As they approached the door, the sound of the helicopter grew louder.

"It's coming back around," Sam said feeling a wave of near nausea. Sam looked at Evie and felt guilty for having gotten her into this.

"They can't see us in here," David said. "Let's just wait till it moves on."

"Don't look so grim, Sam," Evie said. "We've got this. We have a plan, and we have tools. It's going to be OK."

"I wish I felt as confident as you do," Sam said. "Evie, I'm sorry I got you into this. You, too, David."

"You didn't get me into this!" Evie said. I'm the one who found the thumb drive, remember? Besides, I wouldn't have it any other way."

"Ditto," David said. "We're in this together, all for one and one for all!"

"So, we're Musketeers now?" Evie bantered.

David leaned over and peered out the door. "They are flying over the church and turning back along the river trail, heading south. We should be clear to go in just a bit.

David stepped away from the door, just in case, as the helicopter flew within sight. It was beyond the apartments, though, and no one could have seen him. "Are we ready to rock and roll?" David asked and pushed the door open without waiting for an answer.

David led the way, followed by Evie and Sam. Sam felt better if he could see Evie in front of him. Turning left, they walked north, toward the store.

A gun shot pierced the air, and Sam jumped nearly three feet off the ground. Turning to look behind him, Sam saw a security guard with his gun aimed at a surveillance camera. The guard looked puzzled, and Sam realized that he had shot the camera. The crow that had apparently been his target flew back and sat on the camera again.

Apparently Sam's jump had caught the guard's attention. Turning toward Sam, the guard yelled, "Stop or I'll shoot!"

"Run!" Sam yelled, and the three of them took off as fast as they could. One shot rang out, and glass in a school window exploded. Running as hard as he could and trying to stay between Evie and the guard, Sam expected to feel a bullet any second.

They passed the store, and David made a turn to the right, heading east toward the church. Sam looked over his shoulder and saw the guard taking aim, again. Before the guard could fire, the crow perched on the shattered camera swooped down and snatched the guard's revolver. The guard threw up his hands and started to chase them.

The crow dropped the gun and cawed. The guard looked back, turned, and ran for the gun. Before he got to it, the crow swooped down, picked up the gun and dropped it fifty feet farther away. Sam realized he had stopped to watch the spectacle. The guard glared at Sam and pulled out his phone.

"Come on, Sam! What are you waiting for?" Evie's call jolted Sam out of his amazement, and he ran to catch up.

"A crow snatched the guard's gun! When the guard went to pick it up, the crow tossed it farther away!" Sam explained.

"These birds are amazing!" Evie said.

"Amazing or not, I think the guard is alerting the helicopter," Sam said. "We have to find cover!"

"Let's see if we can make it to the woods past the gardens," Evie said, and they started running.

Looking to his right, Sam saw the helicopter bank into a turn. "It looks like they got the call and are headed this way!" he said. "Try to make it to the church before they spot us!"

David turned and aimed for the church. Racing headlong down the hill, Sam could see the helicopter line up and move in their direction. It was gaining speed. "Run faster!" he called.

Bullets began to strafe the ground, coming closer and closer. Evie and David dived for cover to the north side of the church. Sam slid in just behind them and felt dirt hit his face, thrown up by one of the bullets hitting the ground inches from his head. Sam looked up as the helicopter flew by, still accelerating. He saw Daniella looking down at him and felt for the first time ever that he was looking into the face of pure hate.

"It's a good thing the pilot doesn't know what he is doing," David said. "He should have slowed down and hovered right here at us."

Noticing how fast the helicopter was flying, Sam said, "Come on! Let's go!" He jumped up and ran toward the Apache. Evie and David jumped up and followed.

"Sam, why are we chasing the helicopter?" Evie yelled.

"That's a good question," David added.

"Let's try to get under that big oak tree before they turn around. It will hide us!" Sam called back and continued running toward the huge tree that leaned out from the other side of the river. Sam saw the helicopter slowing down to turn and hoped that they would make it in time.

"You know that thing has missiles on it, right?" Sam heard David calling from just behind him.

"The last thing they will expect is for us to run toward them. I'm betting they will think we hid in the church," Sam said, starting to huff and puff.

Evie came up even with Sam, "Hurry up! They will be able to see us soon!" The helicopter was banking into a turn.

As they approached the huge oak, Sam was startled to see something fall out of the tree. He wanted to stop but didn't dare. It was hard to make out the object while running at full speed.

Skidding to a stop under the cover of the tree, Sam saw a vine ladder hanging down. He looked at Evie and David feeling puzzled. David looked up into the tree, "Viviana?"

"Are you just going to stand there all day?" Viviana said urgently.

Sam couldn't believe that there was a raven-haired woman in a deerskin dress standing on the trunk of the tree, beckoning him to climb the ladder. "Hi," was all he could manage. Then he noticed Wingston, Azul, and Canto sitting on a limb over Viviana's shoulder.

The helicopter began approaching, and Sam shooed Evie up the ladder. "You next," he said to David, who wasted no time in scampering up. Sam followed. They were all standing on the trunk of the tree when the helicopter flew over. Viviana knelt down, pulled the vine up, and tied it to a limb with another vine.

"What are you doing here?" David asked, perplexed and anxious.

Over the noise of the helicopter, Viviana explained, "Your little wren is a hero. Canto came and rallied the crows to come help. I had a hunch I might be needed, too."

"Look! This leads across the river! We'll be out of the compound!" Evie said excitedly.

"Let's go!" Sam said and signaled Evie, who was the farthest along the trunk to go.

"Not just yet," Viviana said firmly enough to halt the three, even though they were anxious to get out of danger. The helicopter flew directly overhead and slowed as it approached the church. Flying slowly past the church, it looped around the apartments and came back, making a slow turn right over the tree.

Sam began to feel panicky until he realized that the pilot was maneuvering to hover in front of the church. Viviana said, "Now!" and flicked her hand signaling for Evie to take off along the trunk.

Walking as quickly as they could, they made their way out of the canopy and onto the trunk over the river. Just as Sam was in the middle of the river, glass and wood exploded, startling him. Viviana had to grab him to keep him from falling. Looking over his shoulder, Sam saw the helicopter strafing the church.

David stopped and stared in disbelief. "That's just sick," he said.

"I'm glad we ran for the tree and not into the church," Evie said. "You saved our lives, Sam!"

"We'll have time to celebrate later, but only if we get moving before they see us," Viviana commanded.

Evie, David, Sam, and then Viviana scampered across the trunk and into the dense forest. Once he felt sufficiently concealed, Sam stopped and looked back. A score of guards were converging on the church. The helicopter had stopped firing and hovered while the guards entered the building to search.

"Lady and gentlemen," Viviana said, "we have to keep moving. It won't take long to discover you are not there. I expect they will send out drones, next."

One stepped out of the church, looked up at the helicopter, and shook his head. The helicopter pulled away and resumed searching.

"When I say down, I want everyone to drop to all fours and put heads down, like this," Viviana said, demonstrating. "The drones will identify the infrared image as a deer instead of a human. Follow me!"

Viviana led the way up the side of the mountain along a barely discernible trail. After a fifty-yard climb, they came to a deer trail.

"This is the trail I followed the other day when I was trying to get away from the guards," David said.

A crow landed on a limb in front of Viviana and cawed. "Drop!" she said. "And keep quiet."

The others did as she directed. Sam felt silly until he heard the whir of a large drone between him and the river. He raised his head, trying to imitate a deer that had heard something, and could see the drone flying north.

When the crow flew off, Viviana said, "It's clear. Let's go."

Chapter 43

Viviana continued to lead the group along the deer trail. The trail climbed rather steeply as it led northeast and rounded to the back side of Crow Mountain. Viviana signaled them to drop into deer position twice more.

Sam marveled as they passed rhododendron thickets, fern-covered slopes sweeping down the mountain, and green logs covered with thick moss. They crossed little streams that trickled and sang as the water danced over the rocks.

"This is absolutely gorgeous!" he said.

Evie and David agreed.

As Sam walked, he noticed something odd happening. His body began to feel lighter. The beauty of the scenery seemed to be transforming him. The tension of being hunted was melting away, and the raw nerves were calming. The farther they walked, the more his spirit seemed to jettison the stress and burdens he had been carrying for the last two years. A strange feeling was settling into his soul. He thought and tried to name it. "Peaceful? Content? Happy?"

With a smile, Sam said, "This mountain air seems to be good for my soul."

"I was thinking the same thing," Evie said. "I haven't felt this good in a long time."

The trek along the deer trail continued for a little over an hour. Stopping, Viviana said, "We have a bit of a climb now. Just follow me."

Viviana began climbing up a very steep mountain slope that was not quite a cliff. She stepped on rhododendron trunks that grew out and up. Sam, David, and Evie looked at each other a little skeptically.

"Ladies first," David said.

Evie quickly followed Viviana up, seeming to have no difficulty at all. David went next, trying to match Evie's footsteps. After David was sufficiently on his way, Sam followed.

Sam found the climb a bit tricky, but had his foot slip off only a couple of times. After about twenty vertical feet, Sam stepped out onto a rock ledge that looked out over the valley below. Mountains ranged into the distance, and the sky was turning an amazing pink in the west.

"Wow!" he said, feeling a bit dizzy.

"Isn't it amazing?" Evie said.

"We have to hurry," Viviana reminded and pulled back a large rhododendron branch to reveal the narrow opening to a cave. "Right this way, please," she said.

Evie, David, and Sam squeezed between the rhododendron and rock face of the mountain and into the narrow opening. Sam was surprised by the smell of lavender as he entered the cave. He was also surprised by the darkness. Sam took off his sunglasses and felt more than saw Viviana squeeze past him.

"Welcome to my home," Viviana said, beaming.

As Sam's eyes adjusted to the dark, he noticed bundles of weeds hanging on the walls.

"The lavender smells delicious," Evie said.

"That helps keep bugs and scorpions away," Viviana explained. She led them down what seemed like a hallway.

Sam caught a number of other scents as he passed the various dried plants but didn't recognize them. Sam's breath caught as he stepped out from the narrow entrance way into a vault the size of a house. Cream-colored boulders lay strewn across the floor, and the ceiling was decorated with crevices, almost like curtains, some thirty feet overhead. His eye caught daylight dropping in from a small opening way up a crevice in the ceiling.

"This is my living room," Viviana stated.

"You mean there is more?" Sam said, astounded.

"So, this is the mysterious place you would never let me see," David added. "It is just, wow!"

Sam's jaw dropped as he saw people step out from a crevice in the back of the room. "Arnie?" Sam said in disbelief.

Arnie was followed by Christie, who was holding Brittany.

"What? How did you get here?" Sam said, not believing his eyes.

"We got to parachute!" Arnie said.

Christie went on to explain, "Zeke Starke picked us up and took us on a helicopter. I thought we were dead, but he said that he was sick of Mitch Carter, MC2, and how they were treating us. He told us how Viviana rescued Brittany. He is incredibly grateful, because in rescuing her, he said she saved him, too."

"Yeah," Arnie added. "He put parachutes on us, told us what to do, and we jumped. It was incredible!"

"More like terrifying," Christie said. "We survived but had no idea what to do next. Zeke said Viviana would probably find us, and sure enough after about an hour she appeared!"

"The crows, again, I suppose," Sam said.

"Of course," Viviana agreed.

"Anyway, she brought us back here, and I have never been so happy in my life," Christie said as tears began to fall. She hugged Brittany even closer.

Arnie added, "Zeke said he planned to set the helicopter autopilot so that it would crash in the Atlantic Ocean, and he was going to jump out somewhere between where we jumped and there."

Sam felt a tear start to well up in his eye, too, and he tried to force it to stop. He had been so focused on saving Evie, David, and himself, that he had stuffed the horror of thinking they had failed Arnie and Christie down in a hole somewhere. Yet there they were, alive and well.

That tear worked its way loose, anyway. It was followed by others. Evie came over and put her arm around Sam's shoulder, "What's wrong, Sam?"

It took a moment before Sam could squeak out, "We're all alive! I thought we had failed you and Christie, Arnie. But somehow, here we all are!"

Evie pulled Sam in for a big hug, and he felt a release from the massive burdens of the day. Arnie embraced Christie and Brittany. Sam watched as David looked at Viviana, hesitating.

"Well?" Viviana said.

David took her in his arms, too. Sam saw the biggest smile he had ever seen on David's face. Sam realized he was smiling, too.

Viviana pecked David on the cheek and pulled away. "This is nice, but we do have some organizing to do. I'm afraid I wasn't expecting company for supper."

"No worries," David said. "I never travel without food!" He pulled off his backpack and produced a mound of energy bars and four bottles of water.

A sad, prehistoric caw penetrated the cave and caught everyone's attention.

"Oh no," Viviana said. "You will have to excuse me for a bit." Viviana walked silently out of the cave.

"What is it? What's wrong?" David asked.

Canto, Azul, and Wingston flew out of the cave. David looked at the others with concern on his face and followed Viviana.

"I don't know what's up, but we had better follow, too," Evie said.

Reaching the opening of the cave, Sam could see Viviana sitting cross-legged on the rock just outside. There was silence, other than the sound of birds' wings. As Sam pushed past the rhododendron branch, he could see crows landing everywhere around them in the pinkish twilight. Sam could feel this was a sacred moment. Even Brittany seemed to be affected by the scene and was perfectly quiet.

Sam and the other five sat down on the rock behind Viviana. When the sound of fluttering wings ceased, a crow flew down and landed in the middle of the rock outcropping. The crow leaned its head down and touched the side of its face to the rock for a brief moment, then flew back to its perch. A second crow followed, then a third. Each crow came and touched its cheek to the rock.

Viviana stood, went to the center, and imitated the crows, touching her cheek to the rock. As she walked back toward the group, Sam looked at her pleadingly. She nodded her head, "Yes."

After a few more crows had landed, Sam got up and imitated the behavior, touching his cheek to the rock, which still felt warm from the afternoon sun. In intervals, the others did the same. Even Brittany imitated her mom and touched her cheek to the rock.

The stars had begun to twinkle, and the twilight was replaced by a nearly full moon by the time the crows finished landing on the rock and flew silently away. Sam's legs felt stiff, and his behind was sore from sitting on the rock for so long. Watching Viviana, Sam waited to see what to do next. She waited till all of the crows had flown off before standing. Without a word, they followed Viviana back into the cave.

The cave had darkened noticeably. Sam squinted and could just see Viviana as she moved to the back of the vault and began pulling out something. Sam walked closer and could see a fire ring. Viviana was adding dried grasses and small sticks.

"We'll have light in just a bit," Viviana said. She began scraping something that sounded like metal on metal and sparks flew, flaring up in the grass.

"What is that?" Sam asked.

"I use magnesium to start the fires," Viviana explained as the little flame caught and burned.

"Wow!" Sam said amazed at how quickly she got it going.

The firelight began to dance on the walls of the cave as the flames grew. Sam saw that Viviana had a large pile of sticks of varying sizes stored in a recess by the fire pit. He also realized that the fire pit was directly under the hole through which he had seen daylight.

"Viviana, what was the thing with the crows? It felt like a ceremony." Sam finally had the courage to ask.

"Oh, I didn't explain, did I?" Viviana said. "Apparently, a crow was killed during your escape. The crows gathered to mourn and honor the life that was lost."

"Wow! That was a powerful experience," David said.

"They touch their head to the rock one time for each bird that has died. That is how I know only one was killed," Viviana continued.

"So, it was OK for us to participate?" Evie asked.

"Oh yes. That shows you honor the crow as well. The crows appreciate our participation," Viviana explained.

A soft caw came from over their shoulders and Sam jumped.

"Sorry, I guess I'm still a little edgy," Sam explained. He could see the gleam of several birds' eyes reflecting the growing light from the fire.

"Viviana, what were all of those dried plants we passed on the way in?" Evie asked.

"Herbs," Viviana said. "I use them for medicines."

"Are you sick?" Evie asked.

"Not very often," Viviana said. "The animals come when they are sick, especially the deer. They know I will help."

Sam felt another wave of amazement. He thought, "Who is this woman?" Then, he asked, "You mean they just walk in here like they are going to the doctor?"

"No, they don't come into the cave. They come nearby, usually to the meadow that is up a little higher. Rey tells me they are there."

They heard another caw as Rey sounded his agreement. The fire had grown, and Sam could now see the crow to which

Viviana was referring. Perched nearby were Canto, Azul, and Wingston.

David noticed the birds, too and said, "Wait, how did they get here? When did they get here?"

"They were with us all the way," Viviana said. "You were just too stressed to notice. May I introduce Rey? He is my buddy the crow."

Rey flicked his wings and bobbed his head in greeting.

"It's a pleasure to meet you," Evie said with a smile on her face.

With the fire going well, Viviana stood up. "Let's find bedrooms for everyone," she said. "Sam and Evie, I believe this will be your spot," and she led them off to the right, through a narrow opening and into another cavern that seemed just the size of a bedroom. "You can leave your things here, if you like."

Then Viviana said, "Let's see, David, how about over here?" She showed David to a boulder that required a climb. It led to another boulder that passed into a smaller chamber about ten feet by eight feet. "I hope it's not too small," she said.

"I love it!" David said. "I get to sleep in the loft!" He deposited his backpack. "This will be my pillow," he added. "And I am starving! Let's eat!"

Everyone agreed, and Viviana invited to them to sit near the fire. Sam noticed it was a bit cool and retrieved his and Evie's jackets from their backpacks.

"I'm afraid that I don't have beds, but I do have some deer hides you can use for cover," Viviana said.

"Thanks! That will be great!" Evie responded.

They settled into eating energy bars and talking about the events of the day. After he ate, Sam's body reminded him just how tired he was.

"I don't think I can hold my eyes open any longer!" he said with a yawn. He noticed David's head had slumped over in sleep. "Shall we retire, dear?" Sam said to Evie. Sam lay down close to Evie, pulled the deer hides over them, and was asleep in an instant.

Sam awoke stiff the next morning. Looking over, he saw that Evie was up and gone. He groaned as he got himself up from the floor of the cave. He felt a little disoriented until he saw light coming through what made the doorway into the main vault. Sam walked toward the light and out into the cavern to find Evie and David watching Viviana start a hand-cranked radio.

"Good morning, sleepyhead!" Evie chirruped.

"Good morning. Did I sleep too late?" Sam asked.

"No, the sun just comes up," Viviana said. "I like to listen to the news first thing in the morning. It helps keep me connected with the rest of the world, I guess." She stored the crank handle in its spot and powered up the radio.

"I haven't seen one of these since I was deployed overseas," David said.

"What about Arnie and Christie?" Sam asked.

"They may sleep as long as Brittany will let them," Evie answered.

The radio sputtered with static, then a voice came through, giving the weather for the day. All four took notice when the announcer said, "We have a breaking development out of the National Oceanic and Atmospheric Administration this morning. NOAA Deputy Undersecretary for Operations, Dr. Sonya Feldman, issued a statement this morning that NOAA has evidence that MC2 has tampered with NOAA's climate forecast program, which was being hosted on MC2's supercomputers. The program was altered to keep climate predictions within a moderate range rather than providing the true implications of the data.

"Furthermore, the geographical temperature scale was blanked out over a small area around Salty Ford, West Virginia. Dr. Nashima Jarrard, who is the head of the climate analysis program, stated that preliminary analysis of the true data indicates a hot spot in that area consistent with a large accumulation of radioactive material. A team gathered in the area overnight and reported that they required protective gear due to high radiation levels as far as three quarters of a mile away from the site.

"The team is awaiting the arrival of a specially armored vehicle before they attempt to approach the site. Dr. Feldman stated that no one should attempt to get close to the area, and anyone within a twenty-five-mile radius should evacuate immediately. She said this appears to be the worst nuclear disaster in the history of the planet, and there is the possibility of an explosion due to the extreme heat being generated.

"We have been unable to reach Mitch Carter, the owner of MC2, for comment. We will bring you further developments on this breaking story as they unfold."

Sam felt chills running down his back and shivered. He saw Evie and David sitting there wide-eyed. "No wonder they wanted that thumb drive so badly!" Sam said.

"But how did NOAA get it so quickly?" Evie asked. "Grandpa should have gotten it just yesterday morning!"

Sam thought for a minute and then smiled, "I bet Dad flew it to NOAA himself!" Sam's smile grew even bigger. All of a sudden he jumped up and said, "We did it! We really did it!"

David and Evie jumped up and high-fived him. Viviana joined in the celebration. The noise brought Arnie and Christie out. Sam filled them in on what they had just heard, and Arnie said, "Wow! I had no idea it was that big a deal!"

"Arnie, you are a true hero!" Evie said.

"It looks like we are all heroes!" Arnie replied.

When the celebration calmed down and the six heroes were standing in a circle, Sam said, "Now what do we do?"

Viviana doubled over in laughter. Sam felt puzzled and a little embarrassed by her response. When Viviana finally recovered, she looked at Sam and said, "Now? Now you learn to live!"

A Note from the Author

Thank you so much for reading this novel. I would be grateful if you would take the time to leave a review on the sight from which you purchased this book and/or Goodreads. Reviews help others have a better understanding of whether or not they might like the book and help the author in promoting it.

I initially wanted to write a story that focused on the rising wealth disparity in America and where that might be taking us as a society. As the story progressed in my mind, the characters, particularly Evie, insisted that the story was about them and their struggles to do the right thing in a terrifying situation. So, the idea that we might be headed toward a new form of the feudal system became just the setting for the characters' story.

One of the most consistent comments that I got in the early stages was that people wanted to know more about Viviana. She wanted to tell her story in her own words, so here is a letter she wrote to David.

A LETTER FROM VIVIANA...

My Dear David,

You know that I have grown fond of you, and I feel that this relationship may be getting serious. I haven't been able to give voice to the story of my past for you, but I believe you need to know. It haunts me, but I have learned to live with it. I hope you can learn to live with it, too.

I used to live in Mexico. After my Mom was shot by a member of a drug cartel, my Dad decided to move us to America. I was his only child. While crossing the Rio Grande, my father had a heart attack and drowned. He was my anchor and my rock.

My father was a survival trainer for the Mexican army. He used to take me camping and teach me the same skills he would teach the soldiers. "Just in case you need to know, someday," he would say.

I was seventeen when Papi died. I made it across the river and found my way to my aunt's house about 25 miles from here. After she died, I grew tired of being hunted for deportation. So, I took the skills my father taught me and walked till I found this mountain.

I hope you don't think less of me, now. I know I have fallen in love with you.

I am yours,
Viviana

Also Available from Dwain Cassady

Dwain Cassady is the author of four Advent Devotional studies, if you are interested in a resource to enrich your personal, or a group's, Advent journey. The following are available on Amazon:

"Insights from Matthew: An Advent Journey

"Presence in the Manger: An Advent Journey with Luke

"The Coming Light: An Advent Journey with John

"The Soil of Salvation: An Advent Journey with Isaiah

Made in the USA
Columbia, SC
13 November 2020

24407992R00186